The Free Lances
A Romance of the Mexican Valley

by

Captain Mayne Reid

Double9
BOOKS

The Free Lances
A Romance of the Mexican Valley
by Captain Mayne Reid

ISBN: 978-93-61152-20-7

Published by

DOUBLE 9 BOOKS

2/13-B, Ansari Road
Daryaganj, New Delhi – 110002
info@double9books.com
www.double9books.com
Tel. 011-40042856

This book is under public domain

ABOUT THE AUTHOR

Thomas Mayne Reid, an Irish-American novelist, participated in the Mexican American War. His numerous books on American life discuss colonial policy in the American colonies, the horrors of slave labor, and the lifestyles of American Indians. "Captain" Reid created adventure stories similar to those of Frederick Marryat and Robert Louis Stevenson. They were primarily situated in the American West, Mexico, South Africa, the Himalayas, and Jamaica. He admired Lord Byron. Dion Boucicault turned his anti-slavery novel Quadroon (1856) into a drama called The Octoroon (1859), which was staged in New York. Reid was born in Ballyroney, a hamlet near Katesbridge in County Down, Northern Ireland, as the son of Rev. Thomas Mayne Reid Sr., a senior clerk of the General Assembly of the Presbyterian Church in Ireland, and his wife. Reid's father intended him to become a Presbyterian pastor, so he enrolled at the Royal Belfast Academical Institution in September 1834. He stayed for four years, but lacked the ambition to finish his studies and graduate. He returned to Ballyroney to teach at a school.

CONTENTS

Chapter One
Volunteers for Texas

"I'll go!"

This laconism came from the lips of a young man who was walking along the Levee of New Orleans. Just before giving utterance to it he had made a sudden stop, facing a dead wall, enlivened, however, by a large poster, on which were printed, in conspicuous letters, the words—

"Volunteers for Texas!"

Underneath, in smaller type, was a proclamation, setting forth the treachery of Santa Anna and the whole Mexican nation, recalling in strong terms the Massacre of Fanning, the butchery of Alamo, and other like atrocities; ending in an appeal to all patriots and lovers of freedom to arm, take the field, and fight against the tyrant of Mexico and his myrmidons.

"I'll go!" said the young man, after a glance given to the printed statement; then, more deliberately re-reading it, he repeated the words with an emphasis that told of his being in earnest.

The poster also gave intimation of a meeting to be held the same evening at a certain *rendezvous* in Poydras Street.

He who read only lingered to make note of the address, which was the name of a noted *café*. Having done this, he was turning to continue his walk when his path was barred by a specimen of humanity, who stood full six foot six in a pair of alligator leather boots, on the *banquette* by his side, "So ye're goin', air ye?" was the half-interrogative speech that proceeded from the individual thus confronting him.

"What's that to you?" bluntly demanded the young fellow, his temper a little ruffled by what appeared an impertinent obstruction on the part of some swaggering bully.

"More'n you may think for, young 'un," answered the booted Colossus, still standing square in the way; "more'n you may think for, seein' it's through me that bit o' paper's been put up on that 'ere wall."

"You're a bill-sticker, I suppose?" sneeringly retorted the "young 'un."

"Ha! ha! ha!" laughed the giant, with a cachinnation that resembled the neighing of a horse. "A bill-sticker, eh! Wal; I likes that. An' I likes yur grit, too, young feller, for all ye are so sassy. But ye needn't git riled, an' I reckon ye won't, when I tell ye who I am."

"And who are you; pray?"

"Maybe ye mount a hearn o' Cris Rock?"

"What! Cris Rock of Texas? He who at Fanning's—"

"At Fannin's massacree war shot dead, and kim alive agin."

"Yes," said the interrogator, whose interrogatory referred to the almost miraculous escape of one of the betrayed victims of the Goliad butchery.

"Jess so, young feller. An' since ye 'pear to know somethin' 'bout me, I needn't tell ye I ain't no *bill-sticker*, nor why I 'peared to show impartinence by putting in my jaw when I heern ye sing out, 'I'll go.' I thort it wouldn't need much introduxshun to one as I mout soon hope to call kumarade. Yer comin' to the rendyvoo the night, ain't ye?"

"Yes; I intend doing so."

"Wal, I'll be there myself; an' if ye'll only look high enough, I reck'n ye kin sight me 'mong the crowd. 'Tain't like to be the shortest thar," he added, with a smile that bespoke pride in his superior stature, "tho' ye'll see some tall 'uns too. Anyhow, jest look out for Cris Rock; and, when foun', that chile may be of some sarvice to ye."

"I shall do so," rejoined the other, whose good humour had become quite restored.

About to bid good-bye, Rock held out a hand, broad as the blade of a canoe-paddle. It was freely taken by the stranger, who, while shaking it, saw that he was being examined from head to foot.

"Look hyar!" pursued the Colossus, as if struck by some thought which a closer scrutiny of the young man's person had suggested; "hev ye ever did any sogerin'? Ye've got the look o' it."

"I was educated in a military school—that's all."

"Where? In the States?"

"No. I am from the other side of the Atlantic."

"Oh! A Britisher. Wal, that don't make no difference in Texas. Thar's all sorts thar. English, ain't ye?"

"No," promptly answered the stranger, with a slight scornful curling of the lip: "I'm an Irishman, and not one of those who deny it."

"All the better for that. Thar's a bit of the same blood somewhar in my own veins, out o' a grandmother, I b'lieve, as kim over the mountains into Kaintuck, 'long wi' Dan Boone an' his lot. So ye've been eddycated at a milintary school, then? D'ye unnerstan' anything about the trainin' o' sogers?"

"Certainly I do."

"Dog-goned, ef you ain't the man we want! How'd ye like to be an officer? I reck'n ye're best fit for that."

"Of course I should like it; but as a stranger among you, I shouldn't stand much chance of being elected. You choose your officers, don't you?"

"Sartin, we eelect 'em; an' we're goin' to hold the eelections this very night. Lookee hyar, young fellur; I like yer looks, an' I've seed proof ye've got the stuff in ye. Now, I want to tell ye somethin' ye oughter to know. I belong to this company that's jest a formin', and thar's a fellur settin' hisself up to be its capting. He's a sort o' half Spanish, half French-Creole, o' Noo-Orleans hyar, an' we old Texans don't think much o' him. But thar's only a few o' us; while 'mong the Orleans city fellurs as are goin' out to, he's got a big pop'larity by standin' no eend o' drinks. He ain't a bad lookin' sort for sogerin', and has seen milintary sarvice, they say. F'r all that, thar's a hangdog glint 'bout his eyes this chile don't like; neither do some o' the others. So, young un, if you'll come down to the rendyvoo in good time, an' make a speech—you kin speechify, can't ye?"

"Oh, I suppose I could say something."

"Wal, you stump it, an' I'll put in a word or two, an' then we'll perpose ye for capting; an' who knows we mayent git the majority arter all? You'er willin' to try, ain't ye?"

"Quite willing," answered the Irishman, with an emphasis which showed how much the proposal was to his mind. "But why, Mr Rock, are you not a candidate yourself? You have seen service, and would make a good officer, I should say."

"Me kandydate for officer! Wal, I'm big enough, thet's true, and ef you like, ugly enuf. But I ain't no ambeeshum thet way. Besides, this chile knows nothin' 'bout *drill*; an' that's what's wanted bad. Ye see, we ain't had much reg'lar sogerin' in Texas. Thar's whar the Mexikins hev the advantage o' us, an' thar's whar you'll hev the same if you'll consent to stan'. You say you will?"

"I will, if you wish it."

"All square then," returned the Texan, once more taking his *protégé* by the hand, and giving it a squeeze like the grip of a grizzly bear. "I'll be on the lookout for ye. Meanwhile, thar's six hours to the good yet afore it git sundown. So go and purpar' yur speech, while I slide roun' among the fellurs, an' do a leetle for ye in the line o' canvassin'."

After a final bruin-like pressure of the hand the giant had commenced striding away, when he came again to a halt, uttering a loud "Hiloo!"

"What is it?" inquired the young Irishman.

"It seems that Cris Rock air 'bout one o' the biggest nummorskulls in all Noo-Orleans. Only to think! I was about startin' to take the stump for a kandydate 'ithout knowin' the first letter o' his name. How wur ye crissened, young fellur?"

"Kearney—Florence Kearney."

"Florence, ye say? Ain't that a woman's name?"

"True; but in Ireland many men bear it."

"Wal, it do seem a little kewrious; but it'll do right slick, and the Kearney part soun's well. I've hern speak o' Kate Kearney; thar's a song 'bout the gurl. Mout ye be any connexshun o' hern?"

"No, Mr Rock; not that I'm aware of. She was a Killarney woman. I was born a little further north on the green island."

"Wal, no matter what part o' it, yur are welkim to Texas, I reck'n, or the States eyther. Kearney—I like the name. It hev a good ring, an' it'll soun' all the better wi' 'Capting' for a handle to 't—the which it shall hev afore ten o'clock this night, if Cris Rock ain't astray in his reck'nin'. But see as ye kum early to the rendyvoo, so as to hev time for a talk wi' the boys. Thar's a somethin' in that; an' if ye've got a ten dollar bill to spare, spend it on drinks all round. Thar's a good deal in that too."

So saying, the Texan strode off, leaving Florence Kearney to reflect upon the counsel so opportunely extended.

Chapter Two
A Lady in the Case

Who Florence Kearney was, and what his motive for becoming a "filibuster," the reader shall be told without much tediousness of detail.

Some six months before the encounter described, he had landed from a Liverpool cotton ship on the Levee of New Orleans. A gentleman by birth and a soldier-scholar by education, he had gone to the New World with the design to complete his boyhood's training by a course of travel, and prepare himself for the enacting the *métier* of a man. That this travel should be westward, over fresh untrodden fields, instead of along the hackneyed highways of the European tourist, was partly due to the counsels of a tutor—who had himself visited the New World—and partly to his own natural inclinations.

In the course of his college studies he had read the romantic history of Cortez's conquest, and his mind had become deeply imbued with the picturesqueness of Mexican scenes; so that among the fancies of his youthful life one of the pleasantest was that of some day visiting the land of Anahuac, and its ancient capital, Tenochtitlan. After leaving college the dream had grown into a determination, and was now in the act of being realised. In New Orleans he was so far on his way. He came thither expecting to obtain passage in a coasting vessel to some Mexican seaport—Tampico or Vera Cruz.

Why he had not at once continued his journey thither was due to no difficulty in finding such a vessel. There were schooners sailing every week to either of the above ports that would have accommodated him, yet still he lingered in New Orleans. His reason for thus delaying was one far from uncommon—this being a lady with whom he had fallen in love.

At first the detention had been due to a more sensible cause. Not speaking the Spanish language, which is also that of Mexico, he knew that while travelling through the latter country he would have to go as one dumb. In New Orleans he might easily obtain a teacher; and having sought soon found one, in the person of Don Ignacio Valverde,—a refugee Mexican gentleman, a victim of the tyrant Santa Anna, who, banished from his country, had been for several years resident in the States as an exile. And an exile in straitened circumstances, one of the hardest conditions of life. Once, in his own country, a wealthy landowner, Don Ignacio was now compelled to give lessons in Spanish to such stray pupils as might chance to present themselves. Among the rest, by chance came Florence Kearney, to whom he had commenced teaching it.

But while the latter was making himself master of the Andalusian tongue, he also learnt to love one who spoke it as purely, and far more sweetly, than Don Ignacio. This was Don Ignacio's daughter.

After parting with Cris Rock, the young Irishman advanced along the Levee, his head bowed forward, with eyes to the ground, as if examining the oyster-shells that thickly bestrewed the path; anon giving his glance to the river, as though stirred by its majestic movement. But he was thinking neither of the empty bivalves, nor the flow of the mighty stream. Nor yet of the speech he had promised to make that same night at the *rendezvous* of filibusters. Instead he was reflecting upon that affair of the heart, from which he had been for some time suffering.

To make known his feelings it is necessary to repeat what passed through his mind after he had separated from the Texan.

"There's something odd in all this," soliloquised he, as he strode on. "Here am I going to fight for a country I care nothing about, and against one with which I have no cause of quarrel. On the contrary, I have come four thousand miles to visit the latter, as a peaceful friendly traveller. Now I propose making entry into it, sword in hand, as an enemy and invader! The native land, too, of her who has taken possession of my heart! Ah! therein lies the very reason: *I have not got hers*. I fear—nay, I am certain of that, from what I saw this morning. Bah! What's the use of thinking about it, or about her? Luisa Valverde cares no more for me than the half-score of others—these young Creole 'bloods,' as they call themselves—who flit like butterflies around her. She's a sweet flower from which all of them wish to sip. Only one will succeed, and that's Carlos Santander. I hate the very sight of the man. I believe him to be a cheat and a scoundrel. No matter to her. The cheat she won't understand; and, if report speak true of her country and race, the scoundrel would scarcely qualify him either. Merciful heavens! to think I should love this Mexican girl, warned as I've been about her countrywomen! 'Tis a fascination, and the sooner I get away from it and her presence, the better it may be for me. Now, this Texan business offers a chance of escaping the peril. If I find she cares not for me, it will be a sort of satisfaction to think that in fighting against her country I may in a way humiliate herself. Ah, Texas! If you find in me a defender, it will not be from any patriotic love of you, but to bury bitter thoughts in oblivion."

The chain of his reflections, momentarily interrupted was after a time continued: "My word," he exclaimed, "there's surely something ominous in my encounter with this Cris Rock! Destiny seems to direct me. Here am I scheming to escape from a thraldom of a siren's smiles, and, to do so, ready to throw myself into the ranks of a filibustering band! On the instant a friend is found—a patron who promises to make me their leader! Shall I refuse the favour, which fortune herself seems to offer? Why should I? It is fate, not chance; and this night at their meeting I shall know whether it is meant in earnest. So, canvass your best for me, Cris Rock; and I shall do my best to make a suitable speech. If our united efforts prove successful, then Texas shall gain a friend, and Luisa Valverde lose *one* of her lovers."

At the conclusion of this speech—half boastful, half bitter—Florence Kearney had reached the hotel where he was stopping—the celebrated "Saint Charles," and entering its grand saloon, sat down to reflect further on the step he was about to take.

Chapter Three
Officering the Filibusters

The volunteer *rendezvous* was in a tavern, better known by the name of "Coffee House," in the street called Poydras. The room which had been chartered for the occasion was of ample dimensions, capable of containing three hundred men. Drawn together by the printed proclamation that had attracted the attention of the young Irishman in his afternoon stroll, two-thirds of the above number had collected, and of these at least one-half were determined upon proceeding to Texas.

It was a crowd composed of heterogeneous elements—such as has ever been, and ever will be, the men who volunteer for a military, more especially a filibustering expedition.

Present in the hall were representatives of almost every civilised nation upon earth. Even some that could scarce boast of civilisation; for among the faces seen around the room were many so covered with beards, and so browned with sun, as to tell of long sojourn in savage parts, if not association with the savages themselves. In obedience to the counsels of the Texan, Florence Kearney—a candidate for command over this motley crew—made early appearance in their midst. Not so early as to find that, on entering the room, he was a stranger to its occupants. Cris Rock had been there before him, along with a half-score of his *confrères*—old Texans of the pure breed—who having taken part in most of the struggles of the young Republic, had strayed back to New Orleans, partly for a spree, and partly to recruit fresh comrades to aid them in propagating that principle which had first taken them to Texas—the "Monroe Doctrine."

To these the young Irishman was at once confidentially introduced, and "stood drinks" freely. He would have done so without care of what was to come of it; since it was but the habit of his generous nation. Nor would this of itself have given him any great advantage, for not long after entering the room, he discovered that not only drinks, but dollars, were distributed freely by the opposition party, who seemed earnestly bent upon making a captain of their candidate.

As yet Kearney had not looked upon his competitor, and was even ignorant of his name. Soon, however, it was communicated to him, just as the man himself, escorted by a number of friends, made his appearance in the room. The surprise of the young Irishman may be imagined; when he saw before him one already known, and too well-known,—his rival in the affections of Luisa Valverde!

Yes; Carlos Santander was also a candidate for the command of the filibusters.

To Kearney the thing was a surprise, and something besides. He knew Santander to be on terms of very friendly and intimate relationship not only with Don Ignacio, but other Mexicans he had met at the exile's house. Strange, that the Creole should be aspiring to the leadership of a band about to invade their country! For it was *invasion* the Texans now talked of, in retaliation for a late raid of the Mexicans to their capital, San Antonio. But these banished Mexicans being enemies of Santa Anna it was after all not so unnatural. By humiliating the Dictator, they would be aiding their own party to get back into power—even though the help came from their hereditary foemen, the squatters of Texas.

All this passed through the mind of the young Irishman, though not altogether to satisfy him. The presence of Santander there, as aspirant for leadership, seemed strange notwithstanding.

But he had no opportunity for indulging in conjectures—only time to exchange frowns at his rival and competitor, when a man in undress uniform—a Texan colonel—who acted as chairman of the meeting, mounting upon a table, cried "Silence!" and, after a short pithy speech, proposed that the election of officers should at once proceed. The proposal was seconded, no one objecting; and, without further parley, the "balloting" began.

There was neither noise nor confusion. Indeed, the assembly was one of the quietest, and without any street crowd outside. There were reasons for observing a certain secrecy in the proceedings; for, although the movement was highly popular all over the States, there were some compromising points of International law, and there had been talk of Government interference.

The election was conducted in the most primitive and simple fashion. The names of the candidates were written upon slips of paper, and distributed throughout the room—only the members who had formed the organisation having the right to vote. Each of them chose the slip bearing the name of him he intended to vote for, and dropped it into a hat carried round for the purpose. The other he threw away, or slipped if to his pocket.

When all had deposited their ballots, the hat was capsized, and the bits of paper shaken out upon the table. The chairman, assisted by two other men, examined the votes and counted them. Then ensued a short interval of silence, broken only by an occasional word of direction from the chairman, with the murmuring hum of the examiners, and at length came in a clear loud voice—that of the Texan colonel—"*The votes are in favour of Kearney! Florence Kearney elected Captain by a majority of thirty-three!*"

A cheer greeted the announcement, in which something like a screech from Cris Rock could be heard above all voices; while the giant himself was seen rushing through the crowd to clasp the hand of his *protégé*, whom he had voluntarily assisted in promoting to a rank above himself.

During the excitement, the defeated candidate was observed to skulk out of the room. Those who saw him go could tell by his look of sullen disappointment he had no intention of returning; and that the filibustering cohort was not likely to have the name, "Carlos Santander," any longer on its roll-call.

He and his were soon forgotten. The lieutenants were yet to be chosen. One after another—first, second, and *brevet*—was proposed, balloted for, and elected in the same way as the captain.

Then there was a choice of sergeants and corporals, till the organisation was pronounced complete. In fine, fell a shower of congratulations, with "drinks all round," and for several successive rounds. Patriotic speeches also, in the true "spread-eagle" style, with applauding cheers, and jokes about Santa Anna and his *cork-leg*; when the company at length separated, after singing the "Star-Spangled Banner."

Chapter Four
An Invitation to Supper

Florence Kearney, parting from his new friends, the filibusters, sauntered forth upon the street.

On reaching the nearest corner he came to a stop, as if undecided which way to turn.

Not because he had lost his way. His hotel was but three blocks off; and he had, during his short sojourn in the Crescent City, become acquainted with almost every part of it. It was not ignorance of the locality, therefore, which was causing him to hesitate; but something very different, as the train of his thoughts will tell.

"Don Ignacio, at least, will expect me—wish me to come, whether she do or not. I accepted his invitation, and cannot well—oh! had I known what I do now—seen what I saw this morning— Bah! I shall return to the hotel and never more go near her!"

But he did not return to his hotel; instead, still stood irresolute, as if the thing were worth further considering.

What made the young man act thus? Simply a belief that Luisa Valverde did not love him, and, therefore, would not care to have him as a companion at supper; for it was to supper her father had asked him. On the day before he had received the invitation, and signified acceptance of it. But he had seen something since which had made him half repent having done so; a man, Carlos Santander, standing beside the woman he loved, bending over her till his lips almost touched her forehead, whispering words that were heard, and, to all appearance, heeded. What the words were Florence Kearney knew not, but could easily guess their nature. They could only be of love; for he saw the carmine on her cheeks as she listened to them.

He had no right to call the young lady to an account. During all his intercourse with Don Ignacio, he had seen the daughter scarce half a score times; then only while passing out and in—to or from his lessons. Now and then a few snatches of conversation had occurred between them upon any chance theme—the weather, the study he was prosecuting (how he wished *she* had been his teacher), and the peculiarities of the New Orleans life, to which they were both strangers. And only once had she appeared to take more than an ordinary interest in his speech. This, when he talked of Mexico, and having come from his own far land, "Irlandesa," with an enthusiastic desire to visit hers, telling her of his intention to do so. On this occasion he had ventured to speak of what he had heard about Mexican banditti; still more of the beauty of the Mexican ladies—naïvely adding that he would no doubt be in less danger of losing his life than his heart.

To this he thought she had listened, or seemed to listen, with more than ordinary attention, looking pensive as she made reply.

"Yes, Don Florencio! you will see much in Mexico likely to give you gratification. 'Tis true, indeed, that many of my countrywomen are fair—some very fair. Among them you will soon forget—"

Kearney's heart beat wildly, hoping he would hear the monosyllable "me." But the word was not spoken. In its place the phrase "us poor exiles," with which somewhat commonplace remark the young Mexican concluded her speech.

And still there was something in what she had said, but more in her manner of saying it, which made pleasant impression upon him—something in her tone that touched a chord already making music in his heart. If it did not give him surety of her love, it, for the time, hindered him from despairing of it.

All this had occurred at an interview he had with her only the day before; and, since, sweet thoughts and hopes were his. But on the same morning they were shattered—crushed out by the spectacle he had witnessed, and the interpretation of those whispered words he had failed to hear. It had chased all hope out of his heart, and sent him in wild, aimless strides along the street, just in the right frame of mind for being caught by that call which had attracted his eyes on the poster—

"Volunteers for Texas." And just so had he been caught; and, as described, entered among the filibustering band to be chosen its chief. To the young Irishman it was a day of strange experiences, varying as the changes of a kaleidoscope; more like a dream than reality; and after reflecting upon it all, he thus interrogated himself—

"Shall I see her again, or not? Why not? If she's lost, she cannot be worse lost by my having another interview with her. Nor could I feel worse than I do now. Ah! with this laurel fresh placed upon my brow! What if I tell her of it—tell her I am about to enter her native land as an invader? If she care for her country, that would spite her; and if I find she cares not for me, her spite would give me pleasure."

It was not an amiable mood for a lover contemplating a visit to his sweetheart. Still, natural enough under the circumstances; and Florence Kearney, wavering no longer, turned his steps towards that part of the city where dwelt Don Ignacio Valverde.

Chapter Five
A Studied Insult

In a small house of the third Municipality, in the street called Casa Calvo, dwelt Don Ignacio Valverde. It was a wooden structure—a frame dwelling—of French-Creole fashion, consisting of but a single story, with casement windows that opened on a verandah, in the Southern States termed *piazza*; this being but little elevated above the level of the outside street. Besides Don Ignacio and his daughter, but one other individual occupied the house—their only servant, a young girl of Mexican nativity and mixed blood, half white, half Indian—in short, a *mestiza*. The straitened circumstances of the exile forbade a more expensive establishment. Still, the insignia within were not those of pinched poverty. The sitting-room, if small, was tastefully furnished, while, among other chattels speaking of refinement, were several volumes of books, a harp and a guitar, with accompaniment of sheets of music. The strings of these instruments Luisa Valverde knew how to touch with the skill of a professional, both being common in her own country.

On that night, when the election of the filibustering officers was being held in Poydras Street, her father, alone with her in the same sitting-room, asked her to play the harp to the accompaniment of a song. Seating herself to the instrument, she obeyed, singing one of those *romanzas* in which the language of Cervantes is so rich. It was, in fact, the old song "El Travador," from which has been filched the music set to Mrs Norton's beautiful lay, "Love not." But on this night the spirit of the Mexican señorita was not with her song. Soon as it was finished, and her father had become otherwise engaged, she stepped out of the room, and, standing in the piazza, glanced through the trellised lattice-work that screened it from the street. She evidently expected some one to come that way. And as her father had invited Florence Kearney to supper, and she knew of it, it would look as if he were the expected one.

If so, she was disappointed for a time, though a visitor made his appearance. The door bell, pulled from the outside, soon after summoned Pepita, the Mexican servant, to the front, and presently a heavy footfall on the wooden steps of the porch, told of a man stepping upon the piazza.

Meanwhile the young lady had returned within the room; but the night being warm, the hinged casement stood ajar, and she could see through it the man thus entering. An air of disappointment, almost chagrin, came over her countenance, as the moonlight disclosed to her view the dark visage of Carlos Santander.

"*Pasa V. adientro, Señor Don Carlos,*" said her father also recognising their visitor through the casement; and in a moment after the Creole stepped into the room, Pepita placing a chair for him.

"Though," continued Don Ignacio, "we did not expect to have the honour of your company this evening, you are always welcome."

Notwithstanding this polite speech, there was a certain constraint or hesitancy in the way it was spoken, that told of some insincerity. It was evident that on that night at least Don Carlos' host looked upon him in the light of an intruder. Evidence of the same was still more marked on the countenance, as in the behaviour of Don Ignacio's daughter. Instead of a smile to greet the new-comer, something like a frown sat upon her beautiful brow, while every now and then a half-angry flash from her large liquid eyes, directed towards him, might have told him he was aught but welcome. Clearly it was not for him she had several times during the same night passed out into the piazza and looked through its lattice-work.

In truth, both father and daughter seemed disturbed by Santander's presence, both expecting one whom, for different reasons, they did not desire him to meet. If the Creole noticed their repugnance, he betrayed no sign of it. Don Carlos Santander, besides being physically handsome, was a man of rare intellectual strength, with many accomplishments, among others the power of concealing his thoughts under a mask of imperturbable coolness. Still, on this night his demeanour was different from its wont. He looked flurried and excited, his eyes scintillating as with anger at some affront lately offered him, and the sting of which still rankled in his bosom. Don Ignacio noticed this, but said nothing. Indeed, he seemed to stand in awe of his guest, as though under some mysterious influence. So was he, and here it may as well be told. Santander, though by birth an American and a native of New Orleans, was of Mexican parentage, and still regarded himself as a citizen of the country of his ancestors. Only to his very intimates was it known that he held a very high place in the confidence of Mexico's Dictator. But Don Ignacio knew this, and rested certain hopes upon it. More than once had Santander, for motives that will presently appear, hinted to him the possibility of a return to his own land, with restoration of the estates he had forfeited. And the exiled patriot, wearied with long waiting, was at length willing to lend an ear to conditions, which, in other days, he might have spurned as humiliating if not actually dishonourable.

It was to talk of these Santander had now presented himself; and his host suspecting it, gave the young lady a side look, as much as to say, "Leave the room, Luisita."

She was but too glad to obey. Just then she preferred a turn upon the piazza; and into this she silently glided, leaving her father alone with the guest who had so inopportunely intruded.

It is not necessary to repeat what passed between the two men. Their business was to bring to a conclusion a compact they had already talked of, though only in general terms. It had reference to the restitution of Don Ignacio's confiscated estates, with, of course, also the ban of exile being removed from him. The price of all this, the hand of his daughter given to Carlos Santander. It was the Creole who proposed these terms, and insisted upon them, even to the humiliation of himself. Madly in love with Luisa Valverde, he suspected that on her side there was no reciprocity of the passion. But he would have her hand if he could not her heart.

On that night the bargain was not destined to reach a conclusion, their conference being interrupted by the tread of booted feet, just ascending the front steps, and crossing the floor of the piazza. This followed by an exchange of salutations, in which the voice of Luisa Valverde was heard mingling with that of a man.

Don Ignacio looked more troubled than surprised. He knew who was there. But when the words spoken outside reached the ears of Carlos Santander, first, in openly exchanged salutations and then whispers seemingly secret and confidential, he could no longer keep his seat, but springing up, exclaimed—

"*Carrai*! It's that dog of an *Irlandes*!"

"Hish!" continued his host. "The Señor Florencio will hear you."

"I wish him to hear me. I repeat the expression, and plainly in his own native tongue. I call him a cur of an Irishman."

Outside was heard a short, sharp ejaculation, as of a man startled by some sudden surprise. It was followed by an appealing speech, this in the softer accents of a woman. Then the casement was drawn abruptly open, showing two faces outside. One, that of Florence Kearney, set in an angry frown; the other, Luisa Valverde's, pale and appealing. An appeal idle and too late, as she herself saw. The air had become charged with the electricity of deadliest anger, and between the two men a collision was inevitable.

Without waiting for a word of invitation, Kearney stepped over the casement sill, and presented himself inside the room. Don Ignacio and the Creole were by this also on their feet; and for a second or so the three formed a strange triangular *tableau*—the Mexican with fear on his face, that of Santander still wearing the expression of insult, as when he had exclaimed, "Cur of an Irishman!" Kearney confronting him with a look of indignant defiance.

There was an interval of silence, as that of calm preceding storm. It was broken by the guest latest arrived saying a few words to his host, but in calm, dignified tone; an apology for having unceremoniously entered the room.

"No need to apologise," promptly rejoined Don Ignacio. "You are here by my invitation, Señor Don Florencio, and my humble home is honoured by your presence."

The Hidalgo blood, pure in Valverde's veins, had boiled up at seeing a man insulted under his roof.

"Thanks," said the young Irishman.

"And now, sir," he continued, turning to Santander and regarding him with a look of recovered coolness, "having made my apology, I require *yours*."

"For what?" asked Santander, counterfeiting ignorance.

"For using language that belongs to the *bagnios* of New Orleans, where, I doubt not, you spend most part of your time."

Then, suddenly changing tone and expression of face, he added—

"Cur of a Creole! you must take back your words!"

"Never! It's not my habit to take, but to give; and to you I give this!"

So saying, he stepped straight up to the Irishman, and spat in his face.

Kearney's heart was on fire. His hand was already on the butt of his pistol; but, glancing behind, he saw that pale appealing face, and with an effort restrained himself, calmly saying to Santander—

"Calling yourself a gentleman, you will no doubt have a card and address. May I ask you to favour me with it, as to-morrow I shall have occasion to write to you? If a scoundrel such as you can boast of having a friend, you may as well give him notice he will be needed. Your card, sir!"

"Take it!" hissed the Creole, flinging his card on the table. Then glaring around, as if his glance would annihilate all, he clutched hold of his hat, bowed haughtily to Don Ignacio, looked daggers at his daughter, and strode out into the street.

Though to all appearance defeated and humbled, he had in truth succeeded in his design, one he had long planned and cherished to bring about,—a duel with Kearney, in which his antagonist should be challenger. This would give him the choice of weapons, which, as he well knew, would ensure to him both safety and success. Without the certainty of this, Carlos Santander would have been the last man to provoke such an encounter; for, with all his air of *bravache*, he was the veriest of cowards.

Chapter Six
"To the Salute!"

The thick "swamp-fog" still hovered above the Crescent City, when a carriage, drawn by two horses, rolled out through one of its suburbs, and on along the Shell Road, and in the direction of Lake Pontchartrain.

It was a close carriage—a hackney—with two men upon the driver's seat, and three inside. Of these last, one was Captain Florence Kearney, and another Lieutenant Francis Crittenden, both officers of the filibustering band, with *titles* not two days old. Now on the way neither to Texas nor Mexico, but to the shore of Lake Pontchartrain, where many an affair of honour has been settled by the spilling of much blood. A stranger in New Orleans, and knowing scarce a soul, Kearney had bethought him of the young fellow who had been elected first-lieutenant, and asked him to act as his second. Crittenden, a Kentuckian, being one of those who could not only stand fire, but *eat* it, if the occasion called, eagerly responded to the appeal; and they were now *en route* along the Shell Road to meet Carlos Santander and whoever he might have with him.

The third individual inside the carriage belonged to that profession, one of whose members usually makes the third in a duel—the doctor. He was a young man who, in the capacity of surgeon, had attached himself to the band of filibusters.

Besides the mahogany box balanced upon his thigh there was another lying on the spare bit of cushion beside him, opposite to where Crittenden sat. It was of a somewhat different shape; and no one who had ever seen a case of duelling pistols could mistake it for aught else—for it was such.

As it had been arranged that swords were to be the weapons, and a pair of these were seen in a corner of the carriage, what could they be wanting with pistols?

It was Kearney who put this question; now for the first time noticing what seemed to him a superfluous armament. It was asked of Crittenden, to whom the pistols belonged, as might have been learnt by looking at his name engraved on the indented silver plate.

"Well," answered the Kentuckian, "I'm no great swordsman myself. I usually prefer pistols, and thought it might be as well to bring a pair along. I didn't much like the look of your antagonist's friend, and it's got into my head that before leaving the ground I may have something to say to *him* on my own account. So, if it come to that, I shall take to the barkers."

Kearney smiled, but said nothing, feeling satisfied that in case of any treachery, he had the right sort of man for his second.

He might have felt further secure, in a still other supporting party, who rode on the box beside the driver. This was a man carrying a long rifle, that stood with the barrel two feet above his shoulders, and the butt rested between his heavily booted feet.

It was Cris Rock, who had insisted on coming along, as he said, to see that the fight was all "fair and square." He too had conceived an unfavourable opinion of both the men to be met, from what he had seen of them at the *rendezvous*; for Santander's second had also been there. With the usual caution of one accustomed to fighting Indians, he always went armed, usually with his long "pea" rifle.

On reaching a spot of open ground alongside the road, and near the shore of the lake, the carriage stopped. It was the place of the appointed meeting, as arranged by the seconds on the preceding day.

Though their antagonists had not yet arrived, Kearney and Crittenden got out, leaving the young surgeon busied with his cutlery and bandage apparatus.

"I hope you won't have to use them, doctor," remarked Kearney, with a light laugh, as he sprang out of the carriage. "I don't want you to practise upon me till we've made conquest of Mexico."

"And not then, I trust," soberly responded the surgeon.

Crittenden followed, carrying the swords; and the two, leaping across the drain which separated the road from the duelling ground, took stand under a tree.

Rock remained firm on the coach-box, still seated and silent. As the field was full under his view, and within range of his rifle, he knew that, like the doctor, he would be near enough if wanted.

Ten minutes passed—most of the time in solemn silence, on the part of the principal, with some anxious thoughts. No matter how courageous a man may be—however skilled in weapons, or accustomed to the deadly use of them—he cannot, at such a crisis, help having a certain tremor of the heart, if not a misgiving of conscience. He has come there to kill, or be killed; and the thought of either should be sufficient to disturb mental equanimity. At such times, he who is not gifted with natural courage had needs have a good cause, and confidence in the weapon to be used. Florence Kearney possessed all three; and though it was his first appearance in a duel, he had no fear for the result. Even the still, sombre scene, with the long grey moss hanging down from the dark cypress trees, like the drapery of a hearse, failed to inspire him with dread. If, at times, a slight nervousness came over him, it was instantly driven off by the thought of the insult he had received—and, perhaps also, a little by the remembrance of those dark eyes he fancied would flash proudly if he triumphed, and weep bitterly were he to suffer discomfiture. Very different were his feelings now from those he experienced less than forty-eight hours before, when he was on his way to the house of Don Ignacio Valverde. That night, before leaving it, he was good as sure he possessed the heart of Don Ignacio's daughter. Indeed, she had all but told him so; and was this not enough to nerve him for the encounter near at hand?

Very near now—close to commencing. The rumbling of wheels heard through the drooping festoonery of the trees, proclaimed that a second carriage was approaching along the Shell Road. It could only be that containing the antagonists. And it was that. In less than ten minutes after, it drew up on the causeway, about twenty paces to the rear of the one already arrived. Two men got out, who, although wrapped in cloaks and looking as large as giants through the thick mist, could be recognised as Carlos Santander and his second. There was a third individual, who, like the young surgeon, remained by the carriage—no doubt a doctor, too,—making the duelling party symmetrical and complete.

Santander and his friend having pulled off their cloaks and tossed them back into the carriage, turned towards the wet ditch, and also leaped over it.

The first performed the feat somewhat awkwardly, drooping down upon the further bank with a ponderous thud. He was a large, heavily built man—altogether unlike one possessing the activity necessary for a good swordsman.

His antagonist might have augured well from his apparent clumsiness, but for what he had heard of him. For Carlos Santander, though having the repute of a swaggerer, with some suspicion of cowardice, had proved himself a dangerous adversary by twice killing his man. His second—a French-Creole, called Duperon—enjoyed a similar reputation, he, too, having been several times engaged in affairs that resulted fatally. At this period New Orleans was emphatically the city of the *duello*—for this speciality, perhaps the most noted in the world.

As already said, Florence Kearney knew the sort of man he had to meet, and this being his own first appearance in a duelling field, he might well have been excused for feeling some anxiety as to the result. It was so slight, however, as not to betray itself, either in his looks or gestures. Confiding in his skill, gained by many a set-to with buttoned foils, and supported, as he was, by the gallant young Kentuckian, he knew nothing that could be called fear. Instead, as his antagonist advanced towards the spot where he was standing, and he looked at the handsome, yet sinister face—his thoughts at the same time reverting to Luisa Valverde, and the insult upon him in her presence—his nerves, not at all unsteady, now became firm as steel. Indeed, the self-confident, almost jaunty air, with which his adversary came upon the ground, so far from shaking them—the effect, no doubt, intended—but braced them the more.

When the new-comers had advanced a certain distance into the meadow, Crittenden, forsaking his stand under the tree, stepped out to meet them, Kearney following a few paces behind.

A sort of quadruple bow was the exchanged salutation; then the principals remained apart, the seconds drawing nigher to one another, and entering upon the required conference.

Only a few words passed between them, as but few were required; the weapons, distance, and mode of giving the word, having all been pre-arranged.

There was no talk of apology—nor thought of it being either offered or accepted. By their attitude, and in their looks, both the challenged and challenger showed a full, firm determination to fight.

Duperon did not seem to care much one way or the other, and the Kentuckian was not the sort to seek conciliation—with an insult such as his captain had received calling for chastisement.

After the preliminaries were passed over, the seconds again separated—each to attend upon his principal.

The young Irishman took off his coat, and rolled back his shirt sleeves up to the elbow. Santander, on the other hand, who wore a red flannel shirt under his ample *sacque,* simply threw aside the latter, leaving the shirt sleeves as they were, buttoned around the wrist.

Everybody was now silent; the hackney-drivers on their boxes, the doctors, the gigantic Texan, all looming large and spectral-like through the still lingering mist, while the streamers of Spanish moss hanging from the cypresses around were appropriate drapery for such a scene.

In the midst of the death-like silence a voice broke in, coming from the top of a tall cypress standing near. Strange and wild, it was enough not only to startle, but awe the stoutest heart. A shrill, continued cachinnation, which, though human-like, could scarce be ascribed to aught human, save the laughter of a maniac.

It frightened no one there, all knowing what it was—the cackling cry of the white-headed eagle.

As it ended, but before its echoes had ceased reverberating among the trees, another sound, equally awe-inspiring, woke the echoes of the forest further down. This, the *whoo-whoo-whooa* of the great southern owl, seemingly a groan in answer to the eagle's laugh.

In all countries, and throughout all ages, the hooting of the owl has been superstitiously dreaded as ominous of death, and might have dismayed our duellists, had they been men of the common kind of courage. Neither were, or seemed not to be; for, as the lugubrious notes were still echoing in their ears, they advanced, and with rapiers upraised, stood confronting each other, but one look on their faces, and one thought in their hearts—"*to kill!*"

Chapter Seven
A Duel "to the Death"

The duellists stood confronting one another, in the position of "salute," both hands on high grasping their swords at hilt and point, the blades held horizontally. The second of each was in his place, on the left hand of his principal, half a pace in advance. But a moment more all were waiting for the word. The second of the challenger had the right to give it, and Crittenden was not the man to make delay.

"*Engage!*" he cried out, in a firm clear voice, at the same time stepping half a pace forward, Duperon doing the same. The movement was made as a precaution against foul play; sometimes, though not always intended. For in the excitement of such a moment, or under the impatience of angry passion, one or other of the principals may close too quickly—to prevent which is the duty of the seconds.

Quick, at the "engage," both came to "guard" with a collision that struck sparks from the steel, proving the hot anger of the adversaries. Had they been cooler, they would have crossed swords quietly. But when, the instant after, they came to *tierce*, both appeared more collected, their blades for a while keeping in contact, and gliding around each other as if they had been a single piece.

For several minutes this cautious play continued, without further sparks, or only such as appeared to scintillate from the eyes of the combatants. Then came a counter-thrust, quickly followed by a counter parry, with no advantage to either.

Long ere this, an observer acquainted with the weapons they were wielding, could have seen that of the two Kearney was the better swordsman. In changing from *carte* to *tierce*, or reversely, the young Irishman showed himself possessed of the power to keep his arm straight and do the work with his wrist, whilst the Creole kept bending his elbow, thus exposing his forearm to the adversary's point. It is a rare accomplishment among swordsmen, but, when present, insuring almost certain victory, that is, other circumstances being equal.

In Kearney's case, it perhaps proved the saving of his life; since it seemed to be the sole object of his antagonist to thrust in upon him, heedless of his own guard. But the long, straight point, from shoulder far outstretched, and never for an instant obliquely, foiled all his attempts.

After a few thrusts, Santander seemed surprised at his fruitless efforts. Then over his face came a look more like fear. It was the first time in his duelling experience he had been so baffled, for it was his first encounter with an adversary who could keep a *straight arm*.

But Florence Kearney had been taught *tierce* as well as *carte*, and knew how to practise it. For a time he was prevented from trying it by the other's impetuous and incessant thrusting, which kept him continuously at guard, but as the sword-play proceeded, he began to discover the weak points of his antagonist, and, with a well-directed thrust, at length sent his blade through the Creole's outstretched arm, impaling it from wrist to elbow.

An ill-suppressed cry of triumph escaped from the Kentuckian's lips, while with eyes directed towards the other second, he seemed to ask—

"Are you satisfied?"

Then the question was formally put.

Duperon looked in the face of his principal, though without much show of interrogating him. It seemed as if he already divined what the answer would be.

"*A la mort!*" cried the Creole, with a deadly emphasis and bitter determination in his dark sinister eyes.

"To the death be it!" was the response of the Irishman, not so calmly, and now for the first time showing anger. Nor strange he should, since he now knew he had crossed swords with a man determined on taking his life.

There was a second or two's pause, of which Santander availed himself, hastily whipping a handkerchief round his wounded arm—a permission not strictly according to the code, but tacitly granted by his gallant antagonist.

When the two again closed and came to guard, the seconds were no longer by their sides. At the words "*à la mort*" they had withdrawn—each to the rear of his principal—the mode of action in a duel to the death. Their *rôle* henceforth was simply to look on, with no right of interference, unless either of the principals should attempt foul play. This, however, could not well occur. By the phrase *"à la mort"* is conveyed a peculiar meaning, well-known to the Orleans duellist. When spoken, it is no longer a question of sword-skill, or who draws first blood; but a challenge giving free licence to kill—whichever can.

In the present affair it was followed by silence more profound and more intense than ever, while the attention of the spectators, now including the seconds, seemed to redouble itself.

The only sound heard was a whistling of wings. The fog had drifted away, and several large birds were seen circling in the air above, looking down with stretched necks, as if they, too, felt interested in the spectacle passing underneath. No doubt they did; for they were vultures, and could see—whether or not they scented it—that blood was being spilled.

Once more, also, from the tree tops came the mocking laughter of the eagle; and out of the depths, through long, shadowy arcades, the mournful hootings of the great white owl—fit music for such fell strife.

Disregarding these ominous sounds—each seeming a death-warning in itself—the combatants had once more closed, again and again crossing sword-blades with a clash that frightened owl, eagle, and vulture, for an instant causing them to withhold their vocal accompaniment.

Though now on both sides the contest was carried on with increased anger, there was not much outward sign of it. On neither any rash sword-play. If they had lost temper they yet had control over their weapons; and their guards and points, though perhaps more rapidly exchanged, displayed as much skill as ever.

Again Kearney felt surprised at the repeated thrusts of his antagonist, which kept him all the time on the defensive, while Santander appeared equally astonished and discomfited by that far-reaching arm, straight as a yardstick, with elbow never bent. Could the Creole have but added six inches to his rapier blade, in less than ten seconds the young Irishman would have had nearly so much of it passed between his ribs.

Twice its point touched, slightly scratching the skin upon his breast, and drawing blood.

For quite twenty minutes the sanguinary strife continued without any marked advantage to either. It was a spectacle somewhat painful to behold, the combatants themselves being a sight to look upon. Kearney's shirt of finest white linen showed like a butcher's; his sleeves encrimsoned; his hands, too, grasping his rapier hilt, the same—not with his own blood, but that of his adversary, which had run back along the blade; his face was spotted by the drops dashed over it from the whirling wands of steel.

Gory, too, was the face of Santander; but gashed as well. Bending forward to put in a point, the Creole had given his antagonist a chance, resulting to himself in a punctured cheek, the scar of which would stay there for life.

It was this brought the combat to an end; or, at all events, to its concluding stroke. Santander, vain of his personal appearance, on feeling his cheek laid open, suddenly lost command of himself, and with a fierce oath rushed at his adversary, regardless of the consequences.

He succeeded in making a thrust, though not the one he intended. For having aimed at Kearney's heart, missing it, his blade passed through the buckle of the young Irishman's braces, where in an instant it was entangled.

Only for half a second; but this was all the skilled swordsman required. Now, first since the fight began, his elbow was seen to bend. This to obtain room for a thrust, which was sent, to all appearance, home to his adversary's heart.

Every one on the ground expected to see Santander fall; for by the force of the blow and direction Kearney's blade should have passed through his body, splitting the heart in twain. Instead, the point did not appear to penetrate even an inch! As it touched, there came a sound like the chinking of coin in a purse, with simultaneously the snap of a breaking blade, and the young Irishman was seen standing as in a trance of astonishment, in his hand but the half of a sword, the other half gleaming amongst the grass at his feet.

It seemed a mischance, fatal to Florence Kearney, and only the veriest dastard would have taken advantage of it. But this Santander was, and once more drawing back, and bringing his blade to *tierce*, he was rushing on his now defenceless antagonist, when Crittenden called "Foul play!" at the same time springing forward to prevent it.

His interference, however, would have been too late, and in another instant the young Irishman would have been stretched lifeless along the sward, but for a second individual who had watched the foul play—one who had been suspecting it all along. The sword of Santander seen flying off, as if struck out of his grasp, and his arm dropping by his side, with blood pouring from the tips of his fingers, were all nearly simultaneous incidents, as also the crack of a rifle and a cloud of blue smoke suddenly spurting up over one of the carriages, and half-concealing the colossal figure of Cris Rock, still seated on the box. Out of that cloud came a cry in the enraged voice of the Texan, with words which made all plain—

"Ye darned Creole cuss! Take that for a treetur an' a cowart! Strip the skunk! He's got sumthin' steely under his shirt; I heerd the chink o' it."

Saying which he bounded down from the box, sprang over the water-ditch, and rushed on towards the spot occupied by the combatants.

In a dozen strides he was in their midst, and before either of the two seconds, equally astonished, could interfere, he had caught Santander by the throat, and tore open the breast of his shirt!

Underneath was then seen another shirt, not flannel, nor yet linen or cotton, but link-and-chain steel!

Chapter Eight
A Disgraced Duellist

Impossible to describe the scene which followed, or the expression upon the faces of those men who stood beside Santander. The Texan, strong as he was big, still kept hold of him, though now at arm's length; in his grasp retaining the grown man with as much apparent ease as though it were but a child. And there, sure enough, under the torn flannel shirt, all could see a doublet of chain armour, impenetrable to sword's point as plate of solid steel.

Explanation this of why Carlos Santander was so ready to take the field in a duel, and had twice left his antagonist lifeless upon it. It explained also why, when leaping across the water-ditch, he had dropped so heavily upon the farther bank. Weighted as he was, no wonder.

By this time the two doctors, with the pair of hackney-drivers, seeing that something had turned up out of the common course, parting from the carriages, had also come upon the ground; the jarveys, in sympathy with Cris Rock, crying, "Shame!" In the Crescent City even a cabman has something of chivalry in his nature—the surroundings teach and invite it—and now the detected scoundrel seemed without a single friend. For he—hitherto acting as such, seeing the imposture, which had been alike practised on himself, stepped up to his principal, and looking him scornfully in the face, hissed out the word "*Lâche!*"

Then turning to Kearney and Crittenden he added—

"Let that be my apology to you, gentlemen. If you're not satisfied with it, I'm willing and ready to take his place—with either of you."

"It's perfectly satisfactory, monsieur," frankly responded the Kentuckian, "so far as I'm concerned. And I think I may say as much for Captain Kearney."

"Indeed, yes," assented the Irishman, adding: "We absolve you, sir, from all blame. It's evident you knew nothing of that shining panoply till now;" as he spoke, pointing to the steel shirt.

The French-Creole haughtily, but courteously, bowed thanks. Then, facing once more to Santander, and repeating the "*Lâche*" strode silently away from the ground.

They had all mistaken the character of the individual, who, despite a somewhat forbidding face, was evidently a man of honour, as he had proved himself.

"What d'ye weesh me to do wi' him?" interrogated the Texan, still keeping Santander in firm clutch. "Shed we shoot him or hang him?"

"Hang!" simultaneously shouted the two hackney-drivers, who seemed as bitter against the disgraced duellist as if he had "bilked" them of a fare.

"So I say, too," solemnly pronounced the Texan; "shootin's too good for the like o' him; a man capable o' sech a cowardly, murderous trick desarves to die the death o' a dog."

Then, with an interrogating look at Crittenden, he added: "Which is't to be, lootenant?"

"Neither, Cris," answered the Kentuckian. "If I mistake not, the *gentleman* has had enough punishment without either. If he's got so much as a spark of shame or conscience—"

"Conshence!" exclaimed Rock, interrupting. "Sech a skunk don't know the meanin' o' the word. Darn ye!" he continued, turning upon his prisoner, and shaking him till the links in the steel shirt chinked, "I feel as if I ked drive the blade o' my bowie inter ye through them steel fixin's an' all."

And, drawing his knife from its sheath, he brandished it in a menacing manner.

"Don't, Rock! Please don't!" interposed the Kentuckian, Kearney joining in the entreaty. "He's not worth anger, much less revenge. So let him go."

"You're right thar, lootenant," rejoined Rock. "He ain't worth eyther, that's the truth. An' 'twould only be puttin' pisen on the blade o' my knife to smear it wi' his black blood. F'r all, I ain't a-gwine to let him off so easy's all that, unless you an' the captain insists on it. After the warmish work he's had, an' the sweat he's put himself in by the wearin' o' two shirts at a time, I guess he won't be any the worse of a sprinkling o' cold water. So here goes to gie it him."

Saying which, he strode off towards the ditch, half-dragging, half-carrying Santander along with him.

The cowed and craven creature neither made resistance, nor dared. Had he done so, the upshot was obvious. For the Texan's blade, still bared, was shining before his eyes, and he knew that any attempt on his part, either to oppose the latter's intention or escape, would result in having it buried between, his ribs. So, silently, sullenly, he allowed himself to be taken along, not as a lamb to the slaughter, but a wolf, or rather dog, about to be chastised for some malfeasance.

In an instant after, the chastisement was administered by the Texan laying hold of him with both hands, lifting him from off his feet, and then dropping him down into the water-ditch, where, weighted with the steel shirt, he fell with a dead, heavy plunge, going at once to the bottom.

"That's less than your desarvin's," said the Texan, on thus delivering his charge. "An' if it had been left to Cris Rock 'twould 'a been *up*, 'stead o' *down*, he'd 'a sent ye. If iver man desarved hangin', you're the model o' him. Ha—ha—ha! Look at the skunk now!"

The last words, with the laugh preceding them, were elicited by the ludicrous appearance which Santander presented. He had come to the surface again, and, with some difficulty, owing to the encumbrance of his under-shirt, clambered out upon the bank. But not as when he went under. Instead, with what appeared a green cloak over his shoulders, the scum of the stagnant water long collecting undisturbed. The hackney-driver—there was but one now, the other taken off by Duperon, who had hired him, their doctor too—joined with Rock in his laughter, while Kearney, Crittenden, and their own surgeon could not help uniting in the chorus. Never had tragic hero suffered a more comical discomfiture.

He was now permitted to withdraw from the scene of it, a permission of which he availed himself without further delay; first retreating for some distance along the Shell Road, as one wandering and distraught; then, as if seized by a sudden thought, diving into the timbered swamp alongside, and there disappearing.

Soon after the carriage containing the victorious party rattled past; they inside it scarce casting a look to see what had become of Santander. He was nothing to them now, at best only a thing to be a matter of ludicrous remembrance. Nor long remained he in their thoughts; these now reverting to Texas, and their necessity for hastening back to the Crescent City, to make start for "The Land of the Lone Star."

Chapter Nine
A Spartan Band

In ancient days Sparta had its Thermopylae, while in those of modern date Sicily saw a thousand men in scarlet shirts make landing upon her coast, and conquer a kingdom defended by a military force twenty or thirty times their number!

But deeds of heroism are not alone confined to the history of the Old World. That of the New presents us with many pages of a similar kind, and Texas can tell of achievements not surpassed, either in valour or chivalry, by any upon record. Such was the battle of San Jacinto, where the Texans were victorious, though overmatched in the proportion of ten to one: such the defence of Fort Alamo, when the brave Colonel Crockett, now world-known, surrendered up his life, alongside the equally brave "Jim Bowie," he who gave his name to the knife which on that occasion he so efficiently wielded—after a protracted and terrible struggle dropping dead upon a heap of foes who had felt its sharp point and keen edge.

Among the deeds of great renown done by the defenders of the young Republic, none may take higher rank, since none is entitled to it, than that known as the battle of Mier. Though they there lost the day—a defeat due to the incapacity of an ill-chosen leader—they won glory eternal. Every man of them who fell had first killed his foeman—some half a score—while of those who survived there was not one so craven as to cry "Quarter!" The white flag went not up till they were overwhelmed and overpowered by sheer disparity of numbers.

It was a fight at first with rifles and musketry at long range; then closer as the hostile host came crowding in upon them; the bullets sent through windows and loopholed walls—some from the flat parapetted roofs of the houses—till at length it became a conflict hand to hand with knife, sword, and pistol, or guns clubbed—being empty, with no time to reload them—many a Texan braining one antagonist with the butt of his piece after having sent its bullet through the body of another!

Vain all! Brute strength, represented by superior numbers, triumphed over warlike prowess, backed by indomitable courage; and the "Mier

Expedition," from which Texas had expected so much, ended disastrously, though ingloriously; those who survived being made prisoners, and carried off to the capital of Mexico.

Of the Volunteer Corps which composed this ill-fated expedition—and they were indeed all volunteers—none gave better account of itself than that organised in Poydras Street, New Orleans, and among its individual members no man behaved better than he whom they had chosen as their leader. Florence Kearney had justified their choice, and proved true to the trust, as all who outlived that fatal day ever after admitted. Fortunately, he himself was among the survivors; by a like good luck, so too were his first-lieutenant Crittenden and Cris Rock. As at "Fanning's Massacre," so at Mier the gigantic Texan performed prodigies of valour, laying around him, and slaying on all sides, till at length wounded and disabled, like a lion beset by a *chevaux-de-frise* of Caffre assegais, he was compelled to submit. Fighting side by side, with the man he had first taken a fancy to on the Levee of New Orleans, and afterwards became instrumental in making captain of his corps—finding this man to be what he had conjecturally believed and pronounced him—of the "true grit"—Cris Rock now felt for Florence Kearney almost the affection of a father, combined with the grand respect which one gallant soul is ever ready to pay another. Devotion, too, so strong and real, that had the young Irishman called upon him for the greatest risk of his life, in any good or honourable cause, he would have responded to the call without a moment's hesitancy or murmur. Nay, more than risk; he would have laid it down, absolutely, to save that of his cherished leader.

Proof of this was, in point of fact, afforded but a short while after. Any one acquainted with Texan history will remember how the Mier prisoners, while being taken to the city of Mexico, rose upon their guards, and mastering them, made their escape to the mountains around. This occurred at the little town of El Salado, and was caused by the terrible sufferings the captives had endured upon the march, added to many insults and cruelties, to which they had been subjected, not only by the Mexican soldiers, but the officers having them in charge. These had grown altogether insupportable, at El Salado reaching the climax.

It brought about the crisis for a long time accumulating, and which the Texans anticipated. For they had, at every opportunity afforded them, talked over and perfected a plan of escape.

By early daybreak on a certain morning, as their guards were carelessly lounging about an idle hour before continuing that toilsome journey, a signal shout was heard.

"Now, boys, up and at them!" were the words, with some others following, which all well understood—almost a repetition of the famous order of Wellington at Waterloo. And as promptly obeyed; for on hearing it the Texans rushed at the soldiers of the escort, wrenched from them their weapons, and with those fought their way through the hastily-formed ranks of the enemy out into the open country.

So far they had succeeded, though in the end, for most of them, it proved a short and sad respite. Pursued by an overwhelming force—fresh troops drawn from the garrisons in the neighbourhood, added to the late escort so shamefully discomfited, and smarting under the humiliation and defeat— the pursuit carrying them through a country to which they were entire strangers—a district almost uninhabited, without roads, and, worse still, without water,—not strange that all, or nearly all, of them were recaptured, and carried back to El Salado.

Then ensued a scene worthy of being enacted by savages, for little better than savages were those in whose custody they were. Exulting fiend-like over their recapture, at first the word went round that all were to be executed; this being the general wish of their captors. No doubt the deed of wholesale vengeance would have been done, and our hero, Florence Kearney, with his companion, Cris Rock, never more have been heard of; in other words, the novel of the "Free Lances" would not have been written. But among those reckless avengers there were some who knew better than to advocate indiscriminate slaughter. It was "a far cry to Loch Awe," all knew; the Highland loch typified not by Texas, but the United States. But the more knowing ones always knew that, however far, the cry might be heard, and then what the result? No mere band of Texan filibusters, ill-organised, and but poorly equipped, to come across the Rio Grande; instead a well-disciplined army in numbers enough for sure retaliation, bearing the banner of the "Stars and Stripes."

In fine, a more merciful course was determined upon; only *decimation* of the prisoners—every tenth man to suffer death.

There was no word about degrees in their guiltiness—all were alike in this respect—and the fate of each was to be dependent on pure blind chance.

When the retaken escapadoes had been brought back to El Salado, they were drawn up in line of single file, and carefully counted. A helmet, snatched from the head of one of the Dragoons guarding them, was made use of as a ballot-box. Into this were thrown a number of what we call French or kidney beans—the *pijoles* of Mexico—in count corresponding to that of the devoted victims. Of these *pijoles* there are several varieties, distinguishable chiefly by their colour. Two sorts are common, the black and white; and these were chosen to serve as tickets in that dread lottery of life and death. For every nine white beans there was a black one; he who drew black would be shot within the hour!

Into the hard soldier's head-piece, appropriate for such purpose, the beans were dropped, and the drawing done as designed. I, who now write of it long after, can truthfully affirm that never in the history of human kind has there been a grander exhibition of man's courage than was that day given at El Salado. The men who exemplified it were of no particular nation. As a matter of course, the main body of the Texans were of American birth, but among them were also Englishmen, Scotchmen, Irishmen, French, and Germans—even some who spoke Spanish, the language of their captors, now their judges, and about to become their executioners. But when that helmet of horrible contents was carried round, and held before each, not one showed the slightest fear or hesitancy to plunge his hand into it, though knowing that what they should bring up between their fingers might be the sealing of their fate. Many laughed and made laughter among their comrades, by some quaint *jeu d'esprit*. One reckless fellow—no other than Cris Rock—as he fearlessly rattled the beans about, cried aloud—

"Wal, boys, I guess it's the tallest gamblin' I've ever took a hand at. But this child ain't afeerd. I was born to good luck, an' am not likely to go under—jest yet."

The event justified his confidence, as he drew *blank*—not *black*, the fatal colour.

It was now Kearney's turn to undergo the dread ordeal; and, without flinching, he was about to insert his hand into the helmet, when the Texan, seizing hold of it, stayed him.

"No, Cap!" he exclaimed; "I'm wownded, putty bad, as ye see,"—(he had received a lance thrust in their struggle with the Guards)—"an' mayent git over it. Thurfor, your life's worth more'n mine. Besides, my luck's good jest now. So let me take your chance. That's allowed, as these skunks hev sayed themselves."

So it was—a declaration having been made by the officer who presided over the drawing—from humane motives as pretended—that any one who could find a substitute might himself stand clear. A grim mockery it seemed; and yet it was not so; since, besides Cris Rock, more than one courageous fellow proposed the same to comrade and friend—in the case of two brothers the elder one insisting upon it.

Though fully, fervently appreciating the generous offer, Florence Kearney was not the man to avail himself of it.

"Thanks, brave comrade!" he said, with warmth, detaching his hand from the Texan's grasp, and thrusting it into the helmet. "What's left of your life yet is worth more than all mine; and my luck may be good as yours—we'll see."

It proved so, a murmur of satisfaction running along the line as they saw his hand drawn out with a white bear between the fingers.

"Thanks to the Almighty!" joyously shouted the Texan, as he made out the colour. "Both o' us clar o' that scrape, by Job! An' as there ain't no need for me dyin' yet, I mean to live it out, an' git well agin."

And get well he did, despite the long after march, with all its exposures and fatigues; his health and strength being completely restored as he stepped over the threshold, entering within his prison-cell in the city of Mexico.

Chapter Ten
The Acordada

One of the most noted "lions" in the City of Mexico is the prison called La Acordada. Few strangers visit the Mexican capital without also paying a visit to this celebrated penal establishment, and few who enter its gloomy portals issue forth from them without having seen something to sadden the heart, and be ever afterwards remembered with repugnance and pain.

There is, perhaps, no prison in the universal world where one may witness so many, and such a variety of criminals; since there is no crime known to the calendar that has not been committed by some one of the gaol-birds of the Acordada.

Its cells, or cloisters—for the building was once a monastery—are usually well filled with thieves, forgers, ravishers, highway robbers, and a fair admixture of murderers; none appearing cowed or repentant, but boldly brazening it out, and even boasting of their deeds of villainy, fierce and strong as when doing them, save the disabled ones, who suffer from wounds or some loathsome disease.

Nor is all their criminal action suspended inside the prison walls. It is carried on within their cells, and still more frequently in the courtyards of the ancient convent, where they are permitted to meet in common and spend a considerable portion of their time. Here they may be seen in groups, most of them ragged and greasy, squatted on the flags, card-playing—and cheating when they can—now and then quarrelling, but always talking loud and cursing.

Into the midst of this mass of degraded humanity were thrust two of the unfortunate prisoners, taken at the battle of Mier—the two with whom our tale has alone to do.

For reasons that need not be told, most of the captives were excepted from this degradation; the main body of them being carried on through the city to the pleasant suburban village of Tacubaya.

But Florence Kearney and Cris Rock were not among the exceptions; both having been consigned to the horrid pandemonium we have painted.

It was some consolation to them that they were allowed to share the same cell, though they would have liked it better could they have had this all to themselves. As it was, they had not; two individuals being bestowed in it along with them.

It was an apartment of but limited dimensions—about eight feet by ten—the cloister of some ancient monk, who, no doubt, led a jolly enough life of it there, or, if not there, in the refectory outside, in the days when the Acordada was a pleasant place of residence for himself and his cowled companions. For his monastery, as "Bolton Abbey in the olden time," saw many a scene of good cheer, its inmates being no anchorites.

Beside the Texan prisoners, its other occupants now were men of Mexican birth. One of them, under more favourable circumstances, would have presented a fine appearance. Even in his prison garb, somewhat ragged and squalid, he looked the gentleman and something more. For there was that in his air and physiognomy, which proclaimed him no common man. Captivity may hold and make more fierce, but cannot degrade, the lion. And just as a lion in its cage seemed this man in a cell of the Acordada. His face was of the rotund type, bold in its expression, yet with something of gentle humanity, seen when searched for, in the profound depths of a dark penetrating eye. His complexion was a clear olive, such as is common to Mexicans of pure Spanish descent, the progeny of the Conquistadors; his beard and moustache coal-black, as also the thick mass of hair that, bushing out and down over his ears, half concealed them.

Cris Rock "cottoned" to this man on sight. Nor liked him much the less when told he had been a robber! Cris supposed that in Mexico a robber may sometimes be an honest man, or at all events, have taken to the road through some supposed wrong—personal or political. Freebooting is less a crime, or at all events, more easy of extenuation in a country whose chief magistrate himself is a freebooter; and such, at this moment, neither more nor less, was the chief magistrate of Mexico, Don Antonio Lopez de Santa Anna.

Beyond the fact, or it might be only suspicion, that Ruperto Rivas was a robber, little seemed to be known of him among the inmates of the Acordada. He had been there only a short while, and took no part in their vulgar, commonplace ways of killing time; instead, staying within his cell. His name had, however, leaked out, and this brought up in the minds of some of his fellow-prisoners certain reminiscences pointing to him as one of the road fraternity; no common one either, but the chief of a band of "salteadores."

Altogether different was the fourth personage entitled to a share in the cell appropriated to Kearney and Cris Rock; unlike the reputed robber as the Satyr to Hyperion. In short, a contrast of the completest kind, both physically and mentally. No two beings claiming to be of human kind could have presented a greater dissimilarity—being very types of the extreme. Ruperto Rivas, despite the shabby habiliments in which the gaol authorities had arrayed him, looked all dignity and grandeur, while El Zorillo—the little fox, as his prison companions called him—was an epitomised impersonation of wickedness and meanness; not only crooked in soul, but in body—being in point of fact an *enano* or dwarf-hunchback.

Previous to the arrival of those who were henceforth to share their cell, this ill-assorted pair had been kept chained together, as much by way of punishment as to prevent escape. But now, the gaol-governor, as if struck by a comical idea, directed them to be separated, and the dwarf linked to the Texan Colossus—thus presenting a yet more ludicrous contrast of couples—while the ex-captain of the filibusters and the reputed robber were consigned to the same chain.

Of the new occupants of the cloister, Cris Rock was the more disgusted with the situation. His heart was large enough to feel sympathy for humanity in any shape, and he would have pitied his deformed fellow-prisoner, but for a deformity of the latter worse than any physical ugliness; for the Texan soon learnt that the hideous creature, whose couch as well as chain he was forced to share, had committed crimes of the most atrocious nature, among the rest murder! It was, in fact, for this last that he was now in the Acordada—a cowardly murder, too—a case of poisoning. That he still lived was due to the proofs not being legally satisfactory, though no one doubted of his having perpetrated the crime. At first contact with this wretch the Texan had recoiled in horror, without knowing aught of his past. There was that in his face which spoke a history of dark deeds. But when this became known to the new denizens of the cell, the proximity of such a monster was positively revolting to them.

Vengeance itself could not have devised a more effective mode of torture. Cris Rock groaned under it, now and then grinding his teeth and stamping his feet, as if he could have trodden the mis-shapen thing into a still more shapeless mass under the heels of his heavy boots.

For the first two days of their imprisonment in the Acordada neither of the Texans could understand why they were being thus punished—as it were to satisfy some personal spite. None of the other Mier prisoners, of whom several had been brought to the same gaol, were submitted to a like degradation. True, these were also chained two and two; but to one another, and not to Mexican criminals. Why, then, had they alone been made an exception? For their lives neither could tell or guess, though they gave way to every kind of conjecture. It was true enough that Cris Rock had been one of the ringleaders in the rising at El Salado, while the young Irishman had also taken a prominent part in that affair. Still, there were others now in the Acordada who had done the same, receiving treatment altogether different. The attack upon the Guards, therefore, could scarce be the cause of what they were called upon to suffer now; for besides the humiliation of being chained to criminals, they were otherwise severely dealt with. The food set before them was of the coarsest, with a scarcity of it; and more than once the gaoler, whose duty it was to look after them, made mockery of their irksome situation, jesting on the grotesque companionship of the dwarf and giant. As the gaol-governor had shown, on his first having them conveyed to their cells, signs of a special hostility, so did their daily attendant. But for what reason neither Florence Kearney nor his faithful comrade could divine.

They learnt it at length—on the third day after their entrance within the prison. All was explained by the door of their cell being drawn open, exposing to view the face and figure of a man well-known to them. And from both something like a cry escaped, as they saw standing without, by the side of the gaol-governor—Carlos Santander.

Chapter Eleven
A Colonel in Full Feather

Yes; outside the door of their cell was Carlos Santander. And in full war panoply, wearing a magnificent uniform, with a glittering sword by his side, and on his head a cocked hat, surmounted by a *panache* of white ostrich feathers!

To explain his presence there, and in such guise, it is necessary to return upon time and state some particulars of this man's life not yet before the reader. As already said, he was a native of New Orleans, but of Mexican parentage, and regarding himself as a Mexican citizen. Something more than a mere citizen, indeed; as, previous to his encounter with Florence Kearney, he had been for a time resident in Mexico, holding some sort of appointment under that Government, or from the Dictator himself—Santa Anna. What he was doing in New Orleans no one exactly knew, though among his intimates there was an impression that he still served his Mexican master, in the capacity of a secret agent—a sort of *procurador*, or spy. Nor did this suspicion do him wrong: for he was drawing pay from Santa Anna, and doing work for him in the States, which could scarce be dignified with the name of diplomacy. Proof of its vile character is afforded by the action he took among the volunteers in Poydras Street. His presenting himself at their rendezvous, getting enrolled in the corps, and offering as a candidate for the captaincy, were all done under instructions, and with a design which, for wickedness and cold-blooded atrocity, was worthy of Satan himself. Had he succeeded in becoming the leader of this ill-fated band, for them the upshot might have been no worse; though it would not have been better; since it was his intention to betray them to the enemy at the first opportunity that should offer. Thwarted in this intent, knowing he could no longer show his face among the filibusters, even though it were but as a private in the ranks; fearing, furthermore, the shame that awaited him in New Orleans soon as the affair of the steel shirt should get bruited about, he had hastily decamped from that place, and, as we now know, once more made his way to Mexico.

Luckily for him, the shirt, or rather under-shirt, business leaked not out; at least not to reach the ears of any one in the Mexican capital.

Nor, indeed, was it ever much known in New Orleans. His second, Duperon, for his own sake not desiring to make it public, had refrained from speaking of it; and their doctor, a close little Frenchman, controlled by Duperon, remained equally reticent; while all those on the other side— Kearney, Crittenden, Rock and the surgeon—had taken departure for Texas on the very day of the duel; from that time forward having "other fish to fry."

But there were still the two hackney-drivers, who, no doubt, had they stayed in the Crescent City in pursuit of their daily avocation, would have given notoriety to an occurrence curious as it was scandalous.

It chanced, however, that both the jarveys were Irishmen; and suddenly smitten with warlike aspirations—either from witnessing the spectacle of the duel, or the gallant behaviour of their young countryman—on that same day dropped the ribbons, and, taking to a musket instead, wore among the men who composed the ill-started expedition which came to grief on the Rio Grande.

So, for the time, Carlos Santander had escaped the brand of infamy due to his dastardly act.

His reappearance on the scene in such grand garb needs little explanation. A fairly brave and skilled soldier, a vainer man than General Antonio Lopez de Santa Anna never wore sword, and one of his foibles was to see himself surrounded by a glittering escort. The officers of his staff were very peacocks in their gaudy adornment, and as a rale, the best-looking of them were his first favourites. Santander, on returning to Mexico, was appointed one of his aides-de-camp, and being just the sort—a showy fellow—soon rose to rank; so that the defeated candidate for a captaincy of Texan Volunteers, was now a colonel in the Mexican Army, on the personal staff of its Commander-in-Chief.

Had Florence Kearney and Cris Rock but known they were to meet this man in Mexico—could they have anticipated seeing him, as he was now, at the door of their prison-cell—their hearts would have been fainter as they toiled along the weary way, and perchance in that lottery of life and death they might have little cared whether they drew black or white.

At the sight of him there rose up all at once in their recollection that scene upon the Shell Road; the Texan vividly recalling how he had ducked the caitiff in the ditch, as how he looked after crawling out upon the bank— mud bedraggled and covered with the viscous scum,—in strange contrast to his splendid appearance now! And Kearney well remembered the same, noting in addition a scar on Santander's cheek—he had himself given— which the latter vainly sought to conceal beneath whiskers since permitted to grow their full length and breadth.

These remembrances were enough to make the heart of the captive Irishman beat quick, if it did not quail; while that of the Texan had like reason to throb apprehensively.

Nor could they draw any comfort from the expression on Santander's face. Instead, they but read there what they might well believe to be their death sentence. The man was smiling, but it was the smile of Lucifer in triumph—mocking, malignant, seeming to say, without spoken word but, for all that, emphatically and with determination—

"I have you in my power, and verily you shall feel my vengeance."

They could tell it was no accident had brought him thither no duty of prison inspection—but the fiendish purpose to flaunt his grandeur before their eyes, and gloat over the misery he knew it would cause them. And his presence explained what had hitherto been a puzzle to them—why they two were being made an exception among their captive comrades, and thrown into such strange fellowship. It must have been to humiliate them; as, indeed, they could now tell by a certain speech which the gaol-governor addressed to Santander, as the cell door turned back upon its hinges.

"There they are, Señor Colonel! As you see, I've had them coupled according to orders. What a well-matched pair!" he added, ironically, as his eyes fell upon Cris Rock and the hunchback. "*Ay Dios*! It's a sight to draw laughter from the most sober-sided recluse that ever lodged within these walls. Ha! ha! ha!"

It drew this from Carlos Santander; who, relishing the jest, joined in the "ha! ha!" till the old convent rang with their coarse ribaldry.

Chapter Twelve
"Do your darndest"

During all this time—only a few seconds it was—the four men within the cell preserved silence; the dwarf, as the door alone was drawn open, having said to the gaol-governor: "*Buenas Dias Excellenza*! you're coming to set us free, aren't you?"

A mere bit of jocular bravado; for, as might be supposed, the deformed wretch could have little hope of deliverance, save by the gallows, to which he had actually been condemned. A creature of indomitable pluck, however, this had not so far frightened him as to hinder jesting—a habit to which he was greatly given. Besides, he did not believe he was going to the *garota*. Murderer though he was, he might expect pardon, could he only find money sufficient to pay the price, and satisfy the conscience of those who had him in keeping.

His question was neither answered nor himself taken notice of; the attention of those outside being now directed upon the other occupants of the cell. Of these only two had their faces so that they could be seen. The third, who was the reputed robber, kept his turned towards the wall, the opened door being behind his back; and this attitude he preserved, not being called upon to change it till Santander had closed his conversation with Cris Rock and Kearney. He had opened it in a jaunty, jeering tone, saying—

"Well, my brave Filibusters! Is this where you are? *Caspita*! In a queer place and queer company, too! Not so nice, Señor Don Florencio, as that you used to keep in the Crescent City. And you, my Texan Colossus! I take it you don't find the atmosphere of the Acordada quite so pleasant as the fresh breezes of prairie-land, eh?"

He paused, as if to note the effect of his irony; then continued—

"So this is the ending of the grand Mier Expedition, with the further invasion of Mexico! Well, you've found your way to its capital, anyhow, if you haven't fought it. And now you're here, what do you expect, pray?"

"Not much o' good from sich a scoundrel as you," responded Rock, in a tone of reckless defiance.

"What! No good from me! An old acquaintance—friend, I ought rather to call myself, after the little scene that passed between us on the shores of Pontchartrain. Come, gentlemen! Being here among strangers you should think yourselves fortunate in finding an old comrade of the filibustering band; one owing you so many obligations. Ah! well; having the opportunity now, I shall try my best to wipe out the indebtedness."

"You kin do your darndest," rejoined Rock in the same sullen tone. "We don't look for marcy at your hands nosomever. It ain't in ye; an if 't war, Cris Rock 'ud scorn to claim it. So ye may do yur crowing on a dunghill, whar there be cocks like to be scared at it. Thar ain't neery one o' that sort hyar."

Santander was taken aback by this unlooked-for rebuff. He had come to the Acordada to indulge in the luxury of a little vapouring over his fallen foes, whom he knew to be there, having been informed of all that had befallen them from Mier up to Mexico. He expected to find them cowed, and eager to crave life from him; which he would no more have granted than to a brace of dogs that had bitten him. But so far from showing any fear, both prisoners looked a little defiant; the Texan with the air of a caged wolf seeming ready to tear him if he showed but a step over the threshold of the cell.

"Oh! very well," he returned, making light of what Rock had said. "If you won't accept favours from an old, and, as you know, tried friend, I must leave you so without them. But," he added, addressing himself more directly to Kearney:

"You, Señor Irlandes—surely you won't be so unreasonable?"

"Carlos Santander," said the young Irishman, looking his *ci-devant* adversary full in the face, "as I proved you not worth thrusting with my sword, I now pronounce you not worth words—even to call you coward,— though that you are from the crown of your head to the soles of your feet. Not even brave when your body is encased in armour. Dastard! I defy you."

Though manifestly stung by the reminder, Santander preserved his coolness. He had this, if not courage—at least a knack of feigning it. But again foiled in the attempt to humble the enemy, and, moreover, dreading exposure in the eyes of the gaol-governor—an old *militario*—should the story of the *steel shirt* come out in the conversation, he desisted questioning the *Tejanos*. Luckily for him none of the others there understood English— the language he and the Texans had used in their brief, but sharp exchange of words. Now addressing himself to the governor, he said—

"As you perceive, Señor Don Pedro, these two gentlemen are old acquaintances of mine, whose present unfortunate position I regret, and would gladly relieve. Alas! I fear the law will take its course."

At which commiserating remark Don Pedro smiled grimly; well aware of the sort of interest Colonel Santander took in the pair of prisoners committed to his care. For the order so to dispose of them he knew to have come from Santander himself! It was not his place, nor was he the kind of man to inquire into motives; especially when these concerned his superiors. Santander was an officer on the staff of the Dictator, besides being a favourite at Court. The gaol-governor knew it, and was subservient. Had he been commanded to secretly strangle the two men thus specially placed in his charge, or administer poison to them, he would have done it without pity or protest. The cruel tyrant who had made him governor of the Acordada knew his man, and had already, as rumour said, with history to confirm it, more than once availed himself of this means to get rid of enemies, personal or political.

During all this interlude the robber had maintained his position and silence, his face turned to the blank wall of the cloister, his back upon all the others. What his motive for this was neither of the Texans could tell; and in all likelihood Santander knew not himself any more who the man was. But his behaviour, from its very strangeness, courted inquiry; and seemingly struck with it, the staff-colonel, addressing himself to the gaol-governor, said—

"By the way, Don Pedro, who is your prisoner, who makes the fourth in this curious quartette? He seems shy about showing his face, which would argue it an ugly one like my own."

A bit of badinage in which Carlos Santander oft indulged. He knew that he was anything but ill-favoured as far as face went.

"Only a gentleman of the road—*un salteador*" responded the governor.

"An interesting sort of individual then," said Santander. "Let me scan his countenance, and see whether it be of the true brigand type—a Mazaroni or Diavolo."

So saying, he stepped inside the cell, and passed on till he could see over the robber's shoulder, who now slightly turning his head, faced towards him. Not a word was exchanged between the two, but from the looks it was clear they were old acquaintances, Santander starting as he recognised the other; while his glance betrayed a hostility strong and fierce as that felt for either Florence Kearney or the Texan. A slight exclamation, involuntary, but telling of anger, was all that passed his lips as his eyes met a pair of other eyes which seemed to pierce his very heart.

He stayed not for more; but turning upon his heel, made direct for the door. Not to reach it, however, without interruption. In his hurry to be gone, he stumbled over the legs of the Texan, that stretched across the cell, nearly from side to side. Angered by the obstruction, he gave them a spiteful kick, then passed on outward. By good fortune fast and far out of reach, otherwise Cris Rock, who sprang to his feet, and on for the entrance, jerking the dwarf after, would in all probability there and then have taken his life.

As it was, the gaol-governor, seeing the danger, suddenly shut the cloister door, so saving it.

"Jest as I've been tellin' ye all along, Cap," coolly remarked Rock, as the slammed door ceased to make resonance; "we shed ha' hanged the skunk, or shot him thar an' then on the Shell Road. 'Twar a foolish thing lettin' him out o' that ditch when I had him in it. Darn the luck o' my not drownin' him outright! We're like to sup sorrow for it now."

Chapter Thirteen
The Exiles Returned

Of the *dramatis personae* of our tale, already known to our reader, Carlos Santander, Florence Kearney, and Cris Rock were not the only ones who had shifted residence from the City of New Orleans to that of Mexico. Within the months intervening two others had done the same—these Don Ignacio Valverde and his daughter. The banished exile had not only returned to his native land, but his property had been restored to him, and himself reinstated in the favour of the Dictator.

More still, he had now higher rank than ever before; since he had been appointed a Minister of State.

For the first upward step on this progressive ladder of prosperity Don Ignacio owed all to Carlos Santander. The handsome *aide-de-camp*, having the ear of his chief, found little difficulty in getting the ban removed, with leave given the refugee—criminal only in a political sense—to come back to his country.

The motive will easily be guessed. Nothing of either friendship or humanity actuated Santander. Alone the passion of love; which had to do not with Don Ignacio—but his daughter. In New Orleans he himself dared no longer live, and so could no more see Luisa Valverde there. Purely personal then; a selfish love, such as he could feel, was the motive for his intercession with the political chief of Mexico to pardon the political criminal. But if he had been the means of restoring Don Ignacio to his country, that was all. True, there was the restitution of the exile's estates, but this followed as a consequence on reinstatement in his political rights. The after honours and emoluments—with the appointment to a seat in the Cabinet—came from the Chief of the State, Santa Anna himself. And his motive for thus favouring a man who had lately, and for long, been his political foe was precisely the same as that which actuated Carlos Santander. The Dictator of Mexico, as famed for his gallantries in love as his gallantry in war—and indeed somewhat more—had looked upon Luisa Valverde, and "saw that she was fair."

For Don Ignacio himself, as the recipient of these favours, much may be said in extenuation. Banishment from one's native land, with loss of property, and separation from friends as from best society; condemned to live in another land, where all these advantages are unattainable, amidst a companionship uncongenial; add to this the necessity of work, whether mental or physical toil, to support life—the *res augustae domi*; sum up all these, and you have the history of Don Ignacio Valverde during his residence in New Orleans. He bore all patiently and bravely, as man could and should. For all he was willing—and it cannot be wondered at that he was—when the day came, and a letter reached him bearing the State seal of the Mexican Republic—for its insignia were yet unchanged—to say that he had received pardon, and could return home.

He knew the man who had procured it for him—Carlos Santander—and had reason to suspect something of the motive. But the mouth of a gift horse must not be too narrowly examined; and Santander, ever since that night when he behaved so rudely in Don Ignacio's house, had been chary in showing his face. In point of fact, he had made but one more visit to the Callé de Casa Calvo here, presenting himself several days after the duel with a patch of court plaister on his cheek, and his arm in a sling. An invalid, interesting from the cause which made him an invalid, he gave his own account of it, knowing there was but little danger of its being contradicted; Duperon's temper, he understood, with that of the French doctor, securing silence. The others were all G.T.T. (gone to Texas), the hack-drivers, as he had taken pains to assure himself. No fear, therefore, of what he alleged getting denial or being called in question.

It was to the effect that he had fought Florence Kearney, and given more and worse wounds than he himself had received—enough of them, and sufficiently dangerous, to make it likely that his adversary would not long survive.

He did not say this to Luisa Valverde—only to her father. When she heard it second hand, it came nigh killing her. But then the informant had gone away—perhaps luckily for himself—and could not further be questioned. When met again in Mexico, months after, he told the same tale. He had no doubt, however, that his duelling adversary, so terribly gashed as to be in danger of dying, still lived. For an American paper which gave an account of the battle of Mier, had spoken of Captain Kearney in eulogistic terms, while not giving his name in the death list; this Santander had read. The presumption, therefore, was of Kearney being among the survivors.

Thus stood things in the city of Mexico at the time the Mier prisoners entered it, as relates to the persons who have so far found place in our story—Carlos Santander, a colonel on the staff of the Dictator; Don Ignacio Valverde, a Minister of State; his daughter, a reigning belle of society, with no aspirations therefor, but solely on account of her beauty; Florence Kearney, late Captain of the Texan filibusters, with Cris Rock, guide, scout, and general skirmisher of the same—these last shut up in a loathsome prison, one linked leg to leg with a robber, the other sharing the chain of a murderer, alike crooked in soul as in body!

That for the Texan prisoners there was yet greater degradation in store—one of them, Kearney, was made aware the moment after the gaol-governor had so unceremoniously shut the door of their cell. The teaching of Don Ignacio in New Orleans had not been thrown away upon him; and this, with the practice since accruing through conversation with the soldiers of their escort, had made him almost a master of the Spanish tongue.

Carlos Santander either did not think of this, or supposed the cloister door too thick to permit of speech in the ordinary tone passing through it. It did, notwithstanding; what he said outside to the governor reaching the Irishman's ear, and giving him a yet closer clue to that hitherto enigma—the why he and Cris Rock had been cast into a common gaol, among the veriest and vilest of malefactors.

The words of Santander were—

"As you see, Señor Don Pedro, the two Tejanos are old acquaintances of mine. I met them not in Texas, but the United States—New Orleans—where we had certain relations; I need not particularise you. Only to say that both the gentlemen left me very much in their debt; and I now wish, above all things, to wipe out the score. I hope I may count upon you to help me!"

There could be no mistaking what he meant. Anything but a repayal of friendly services, in the way of gratitude; instead, an appeal to the gaol-governor to assist him in some scheme of vengeance. So the latter understood it, as evinced by his rejoinder—

"Of course you can, Señor Colonel. Only say what you wish done. Your commands are sufficient authority for me."

"Well," said Santander, after an interval apparently spent in considering, "as a first step, I wish you to give these gentlemen an airing in the street; not alone the Tejanos, but all four."

"*Caspita!*" exclaimed the governor, with a look of feigned surprise. "They ought to be thankful for that."

"They won't, however. Not likely; seeing their company, and the occupation I want them put at."

"Which is?"

"A little job in the *zancas*!"

"In which street?"

"The Callé de Plateros. I observe that its stones are up."

"And when?"

"To-morrow—at midday. Have them there before noon, and let them be kept until night, or, at all events, till the procession has passed. Do you quite understand me?"

"I think I do, Señor Colonel. About their *jewellery*—is that to be on?"

"Every link of it. I want them to be coupled, just as they are now—dwarf to giant, and the two grand gentlemen together."

"*Bueno*! It shall be done."

So closed the curious dialogue, or, if continued, what came after it did not reach the ears of Florence Kearney; they who conversed having sauntered off beyond his hearing. When he had translated what he heard to Cris Rock, the latter, like himself, was uncertain as to what it meant. Not so either of their prison companions, who had likewise listened to the conversation outside—both better comprehending it.

"*Bueno*, indeed!" cried the dwarf, echoing the gaol-governor's exclamation. "It shall be done. Which means that before this time to-morrow, we'll all four of us be up to our middle in mud. Won't that be nice? Ha! ha! ha!"

And the imp laughed, as though, instead of something repulsive, he expected a pleasure of the most enjoyable kind.

Chapter Fourteen
On the Azotea

In the city of Mexico the houses are flat-roofed, the roof bearing the name of *azotea*. A parapetted wall, some three or four feet in height, runs all round to separate those of the adjacent houses from one another when they chance to be on the same level, and also prevent falling off. Privacy, besides, has to do with this protective screen; the azotea being a place of almost daily resort, if the weather be fine, and a favourite lounging place, where visitors are frequently received. This peculiarity in dwelling-house architecture has an oriental origin, and is still common among the Moors, as all round the Mediterranean. Strange enough, the Conquistadors found something very similar in the New World—conspicuously among the Mexicans—where the Aztecan houses were flat or terrace-topped. Examples yet exist in Northern and New Mexico, in the towns of the Pecos Zuñis, and Moquis. It is but natural, therefore, that the people who now call themselves Mexicans should have followed a pattern thus furnished them by their ancestry in both hemispheres.

Climate has much to do with this sort of roof, as regards its durability; no sharp frosts or heavy snows being there to affect it. Besides, in no country in the world is out-door life more enjoyable than in Mexico, the rainy months excepted; and in them the evenings are dry. Still another cause contributes to make the roof of a Mexican house a pleasant place of resort. Sea-coal and its smoke are things there unknown; indeed chimneys, if not altogether absent, are few and far between; such as there are being inconspicuous. In the *siempre-verano* (eternal spring) of Anahuac there is no call for them; a wood fire here and there kindled in some sitting-room being a luxury of a special kind, indulged in only by the very delicate or very rich. In the kitchens, charcoal is the commodity employed, and as this yields no visible sign, the outside atmosphere is preserved pure and cloudless as that which overhung the Hesperides.

A well-appointed azotea is provided with pots containing shrubs and evergreen plants; some even having small trees, as the orange, lime, camellia, ferns, and palms; while here and there one is conspicuous by a *mirador* (belvedere) arising high above the parapet to afford a better view of the surrounding country.

It would be difficult to find landscape more lovely, or more interesting, than that which surrounds the city of Mexico. Look in what direction one will, the eye is furnished with a feast. Plains, verdant and varied in tint, from the light green of the *milpas* (young maize), to the more sombre *maguey* plants, which, in large plantations (magueyals), occupy a considerable portion of the surface; fields of *chili* pepper and frijoles (kidney beans); here and there wide sheets of water between, glistening silver-like under the sun; bounding all a periphery of mountains, more than one of their summits white with never-melting snow—the grandest mountains, too, since they are the Cordilleras of the Sierra Madre or main Andean chain, which here parted by some Plutonic caprice, in its embrace the beautiful valley of Mexico, elevated more than seven thousand feet above the level of the sea.

Surveying it from any roof in the city itself, the scene is one to delight the eye and gladden the heart. And yet on the azotea of a certain house, or rather in the *mirador* above it, stood a young lady, who looked over it without delight in her eye or gladness in her heart. Instead, the impression upon her countenance told of thoughts that, besides being sad, dwelt not on the landscape or its beauties.

Luisa Valverde it was, thinking of another land, beautiful too, where she had passed several years in exile; the last of them marked by an era the sweetest and happiest of her life. For it was there she first loved; Florence Kearney being he who had won her heart. And the beloved one—where was he now? She knew not; did not even know whether he still lived. He had parted from her without giving any clue, though it gave pain to her—ignorant of the exigencies which had ruled his sudden departure from New Orleans. He had told her, however, of his becoming captain of the volunteer band; which, as she soon after became aware, had proceeded direct to Texas. Furthermore, she had heard all about the issue of the ill-fated expedition; of the gallant struggle made by the men composing it, with the havoc caused in their ranks; of the survivors being brought on to the city of Mexico, and the cruel treatment they had been submitted to on the march; of their daring attempt to escape from the Guards, its successful issue for a time, till their sufferings among the mountains compelled them to a second surrender—in short, everything that had happened to that brave band of which her lover was one of the leaders.

She had been in Mexico throughout all this; for shortly after the departure of the volunteers for Orleans, her father had received the pardon we have spoken of. And there she had been watching the Mier Expedition through every step of its progress, eagerly collecting every scrap of information relating to it published in the Mexican papers; with anxious heart, straining her ears over the lists of killed and wounded. And when at length the account came of the shootings at El Salado, apprehensively as ever scanned she that death-roll of nigh twenty names—the *decimated*; not breathing freely until she had reached the last, and saw that no more among these was his she feared to find.

So far her researches were, in a sense, satisfactory. Still, she was not satisfied. Neither to read or hear word of him—that seemed strange; was so in her way of thinking. Such a hero as he, how could his name be hidden? Gallant deeds were done by the Tejanos, their Mexican enemies admitted it. Surely in these Don Florencio had taken part, and borne himself bravely? Yes, she was sure of that. But why had he not been mentioned? And where was he now?

The last question was that which most frequently occupied her mind, constantly recurring. She could think of but one answer to it; this saddening enough. He might never have reached the Rio Grande, but perished on the way. Perhaps his life had come to an inglorious though not ignominious end—by disease, accident, or other fatality—and his body might now be lying in some lonely spot of the prairies, where his marching comrades had hastily buried it.

More than once had Luisa Valverde given way to such a train of reflection during the months after her return to Mexico. They had brought pallor to her cheeks and melancholy into her heart. So much, that not all the honours to which her father had been restored—not all the compliments paid to herself, nor the Court gaieties in which she was expected to take part—could win her from a gloom that seemed likely to become settled on her soul.

Chapter Fifteen
Waiting and Watching

As a rule, people of melancholy temperament, or with a sorrow at the heart, give way to it within doors in the privacy of their own apartments. The daughter of Don Ignacio had been more often taught to assuage hers upon the house-top, to which she was accustomed to ascend daily, staying there for hours alone. For this she had opportunity; her father, busied with State affairs, spending most of his time—at least during the diurnal hours—at Government headquarters in the *Palacio*.

On this day, however, Luisa Valverde mounted up to the azotea with feelings, and under an impulse, very different from that hitherto actuating her. Her behaviour, too, was different. When she made her way up and took stand inside the mirador, her eyes, instead of wandering all around, or resting dreamily on the landscape, with no care for its attractions, were turned in a particular direction, and became fixed upon a single point. This was where the road, running from the city to Tacubaya, alongside the aqueduct of Chapultepec, parts from the latter, diverging abruptly to the left. Beyond this point the causeway, carried on among maguey plants, and Peruvian pepper trees, cannot be seen from the highest house-top in the city.

Why on this day, more than any other, did the young lady direct her glance to the bend in the road, there keeping it steadfast? For what reason was the expression upon her countenance so different from that of other days? No listless look now; instead, an earnest eager gaze, as though she expected to see some one whose advent was of the greatest interest to her. It could only be the coming of some one, as one going would have been long since visible by the side of the aqueduct.

And one she did expect to come that way; no grand cavalier on prancing steed, but a simple pedestrian—in short, her own servant. She had sent him on an errand to Tacubaya, and was now watching for, and awaiting his return. It was the nature of his errand which caused her to look for him so earnestly.

On no common business had he been despatched, but one of a confidential character, and requiring tact in its execution. But José, a *mestizo* whom she had commissioned, possessed this, besides having her confidence, and she had no fear of his betraying her. Not that it was a life or death matter; only a question of delicacy. For his errand was to inquire, whether among the Texan prisoners taken to Tacubaya one was called Florence Kearney.

As it was now the third day after their arrival in Mexico, it may be wondered why the young lady had not sought this information before. The explanation is easy. Her father owned a country house in the environs of San Augustine, some ten miles from the city; and there staying she had only the day before heard that the captive train, long looked-for, had at length arrived. Soon as hearing it, she had hastened her return to town, and was now taking steps to ascertain whether her lover still lived.

She did not think of making inquiry at the Acordada, though a rumour had reached her that some of the prisoners were there. But surely not Don Florencio! If alive, it was not likely he would be thus disgraced: at least she could not believe it. Little dreamt she of the malice that was moving, and in secret, to degrade in her eyes the man who was uppermost in her thoughts.

And as little suspected she when one of the house domestics came upon the azotea and handed her a large ornamental envelope, bearing the State arms, that it was part of the malignant scheme.

Breaking it open she drew out an embossed and gilded card—a ticket. It came from the Dictator, inviting Doña Luisa Valverde to be present in a grand procession, which was to take place on the following day; intimating, moreover, that one of the State carriages would be at the disposal of herself and party.

There were but few ladies in the city of Mexico who would not have been flattered by such an invitation; all the more from the card bearing the name, Antonio Lopez de Santa Anna, signed by himself, with the added phrase "con estima particular."

But little cared she for the flattery. Rather did it cause her a feeling of disgust, with something akin to fear. It was not the first time for the ruler of Mexico to pay compliments and thus press his attentions upon her.

Soon as glanced over, she let the despised thing fall, almost flinging it at her feet; and once more bent her eyes upon the Tacubaya Road, first carrying her glance along the side of the aqueduct to assure herself that her messenger had not in the meanwhile rounded the corner.

He had not, and she continued to watch impatiently; the invitation to ride in the State carriage being as much out of her mind as though she had never received it.

Not many minutes longer before being intruded on. This time, however, by no domestic; instead a lady—like herself, young and beautiful, but beauty of an altogether different style. Though of pure Spanish descent, Luisa Valverde was a *güera*; her complexion bright, with hair of sunny hue. Such there are in Mexico, tracing their ancestry to the shores of Biscay's famous bay.

She who now appeared upon the azotea was dark; her skin showing a tinge of golden brown, with a profusion of black hair plaited and coiled as a coronet around her head. A crayon-like shading showed upon her upper lip—which on that of a man would have been termed a moustache—rendering whiter by contrast teeth already of dazzling whiteness; while for the same reason, the red upon her cheeks was of the deep tint of a damask rose. The tones of all, however, were in perfect harmony; and distributed over features of the finest mould produced a face in which soft feminine beauty vied with a sort of savage picturesqueness, making it piquantly attractive.

It was altogether a rare bewitching face; part of its witchery being due to the *raza Andalusiana*—and beyond that the Moriscan—but as much of it coming from the ancient blood of Anahuac—possibly from the famed Malinche herself. For the young lady delineated was the Condes Almonté—descended from one of Conquistadors who had wedded an Aztec princess—the beautiful Ysabel Almonté whose charms were at the time the toast of every *cercle* in Mexico.

Chapter Sixteen
A Mutual Misapprehension

Luisa Valverde and Ysabel Almonté were fast friends—so fondly intimate that scarcely a day passed without their seeing one another and exchanging confidences. They lived in the same street; the Condesa having a house of her own, though nominally owned by her grand-aunt and guardian. For, besides being beautiful and possessed of a title—one of the few still found in Mexico, relics of the old *régime*—Ysabel Almonté was immensely rich; had houses in the city, *haciendas* in the country, property everywhere. She had a will of her own as well, and spent her wealth according to her inclinations, which were all on the side of generosity, even to caprice. By nature a lighthearted, joyous creature, gay and merry, as one of the bright birds of her country, it was a rare thing to see sadness upon her face. And yet Luisa Valverde, looking down from the mirador, saw that now. There was a troubled expression upon it, excitement in her eyes, attitude, and gestures, while her bosom rose and fell in quick pulsations. True, she had run up the *escalera*—a stair of four flights—without pause or rest; and that might account for her laboured breathing. But not for the flush on her cheek, and the sparkle in her eyes. These came from a different cause, though the same one which had carried her up the long stairway without pausing to take breath.

She had not enough now left to declare it; but stood panting and speechless.

"*Madre de Dios*!" exclaimed her friend in an accent of alarm. "What is it, Ysabel?"

"*Madre de Dios*! I say too," gasped the Condesa. "Oh, Luisita! what do you think?"

"What?"

"They've taken him—they have him in prison!"

"He lives then—still lives! Blessed be the Virgin!"

Saying which Luisa Valverde crossed her arms over her breast, and with eyes raised devotionally towards heaven, seemed to offer up a mute, but fervent thanksgiving.

"Still lives!" echoed the Condesa, with a look of mingled surprise and perplexity.

"Of course he does; surely you did not think he was dead!"

"Indeed I knew not what to think—so long since I saw or heard of him. Oh, I'm so glad he's here, even though in a prison; for while there's life there's hope."

By this the Condesa had recovered breath, though not composure of countenance. Its expression alone was changed from the look of trouble to one of blank astonishment. What could her friend mean? Why glad of his being in a prison? For all the while she was thinking of a *him*.

"Hope!" she ejaculated again as an echo, then remaining silent, and looking dazed-like.

"Yes, Ysabel; I had almost despaired of him. But are you sure they have him here in prison? I was in fear that he had been killed in battle, or died upon the march, somewhere in those great prairies of Texas—"

"*Carramba!*" interrupted the young Countess, who, free of speech, was accustomed to interlarding it with her country forms of exclamation. "What's all this about prairies and Texas? So far as I know, Ruperto was never there in his life."

"Ruperto!" echoed the other, the joy which had so suddenly lit up her features as suddenly returning to shadow. "I thought you were speaking of Florencio."

They understood each other now. Long since had their love secrets been mutually confessed; and Luisa Valverde needed no telling who Ruperto was. Independent of what she had lately learned from the Condesa, she knew him to be a gentleman of good family, a soldier of some reputation; but who—as once her own father—had the misfortune to belong to the party now out of power; many of them in exile, or retired upon their estates in the country—for the time taking no part in politics. As for himself, he had not been lately seen in the city of Mexico, though it was said he was still in the country; as rumour had it, hiding away somewhere among the mountains. And rumour went further, even to the defiling of his fair name. There were reports of his having become a robber, and that, under another name, he was now chief of a band of *salteadores*, whose deeds were oft heard of on the Acapulco Road, where this crosses the mountains near that place of many murders—the Cruz del Marques.

Nothing of this sinister tale, however, had reached the ears of Don Ignacio's daughter. Nor till that day—indeed that very hour—had she, more interested in him, heard aught of it. Hence much of the wild excitement under which she was labouring.

"Forgive me, Ysabel!" said her friend, opening her arms, and receiving the Countess in sympathetic embrace; "forgive me for the mistake I have made."

"Nay, 'tis I who should ask forgiveness," returned the other, seeing the misapprehension her words had caused, with their distressing effect. "I ought to have spoken plainer. But you know how much my thoughts have been dwelling on dear Ruperto."

She did know, or should, judging by herself, and how hers had been dwelling on dear Florencio.

"But, Ysabel: you say they made him a prisoner! Who has done that, and why?"

"The soldiers of the State. As to why, you can easily guess. Because he belongs to the party of Liberals. That's why, and nothing else. But they don't say so. I've something more to tell you. Would you believe it, Luisita, that they accuse him of being a *salteador*?"

"I can believe him accused of it—some of those in power now are wicked enough for anything—but not guilty. You remember we were acquainted with Don Ruperto, before that sad time when we were compelled to leave the country. I should say he would be the last man to stain his character by becoming a robber."

"The very last man! Robber indeed! My noble Ruperto the purest of patriots, purer than any in this degenerate land. *Ay-de-mi!*"

"Where did they take him, and when?"

"Somewhere near San Augustin, and I think, several days ago, though I've only just heard of it."

"Strange that. As you know, I've been staying at San Augustin for the last week or more; and there was no word of such a thing there."

"Not likely there would be; it was all done quietly. Don Ruperto has been living out that way up in the mountains, hiding, if you choose to call it. I know where, but no matter. Too brave to be cautious he had come down to San Augustin. Some one betrayed him, and going back he was waylaid by the soldiers, surrounded, and made prisoner. There must have been a whole host of them, else they'd never have taken him so easily. I'm sure they wouldn't and couldn't."

"And where is he now, Ysabel?"

"In prison, as I've told you."

"But what prison?"

"That's just what I'm longing to know. All I've ye heard is that he's in a prison under the accusation of being a highwayman. *Santissima!*" she added, angrily stamping her tiny foot on the tesselated flags. "They who accuse him shall rue it. He shall be revenged on them. I'll see justice done him myself. Ah! that will I, though it costs me all I'm worth. Only to think—Ruperto a robber! My Ruperto! *Valga me Dios!*"

By this, the two had mounted up into the mirador—the Señorita Valverde having come down to receive her visitor. And there, the first flurry of excitement over, they talked more tranquilly, or at all events, more intelligibly of the affairs mutually affecting them. In those there was much similarity, indeed, in many respects a parallelism. Yet the feelings with which they regarded them were diametrically opposite. One knew that her lover was in prison, and grieved at it; the other hoped hers might be the same, and would have been glad of it!

A strange dissimilitude of which the reader has the key.

Beyond what she had already said, the Condesa had little more to communicate, and in her turn became the questioner.

"I can understand now, *amiga mia*, why you spoke of Don Florencio. The Tejano prisoners have arrived, and you are thinking he's amongst them? That's so, is it not?"

"Not thinking, but hoping it, Ysabel."

"Have you taken any steps to ascertain?"

"I have."

"In what way?"

"I've sent a messenger to Tacubaya, where I'm told they've been taken."

"Not all. Some of them have been sent elsewhere. One party, I believe, is shut up in the Acordada."

"What! in that fearful place? among those horrid wretches—the worst criminals we have! The Tejans are soldiers—prisoners of war. Surely they do not deserve such treatment?"

"Deserve it or not, some of them are receiving it. That grand gentleman, Colonel Carlos Santander—your friend by the way—told me so."

The mention of Santander's name, but more a connection with the subject spoken of, produced a visible effect on Luisa Valverde. Her cheek seemed to pale and suddenly flashed red again. Well she remembered, and vividly recalled, the old enmity between him and Don Florencio. Too well, and a circumstance of most sinister recollection as matters stood now. She had thought of it before; was thinking of it all the time, and therefore the words of the Condesa started no new train of reflection. They but intensified the fear she had already felt, for a time holding her speechless.

Not noticing this, and without waiting a rejoinder, the other ran on, still interrogating:

"Whom have you trusted with this delicate mission, may I ask?"

"Only José?"

"Well; José, from what I've seen of him, is worthy of the trust. That is so far as honesty is concerned, and possibly cleverness. But, *amiga mia*, he's only a humble servitor, and out there in Tacubaya, among the garrison soldiers, or if it be in any of the prisons, he may experience a little difficulty in obtaining the information you seek. Did you give him any money to make matters easy?"

"He has my purse with him, with permission to use it as he may see best."

"Ah! then you may safely expect his bringing back a good account, or at all events one that will settle the question you wish to have settled. Your purse should be a key to Don Florencio's prison—if he be inside one anywhere in Mexico."

"Oh! I hope he is."

"Wishing your *amanti* in a prison! That would sound strange enough, if one didn't understand it."

"I'd give anything to know him there—all I have to be assured he still lives."

"Likely enough you'll soon hear. When do you expect your messenger to be back?"

"At any moment. He's been gone many hours ago. I was watching for him when you came up—yonder on the Tacubaya Road. I see nothing of him yet, but he may have passed while we've been talking."

"*Muy amiga mia*! How much our doings this day have been alike. I, too, have despatched a messenger to find out all about Ruperto, and am now awaiting his return. I ran across to tell you of it. And now that we're together let us stay till we know the worst or the best. God help us both; for, to make use of the phrase I've heard among *marineros*, we're 'both in the same boat.'

What is this?" she added, stooping, and taking up the gilded card which had been all the while lying upon the floor. "Oh, indeed! Invitation to an airing in one of the State carriages—with such a pretty compliment appended! How free El Excellentissimo is with his flattery. For myself I detest both him and it. You'll go, won't you?"

"I don't wish it."

"No matter about wishing; I want you. And so will your father, I'm sure."

"But why do you want me?"

"Why, so that you may take me with you."

"I would rather wait till I hear what father says."

"That's all I ask, *amiga*. I shall be contented with his dictum, now feeling sure—"

She was interrupted by the pattering of feet upon the stone stairway; two pairs of them, which told that two individuals were ascending. The heavy tread proclaimed them to be men. Presently their faces showed over the baluster rail, and another step brought them upon the roof. Both ladies regarding them with looks of eager inquiry, glided down out of the mirador to meet them.

For they were the two messengers that had been despatched separately, though on errands so very similar.

Returning, they had met by the front door, and entered the house together. Each having had orders to deliver his report, and without delay, was now acting in obedience to them.

Two and two they stood upon the azotea,—the men, hat in hand, stood in front of their respective mistresses; not so far apart, but that each mistress might have heard what the servant of the other said; for on their part there was no wish or reason for concealment.

"Señorita," reported José, "the gentleman you sent me to inquire about is not in Tacubaya."

Almost a cry came from Luisa Valverde's lips, as with paled cheek, she said,—"You've not heard of him, then?" But the colour quickly returned at the answer,—"I have, Señorita; more, I have seen him."

"Seen Don Florencio! Where? Speak, quick, José!"

"In the Acordada!"

"In the Acordada!" in still another voice—that of the Condesa speaking in a similar tone, as though it were an echo; for she, too, had just been told that her lover was in the same gaol.

"I saw him in a cell, my lady," continued the Countess's man, now taking precedence. "They had him coupled to another prisoner—a Tejano."

"He was in one of the cells, Señorita," spoke José, also continuing his report, "chained to a robber."

Chapter Seventeen
Por Las Zancas

In all cities there is a street favoured by fashion. This in Mexico is the Callé de Plateros (street of the silversmiths), so called because there the workers in precious metals and dealers in bijouterie "most do congregate."

In this street the *jovenes dorados* (gilded youth) of modern Tenochtitlan strolled in tight-fitting patent leather boots, canary-coloured kid gloves, cane in hand, and quizzing-glass to the eye. There, too, the señoras and señoritas go shopping bareheaded, with but the shawl thrown over the crown hood-fashion.

When out only for promenade, none of these linger long in the street of the silversmiths. They but pass through it on their way to the *Alameda*, a sort of half-park, half-garden, devoted to the public use, and tastefully laid out in walks, terraces, and parterres with flowers, and fountains; grand old evergreen trees overshadowing all. For in that summery clime shade, not sun, is the desideratum. Here the *jovenes dorados* spent part of the afternoons sauntering along the arcaded walks, or seated around the great fountain watching the play of its crystal waters. But with an eye to something besides—the señoritas, who are there, too, flirting the fans with a dexterity which speaks of much practice—speaks of something more. Not every movement made by these rustling segments of circles is intended to create currents of air and cool the heated skin. Many a twist and turn, watched with anxious eyes, conveys intelligence interesting as words never spoken. In Mexico many a love tale is told, passion declared, jealous pang caused or alleviated, by the mute languages of fans and fingers.

Though the Callé de Plateros terminates at the gate of the Alameda, the same line of street is continued half a mile further on, to the fashionable drive of the *Pasco Nuevo*, sometimes called Pasco de Buccareli, from the Viceroy who ruled New Spain when it was laid out. It is the Rotten Row of Mexico, for it is a ride as well as a drive; and at a certain hour of the afternoon a stream of carriages, with strings of horsemen, may be seen tending towards it, the carriages drawn, some of them by mules, others by the small native horses, and a distinguished few by large English or American animals, there known as *frisones*. It is the top thing to have a pair of "*frisones*."

In the carriages, the señoras and señoritas are seen attired in their richest robes—full evening dress—bare-armed and bareheaded, their hair, usually black, ablaze with jewels or entwined with flowers fresh picked—the sweet-scented suchil, the white star-like jasmine, and crimson grenadine. Alongside ride the cavaliers, in high-peaked, stump-leather saddles, their steeds capering and prancing; each rider, to all appearance, requiring the full strength of his arms to control his mount, while insidiously using his spurs to render the animal uncontrollable. The more it pitches and plunges the better he is pleased, provided the occupants of the carriages have their eyes on him.

Every day in the year—except during the week of *Guaresma* (Lent), when capricious fashion takes him to the Paseo Viejo, or *Lav Vigas*, on the opposite side of the city—can this brilliant procession be seen moving along the Callé de Plateros, and its continuation, the Callé de San Francisco.

But in this same thoroughfare one may often witness a spectacle less resplendent, with groups aught but gay. Midway along the street runs a deep drain or sewer, not as in European cities permanently covered up, but loosely flagged over, the flags removable at will. This, the *zanca*, is more of a stagnant sink than a drainage sewer; since from the city to the outside country there is scarce an inch of fall to carry off the sewage. As a consequence it accumulates in the zancas till they are brimming full, and with a stuff indescribable. Every garbage goes there—all the refuse of household product is shot into them. At periodical intervals they are cleared out, else the city would soon be a-flood in its own filth. It is often very near it, the blue black liquid seen oozing up between the flagstones that bridge over the zancas, filling the air with a stench intolerable. Every recurring revolution make the municipal authorities of Mexico careless about their charge and neglectful of their duties. But when the scouring-out process is going on, the sights are still more offensive, and the smells too. Then the flags are lifted and laid on one side—exposing all the impurity—while the stuff is tossed to the other, there to lie festering for days, or until dry enough to be more easily removed. For all it does not stop the circulation of the carriages. The grand dames seated in them pass on, now and then showing a slight contortion in their pretty noses. But they would not miss their airing in the Paseo were it twenty times worse—that they wouldn't. To them, as to many of their English sisterhood in Hyde Park, the afternoon drive is everything—to some, as report says, even more than meat or drink; since they deny themselves these for the keeping of the carriage.

It may be imagined that the scouring-out of the zancas is a job for which labourers are not readily obtained.

Even the *pelado* turns up his nose at it, and the poorest proletarian will only undertake the task when starvation is staring him in the face. For it is not only dirty, but deemed degrading. It is, therefore, one of the travaux-forces which, as a matter of necessity, falls to the lot of the "gaol-bird." Convicts are the scavengers; criminals sentenced to long periods of imprisonment, of whom there are often enough in the *carceles* of Mexico to clean out all the sewers in the country. Even by these it is a task looked upon with repugnance, and usually assigned to them as a punishment for prison derelictions. Not that they so much regard the dirt or the smells; it is the toil which offends them—the labour being hard, and often requiring to be done under a hot, broiling sun.

To see them is a spectacle of a rather curious kind, though repulsive. Coupled two and two—for the precaution is taken, and not unfrequently needed—to keep their leg-chains on; up in mud to the middle of their bodies, and above bespattered with it—such mud too! many of them with faces that, even when clean, are aught but nice to look at; their eyes now flashing fierce defiance, now bent down and sullen, they seem either at enmity or out of sorts with all mankind. Some among them, however, make light of it, bandy words with the passers-by, jest, laugh, sing, shout, and swear, which to a sensitive mind but makes the spectacle more sad.

All this understood, it may well be conceived with what anxiety Florence Kearney listened to that snatch of dialogue between Santander and the gaol-governor outside the cell. He did not even then quite comprehend the nature of what was intended for them. But the sharer of his chain did, who soon after made it all known to him, he passing the knowledge on to Cris Rock. So when, on the next morning, the governor again presented himself at the door of their cell, saying:

"Now, gentlemen, get ready to take a little exercise,"—they knew what sort of exercise was meant.

He, however, believing them ignorant of it—for he was not aware they had overheard his out-door speech with Santander, added ironically:

"It's a special favour I'm going to give you—at the request of Señor Colonel Santander, who, as I've seen, takes a friendly interest in some of you. For your health's sake, he has asked me to give you a turn upon the streets, which I trust you will enjoy and get benefit by."

Don Pedro was a born joker, and felt conceit in his powers as a satirist. In the present instance his irony was shaftless, being understood.

The dwarf was the only one who deigned rejoinder.

"Ha, ha, ha!" he yelled in his wild unearthly way. "Turn *upon* the streets! That's fine for you, Don Pedro. A turn *under* the streets—that's what you mean, isn't it?"

He had been long enough in the gaol-governor's charge to know the latter's name, and was accustomed to address him thus familiarly. The deformed creature was fearless from his very deformity, which in a way gave him protection.

"*Vayate Zorillo*," returned the Governor, slightly put out and evidently a little nettled, "you're too fond of jesting—or trying. I'll take that out of you, and I mean to give you a lesson in good manners this very day." Then fixing his eyes upon Rivas, he added: "Señor Don Ruperto, I should be only too happy to let you off from the little excursion your prison companions are about to make and save you the fatigue. But my orders are rigorous. They come from the highest quarter, and I dare not disobey them."

This was all pure irony, intended but to torment him; at least so the robber seemed to understand it. For, instead of accepting it in a friendly sense, he turned savagely on his tormentor, hissing out:

"I know you daren't disobey them, dog that you are! Only such as you would be governor of a gaol like this: you, who turned coat and disgraced the sword you wore at Zacatecas. Do your worst, Don Pedro Arias! I defy you."

"*Cascaras*! how swelling big you talk, Señor Captain Rivas! Ah! well. I'll let a little of the wind out of you too, before you bid good-bye to the Acordada. Even the Condesa, grand dame though she is, won't be able to get you clear of my clutches so easy as you may be thinking. La Garrota is the lady likeliest to do that."

After thus spitefully delivering himself, he called to some prison warders in waiting in the court outside, and commanded them to come up to him.

"Here," he directed, "take these two pairs and hand them over to the guard at the gate. You know what for, Dominguez?" The half interrogatory was addressed to a big, hulking fellow, chief of the turnkeys, who looked all Acordada.

"*Por cierto, Señor Gobernador*," he rejoined with a significant look, after giving the prison salute to his superior. "I know all about it."

"See, moreover, that they be kept all day at it; that's my orders."

"Sure will I, Señor," was the compliant rejoinder.

After which the man twitted with turning his coat, turned his back upon the place where he had been so ungraciously received, going off to more agreeable quarters.

"Now, gentlemen!" said the gaoler, stepping up to the door of the cell, "*Por las zancas!*"

Chapter Eighteen
Tyrant and Tool

El Excellentissimo Illustrissimo General Don José Antonio Lopez de Santa Anna.

Such the twice sesquipedalian name and title of him who at this time wielded the destinies of Mexico. For more than a quarter of a century this man had been the curse of the young Republic—its direst, deadliest bane. For although his rule was not continuous, its evil effects were. Unfortunately, the demoralisation brought about by despotism extends beyond the reign or life of the despot; and Santa Anna had so debased the Mexican people, both socially and politically, as to render them unfitted for almost any form of constitutional government. They had become incapable of distinguishing between the friends of freedom and its foes; and in the intervals of Liberal administration, because the Millennium did not immediately show itself, and make all rich, prosperous, and happy, they leaped to the conclusion that its failure was due to the existing *régime*, making no account or allowance for the still uncicatrised wounds of the body politic being the work of his wicked predecessor.

This ignorance of political cause and effect is, alas! not alone confined to Mexico. There is enough of it in England, too, as in every other nation. But in the earlier days of the Mexican Republic, the baneful weed flourished with unusual vigour and rankness—to the benefit of Antonio Lopez de Santa Anna, and the blight of his country. Deposed and banished so many times that their number is not easily remembered, he was ever brought back again—to the wonder of people then, and the puzzle of historians yet. The explanation, however, is simple enough. He reigned through corruption that he had himself been instrumental in creating; through militarism and an abominable *Chauvinism*—this last as effective an instrument as the oppressor can wield. *Divide et impera* is a maxim of despotic state-craft, old as despotism itself; "flatter and rule" is a method equally sure, and such Santa Anna practised to its full. He let pass no opportunity of flattering the national vanity, which brought the Mexican nation to shame, with much humiliation—as the French at a later period, and as it must every people that aims at no higher standard of honour than what may be derived from self-adulation.

At the time I am writing of, the chief of the Mexican Republic was aiming at "Imperium"—eagerly straining for it. Its substance he already had, the "Libertas" having been long since eliminated from his system of government, and trodden under foot. But the title he had not acquired yet. He yearned to wear the purple, and be styled "Imperador," and in order to prepare his subjects for the change, already kept a sort of Imperial court, surrounding it with grand ceremonials. As a matter of course, these partook of a military character, being himself not only political head of the State, but commander-in-chief of its armies. As a consequence, *Palacio*, his official residence was beset with soldier-guards, officers in gorgeous uniforms loitering about the gates, or going out and in, and in the Plaza Grande at all times exhibiting the spectacle of a veritable Champ de Mars. No one passing through the Mexican metropolis at this period would have supposed it the chief city of a Republic.

On that same day in which Carlos Santander had shown himself at the Acordada, only at an early hour, the would-be Emperor was seated in his apartment of the palace in which he was wont to give audience to ordinary visitors. He had got through the business affairs of the morning, dismissed his Ministers, and was alone, when one of the aides-de-camp in attendance entered with a card, and respectfully saluting him, laid it on the table before him.

"Yes; say I can see him. Tell him to come in," he directed, soon as reading the name on the card.

In the door, on its second opening, appeared Carlos Santander, in the uniform of a colonel of Hussars, gold bedizened, and laced from collar to cuffs.

"Ah! Señor Don Carlos!" exclaimed the Dictator in a joyous, jocular way, "what's your affair? Coming to tell me of some fresh conquest you've made among the *muchachas*? From your cheerful countenance I should say it's that."

"Excellentissimo!"

"Oh! you needn't deny, or look so demure about it. Well, you're a lucky fellow to be the lady killer I've heard say you are."

"Your Excellency, that's only say-say; I ought rather to call it slander. I've no ambition to be thought such a character. Quite the reverse, I assure you."

"If you could assure me, but you can't. I've had you long enough under my eye to know better. Haven't I observed your little flirtations with quite half a score of our señoritas, among them a very charming young lady you met in Louisiana, if I mistake not?"

Saying this, he fixed his eyes on Santander's face in a searching, interrogative way, as though he himself felt more than a common interest in the charming young lady who had been met in Louisiana.

Avoiding his glance, as evading the question, the other rejoined—

"It is very good of your Excellency to take such interest in me, and I'm grateful. But I protest—"

"Come, come! *amigo mio!* No protestations. 'Twould only be adding perjury to profligacy. Ha, ha, ha!"

And the grand dignitary leaned back in his chair, laughing. For it was but badinage, and he in no way intended lecturing the staff-colonel on his morality, nor rebuking him for any backslidings. Instead, what came after could but encourage him in such wise, his chief continuing—

"Yes, Señor Don Carlos, I'm aware of your *amourettes*, for which I'm not the man to be hard upon you. In that regard, I myself get the credit—so rumour says—of living in a glass house, so I cannot safely throw stones. Ha, ha!"

The tone of his laugh, with his self-satisfied look, told of his being aught but angry with rumour for so representing him.

"Well, Excellentissimo," here put in the subordinate, "it don't much signify what the world says, so long as one's conscience is clear."

"*Bravo—bravissimo!*" exclaimed the Most Excellent. "Ha, ha, ha!" he continued, in still louder cachinnation. "Carlos Santander turned moralist! And moralising to me! It's enough to make a horse laugh. Ha, ha, ha!"

The staff-colonel appeared somewhat disconcerted, not knowing to what all this might be tending. However, he ventured to remark—

"I am glad to find your Excellency in such good humour this morning."

"Ah! that's because you've come to ask some favour from me, I suppose." Santa Anna had a habit of interlarding his most familiar and friendly discourse with a little satire, sometimes very disagreeable to those he conversed with. "But never mind," he rattled on, "though I confess some surprise at your hypocrisy, which is all thrown away upon me, *amigo!* I don't at all wonder at your success with the señoritas. You're a handsome fellow, Don Carlos; and if it weren't for that scar on your cheek— By the way, you never told me how you came by it. You hadn't it when you were last with us."

The red flushed into Santander's face, and up over his forehead to the roots of his hair. He had told no one in Mexico, nor anywhere else, how he came by that ugly thing on his jaw, which beard could not conceal, and which he felt as a brand of Cain.

"It's a scar of a sword-cut, your Excellency. I got it in a duel."

"Ah! An honourable wound, then. But where?"

"In New Orleans."

"Just the place for that sort of thing, as I know, having been there myself." (Santa Anna had made a tour of the States, on *parole*, after the battle of San Jacinto, where he was taken prisoner.) "A very den of duellists is Nuevo Orleans; many of them *maîtres d'éscrime*. But who was your antagonist? I hope you gave him as good as you got."

"I did, your Excellency; that, and more."

"You killed him?"

"Not quite. I would have done so, but that my second interposed, and persuaded me to let him off."

"Well, he hasn't let you off, anyhow. What was the quarrel about? *Carrai*! I needn't ask; the old orthodox cause—a lady, of course?"

"Nay; for once your Excellency is in error. Our *desajio* originated in something quite different."

"What thing?"

"An endeavour on my part to do a service to Mexico and its honoured ruler."

"Oh, indeed! In what way, Señor Colonel?"

"That band of *filibusteros*, of which, as your Excellency will remember—"

"Yes—yes," interrupted Santa Anna impatiently. He evidently knew all about that, and preferred hearing no more of it. "It was one of the *filibusteros* you fought with, I suppose?"

"Yes, Excellentissimo; the one they chose for their captain."

"You were angry at his being preferred to yourself, and so called him out? Well, that was cause enough to a man of your mettle. But what became of him afterwards? Was he among those at Mier?"

"He was."

"Killed there?"

"No, your Excellency; only taken prisoner."

"Shot at Salado?"

"Neither that, Excellentissimo."

"Then he must be here?"

"He is here, your Excellency."

"What's his name?"

"Kearney—Florence Kearney, *un Irlandes*."

A peculiar expression came over Santa Anna's features, a sort of knowing look, as much as to say the name was not new to him. Nor was it. That very morning, only an hour before, Don Ignacio Valverde had audience of him on a matter relating to this same man—Florence Kearney; in short, to obtain clemency for the young Irishman—full pardon, if possible. But the Minister had been dismissed with only vague promises. His influence at court was still not very great, and about the motive for his application—as also who it originated from—Santa Anna had conceived suspicions.

Of all this he said nothing to the man before him now, simply inquiring—

"Is the *Irlandes* at Tacubaya?"

"No, your Excellency; he's in the Acordada."

"Since you had the disposal of the Tejano prisoners, I can understand that," returned the Dictator, with a significant shrug. "It's about him, then, you're here, I suppose. Well, what do you want?"

"Your authority, Excellentissimo, to punish him as he deserves."

"For making that tracing on your cheek, eh? You repent not having punished him more at the time when you yourself had the power? Isn't it so, Señor Colonel?"

Santander's face reddened, as he made reply—

"Not altogether, your Excellency. There's something besides, for which he deserves to be treated differently from the others."

Santa Anna could have given a close guess at what the exceptional something was. To his subtle perception a little love drama was gradually being disclosed; but he kept his thoughts to himself, with his eyes still searchingly fixed on Santander's face.

"This Kearney," continued the latter, "though an Irishman, is one of Mexico's bitterest enemies, and especially bitter against your Excellency. In a speech he made to the *filibusteros*, he called you a usurper, tyrant, traitor to liberty and your country—ay, even coward. Pardon me for repeating the vile epithets he made use of."

Santa Anna's eyes now scintillated with a lurid sinister light, as if filled with fire, ready to blaze out. In the American newspapers he had often seen his name coupled with such opprobrious phrases, but never without feeling savagely wrathful. And not the less that his own innate consciousness told him it was all as said.

"*Chingara!*" he hissed out, for he was not above using this vulgar exclamation. "If it is true what you say, Don Carlos, as I presume it is, you can do as you like with this dog of an *Irlandes!* have him shot, or have him despatched by *La Garrota*, whichever seems best to you. But no—stay! That won't do yet. There's a question about these Tejanos with the United States Minister; and as this Kearney is an Irishman, and so a British subject, the representative of that country may make trouble too. So till all this is settled, the *Irlandes* mustn't be either shot or garrotted. Instead, let him be treated tenderly. You comprehend?"

The staff-colonel did comprehend; the emphasis on the "tenderly" made it impossible for him to mistake the Dictator's meaning, which was just as he desired it. As he passed out of the presence, and from the room, his countenance was lit up, or rather darkened, by an expression of fiendish triumph. He now had it in his power to humiliate them who had so humbled him.

"Quite a little comedy!" soliloquised Santa Anna, as the door closed on his subordinate, "in which, before it's played out, I may myself take a part. She's a charming creature, this Señorita Valverde. But, ah! nothing to the Condesa. That woman—witch, devil, or whatever I may call her—bids fair to do what woman never did—make a fool of Lopez de Santa Anna."

Chapter Nineteen
A Wooden-Legged Lothario

For some time the Dictator remained in his seat lighting cigarrito after cigarrito, and puffing away at them furiously. The look of light frivolity had forsaken his face, which was now overcast with gloom.

At this time, as said, he wielded supreme unlimited power over the Mexican people—even to life and death. For although he might not recklessly or openly decree this, he could bring it about secretly—by means which, if rumour spoke true, he had more than once made use of. Indeed, there stood against his name more than one well-confirmed record of assassination.

Thought of this may have had something to do with the cloud that had come over his features; though not for any qualms of conscience for the murders he may have committed or hired others to commit. More likely a fear that he himself might some day meet a similar fate; like all despots he dreaded the steel of the assassin. By his corrupt administration, he had encouraged bravoism till it had become a dangerous element in the social life of his country—almost an institution—and it was but natural he should fear the bravo's blade turned against himself.

Another apprehension may at this time have been troubling him. Although to all appearance secure in the dictatorial chair, with a likelihood of his soon converting it into a real throne, he had his misgivings about this security. By imprisonments, executions, banishments, and confiscations, he had done all in his power to annihilate the Liberal party. But though crushed and feeble now, its strength was but in abeyance, its spirit still lived, and might again successfully assert itself. No man knew this better than he himself; and no better teacher could he have had than his own life's history, with its alternating chapters of triumph and defeat. Even then there was report of a *pronunciamento* in one of the northern cities of the Republic—the State, by a polite euphemism, being still so designated. Only a faint "gritto" it was, but with a tone that resembled the rumbling of distant thunder, which might yet be heard louder and nearer.

Little, however, of matters either revolutionary or political was he thinking now. The subject uppermost in his mind was that latent on his lips—woman. Not in a general way, but with thoughts specially bent upon one of them, or both, with whose names he had just been making free. As his soliloquy told, a certain "Condesa" had first place in his reflections, she being no other than the Condesa Almonté. In his wicked way he had made love to this young lady, as to many others; but, unlike as with many others, he had met repulse. Firm, though without indignation, his advances not yet having gone so far, nor been so bold, as to call for this. He had only commenced skirmishing with her; a preliminary stroke of his tactics being that invitation to ride in the State carriage extended to Doña Luisita Valverde, while withheld from the Countess—an astute manoeuvre on his part, and, as he supposed, likely to serve him. In short, the old sinner was playing the old game of "piques." Nor did he think himself so ancient as to despair of winning at it. In such contests he had too often come off victorious, and success might attend upon him still. Vain was he of his personal appearance, and in his earlier days not without some show of reason. In his youth Santa Anna would claim to be called, if not handsome, a fairly good-looking man. Though a native Mexican, a *Vera-cruzano*, he was of pure Spanish race and good blood—the boasted *sangre-azul*. His features were well formed, oval, and slightly aquiline, his complexion dark, yet clear, his hair and moustaches black, lustrous, and profuse. But for a sinister cast in his eyes, not always observable, his countenance would have been pleasing enough. As it was he prided himself upon it even now that he was well up in years, and his hair becoming silvered. As for the moustaches, black pomatum kept them to their original colour.

One thing soured him, even more than advancing age—his wooden leg. 'Tis said he could never contemplate that without an expression of pain coming over his features, as though there was gout in the leg itself giving him a twinge. And many the time—nay, hundreds of times—did he curse Prince de Joinville. For it was in defending Vera Cruz against the French, commanded by the latter, he had received the wound, which rendered amputation of the limb necessary. In a way he ought to have blessed the Prince, and been grateful for the losing of it rather than otherwise. Afterwards the mishap stood him in good stead; at election times when he was candidate for the Chief Magistracy of the State. Then he was proud to parade the artificial limb; and did so to some purpose. It was, indeed, an important element in his popularity, and more than once proved an effective aid to his reinstatement. With a grim look, however, he regarded it now. For though it had helped him politically, he was not thinking of politics, and in what he was thinking about he knew it an obstruction. A woman to love a man with a wooden leg! And such a woman as Ysabel Almonté! Not that he put it to himself in that way; far from it. He had still too good an opinion, if not of his personal appearance, at least of his powers otherwise, and he even then felt confident of success. For he had just succeeded in removing another obstacle which seemed likely to be more in his way than the wooden leg. He had but late come to know of it; but as soon as knowing, had taken measures to avert the danger dreaded—by causing the imprisonment of a man. For it was a man he feared, or suspected, as his competitor for the affections of the Condesa. It had cost him no small trouble to effect this individual's arrest, or rather capture. He was one of the proscribed, and in hiding; though heard of now and then as being at the head of a band of *salteadore*—believed to have turned highwayman.

But he had been taken at length, and was at that moment in the gaol of the Acordada; which Santa Anna well knew, having himself ordered his incarceration there, and given other instructions regarding him to the gaol-governor, who was one of his creatures.

After sitting for some time, as he stretched out his hand, and held the end of his paper cigar to the red coals burning in a *brazero* on the table before him, the frown upon his features changed to a demoniac smile. Possibly from the knowledge that this man was now in his power. Sure was he of this; but what would he not have given to be as sure of her being so too!

Whether his reflections were sweet or bitter, or which predominated, he was not permitted longer to indulge in them. The door again opening—after a tap asking permission to enter—showed the same aide-de-camp. And on a similar errand as before, differing only in that now he placed two cards on the table instead of one; the cards themselves being somewhat dissimilar to that he had already brought in.

And with altogether a different air did Santa Anna take them up for examination. He was enough interested at seeing by their size and shape that those now desiring an audience of him were ladies. But on reading the names, his interest rose to agitation, such as the aide-de-camp never before had seen him exhibit, and which so much astonished the young officer that he stood staring wonderingly, if not rudely, at the grand dignitary, his chief. His behaviour, however, was not noticed, the Dictator's eyes being all upon the cards. Only for an instant though. If he gave ready reception to his late visitor, still readier did he seem desirous of according it to those now seeking speech with him.

"Conduct the ladies in," was his almost instantaneous command, as quickly retracted. For soon as spoken he countermanded it; seemingly from some afterthought which, as a codicil, had suddenly occurred to him. Then followed a chapter of instructions to the aide-de-camp, confidential, and to the effect that the ladies were not to be immediately introduced. He was to keep them in conversation in the ante-chamber outside, till he should hear the bell.

Judging by his looks as he went out the young subaltern was more than satisfied with the delay thus enjoined upon him. It was aught but a disagreeable duty; for, whether acquainted with the ladies who were in waiting, or not, he must have seen that both were bewitchingly beautiful — one being Luisa Valverde, the other Ysabel Almonté.

Chapter Twenty
A Pair of Beautiful Petitioners

Soon as the aide-de-camp had closed the door behind him, Santa Anna sprang up from his seat and hastily stumped it to a large cheval glass which stood on one side of the room. Squaring himself before this he took survey of his person from crown to toes. He gave a pull or two at his moustaches, twisting their points, and turning them upward along his cheeks. Then running his fingers comb-like through his hair, he gave that also a jaunty set. In fine, straightening himself in his gold-braided uniform frock, with a last glance down to his feet—this resulting in a slight grimace—he returned to the state chair and reseated himself.

With all his gallantry and politeness—and to these he made much pretension—it was not his custom to receive lady visitors standing. In the upright attitude the artificial leg made him look stiff, and he preferred stowing it away under the table. Besides, there was his dignity, as the grand figure-head of the nation, which he now wished to have its full effect. Leaning forward, he gave a downward blow to the spring of the table bell; then assuming an attitude of expectant grandeur, sate expectant. This time the aide-de-camp required no passing to and fro; and the door again opening, the ladies were ushered into the august presence.

In their air and manner they betrayed agitation too, while the serious expression upon their features told they were there on no trivial errand.

"Pray be seated, ladies," said the Dictator, after exchanging salutations with them. "'Tis not often the Condesa Almonté honours the Palacio with her presence, and for the Señorita Valverde, were it not for official relations with her father, I fear we should see even less of her than we do."

While speaking he pointed to a couple of couch chairs that stood near the table.

They sat down rather hesitatingly, and slightly trembling. Not that either would have been at all timid had the occasion been a common one. Both were of Mexico's best blood, the Condesa one of the old *noblesse* who hold their heads higher even than the political chief of the State, when he chances to be—as more than once has occurred—an adventurer of humbler birth. Therefore, it was not any awe of the great dignitary that now unnerved them, but the purpose for which they were seeking speech with him. Whether Santa Anna guessed it, or not, could not be told by his looks. An experienced diplomatist, he could keep his features fixed and immovable as the Sphinx, or play them to suit the time and the tune. So, after having delivered himself, as above, with the blandest of smiles upon his face, he remained silent, awaiting the rejoinder.

It was the Condesa who made it.

"Your Excellency," she said, doing her utmost to look humble; "we have come to beg a favour from you."

A gratified look, like a gleam of light, illuminated Santa Anna's swarthy features. Ysabel Almonté begging favours from him! What better could he have wished? With all his command of features he but ill-concealed the triumph he now felt. It flashed up in his eyes as he said respondingly —

"A favour you would ask? Well, if it be within my power to grant it, neither the Condesa Almonté, nor the Doña Luisa Valverde need fear refusal. Be frank, then, and tell me what it is."

The Countess, with all her courage, still hesitated to declare it. For despite the ready promise of compliance, she did fear a refusal; since it had been asked for that same morning and though not absolutely refused, the answer left but little hope of its being conceded.

As is known, at an earlier hour Don Ignacio had paid a visit to the Palacio, to seek clemency for a prisoner-of-war, Florence Kearney. But pardon for a state prisoner was also included in his application — that being Ruperto Rivas. Of all this the ladies were well aware, since it was at their instigation, and through their importunity, he had acted. It was only, therefore, by the urgency of a despairing effort, as a *dernier ressort*, these had now sought the presence as petitioners, and naturally they dreaded denial. Noting the Condesa's backwardness — a thing new but not displeasing to him, since it gave promise of influence over her — Santa Anna said interrogatively:

"Might this favour, as you are pleased to term it, have ought to do with a request lately made to me by Don Ignacio Valverde?"

"'Tis the same, your Excellency," answered the Countess, at length recovering spirit, but still keeping up the air of meek supplication she had assumed.

"Indeed!" exclaimed the Dictator, adding, "that grieves me very much."

He made an attempt to look sorry, though it needed none for him to appear chagrined. This he was in reality, and for reasons intelligible.

Here were two ladies, both of whom he had amatory designs upon, each proclaiming by her presence—as it were telling him to his teeth, the great interest she felt in another—that or she would not have been there!

"But why, Excellentissimo?" asked the Countess, entreatingly. "What is there to grieve you in giving their freedom to two men—gentlemen, neither of whom has been guilty of crime, and who are in prison only for offences your Excellency can easily pardon?"

"Not so easily as you think, Condesa. You forget that I am but official head of the State, and have others to consult—my Ministers and the Congress—in affairs of such magnitude. Know, too, that both these men for whom you solicit pardon have been guilty of the gravest offences; one of them, a foreigner, an enemy of our country, taken in arms against it; the other, I am sorry to say, a citizen, who has become a rebel, and worse still, a robber!"

"'Tis false!" exclaimed the Countess, all at once changing tone, and seeming to forget the place she was in and the presence. "Don Ruperto Rivas is no robber; never was, nor rebel either; instead, the purest of patriots!"

Never looked Ysabel Almonté lovelier than at that moment—perhaps never woman. Her spirit roused, cheeks red, eyes sparkling with indignation, attitude erect—for she had started up from her chair—she seemed to be the very impersonation of defiance, angry, but beautiful. No longer meek or supplicating now. Instinct or intuition told her it would be of no use pleading further, and she had made up her mind for the worst.

The traits of beauty which her excitement called forth, added piquancy to her natural charms, and inflamed Santa Anna's wicked passions all the more. But more than any of them revenge. For now he knew how much the fair petitioner was interested in the man whose suit she had preferred. With a cold cynicism—which, however, cost him an effort—he rejoined:

"That, perhaps, is your way of thinking, Condesa. But it remains to be proved—and the prisoner you speak of shall have an opportunity of proving it—with his innocence in every respect. That much I can promise you. The same for him," he added, turning to Luisa Valverde, "in whom, if I mistake not, the Doña Luisa is more especially interested. These *gentlemen* prisoners shall have a fair trial, and justice done them. Now, ladies! can you ask more of me?"

They did not; both seeing it would be to no purpose. Equally purposeless to prolong the interview; and they turned toward the door, the daughter of Don Ignacio leading where she had before followed.

This was just as Santa Anna wished it. Seemingly forgetful of his cork-leg, and the limp he took such pains to conceal, he jerked himself out of his chair and hurried after—on a feigned plea of politeness. Just in time to say to the Countess in a hurried, half-whisper:—

"If the Condesa will return, and prefer her request *alone*, it may meet with more favour."

The lady passed on, with head held disdainfully, as though she heard but would not heed. She did hear what he said, and it brought a fresh flush upon her cheek, with another flash of anger in her eyes. For she could not mistake his meaning, and knew it was as the serpent whispering into the ear of Eve.

Chapter Twenty One
A Woman's Scheme

"My poor Ruperto is indeed in danger! Now I am sure of it. Ah, even to his life! And I may be the cause of his losing it."

So spoke the Countess Almonté half in soliloquy, though beside her sat her friend Luisa Valverde. They were in a carriage on return from their fruitless visit to the Dictator. It was the Countess' own landau which had remained waiting for them outside the Palace gates.

The other, absorbed with her own anxieties, might not have noticed what was said but for its nature. This, being in correspondence with what was at the moment in her own mind, caught her ear, almost making her start. For she, too, was thinking of a life endangered, and how much that danger might be due to herself. It was not poor Ruperto's life, but poor Florencio's.

"You the cause, Ysabel!" she said, not in surprise, save at the similarity of their thoughts. "Ah! yes; I think I comprehend you."

"If not, *amiga*, don't ask explanation of it now. It's a hateful thing, and I dislike to think, much more speak of it. Some other time I'll tell you all. Now we've work to do—a task that will take all our energies—all our cunning to accomplish it. However is it to be done? *Valga me Dios!*"

To her interrogatory she did not expect reply. And the desponding look of Luisa Valverde showed she had none to give that would be satisfactory; for she quite understood what was the task spoken of, and equally comprehended the difficulty of its accomplishment. Perplexed as the Countess herself, and possibly more despairing, she could but echo the exclamatory words—

"How indeed! *Valga me Dios.*"

For a while they sat without further exchange of speech, both buried in thought. Not long, however, when the Countess again spoke, saying—

"You're not good at dissembling, Luisita; I wish you were."

"*Santissima!*" exclaimed her friend, alike surprised at the remark as at its abruptness. "Why do you wish that Ysabel?"

"Because I think I know a way by which something might be done—if you were but the woman to do it."

"Oh, Ysabelita! I will do anything to get Florencio out of prison."

"It isn't Florencio I want you to get out, but Ruperto. Leave the getting out of Florencio to me."

Still more astonished was Don Ignacio's daughter. What could the countess mean now? She put the question to her thus—

"What is it you desire me to do?"

"Practise a little deception—play the coquette—that's all."

It was not in Luisa Valverde's nature. If she had many admirers, and she had—some of them over head and ears in love with her—it was from no frivolity, or encouragement given them, on her part. From the day Florence Kearney first made impression upon her heart, it had been true to him, and she loyal throughout all. So much that people thought her cold, some even pronouncing her a prude. They knew not how warmly that heart beat, though it was but for one. Thinking of this one, however, what the countess proposed gave her a shock, which the latter perceiving, added, with a laugh—

"Only for a time, *amiga mia*. I don't want you to keep it up till you've got a naughty name. Nor to make fools of all the fine gentlemen I see dangling around you. Only one."

"Which one?"

She was not averse to hearing what the scheme was, at all events. How could she be, in view of the object aimed at?

"A man," pursued the Countess, "who can do more for us than your father; more than we've been able to do ourselves."

"Who is he?"

"Don Carlos Santander, colonel of Hussars on the staff—aide-de-camp and adjutant to El Excellentissimo in more ways than military ones—some not quite so honourable, 'tis said. Said also, that this staff-colonel, for reasons nobody seems to know, or need we care, has more influence at Court than almost any one else. So what I want you to do is to utilise this influence for our purpose, which I know you can."

"Ah, Ysabelita! How much you are mistaken, to think I could influence him to that! Carlos Santander would be the last man to help me in procuring pardon for Florencio—the very last. You know why."

"Oh yes; I know. But he may help me in procuring pardon for Ruperto. Luckily my good looks, if I have any, never received notice from the grand colonel, who has eyes only for you; so he's not jealous of Ruperto. As the obsequious servant of his master, hostile to him no doubt; but that might be overcome by your doing as I should direct."

"But what would you have me do."

"Show yourself *complaisant* to the Colonel. Only in appearance, as I've said; and only for a time till you've tried your power over him, and see with what success."

"I'm sure it would fail."

"I don't think it would, *amiga mia*; and will not, if you go about it according to instructions. Though it may cost you some unpleasantness, Luisita, and an effort, you'll make it for my sake, won't you? And as a reward," pursued the Countess, as if to render her appeal more surely effective, "I shall do as much for you, and in a similar way. For I, too, intend counterfeiting complacency in a certain quarter, and in the interest of a different individual—Don Florencio. Now, you understand me?"

"Not quite yet."

"Never mind. I'll make it more plain by-and-by. Only promise me that you'll do—"

"Dearest Ysabelita! I'd do anything for you."

"And Don Florencio. I thought that would secure your consent. Well, *mil mil gracias*! But what a game of cross-purposes we'll be playing; I for you, and you for me, and neither for ourselves! Let us hope we may both win."

By this the carriage had stopped in front of the Casa Valverde to set down Doña Luisa. The Countess alighted also, ordering the horses home. It was but a step to her own house, and she could walk it. For she had something more to say which required saying there and then. Passing on into the *patio*, far enough to be beyond earshot of the "cochero," and there stopping, she resumed the dialogue at the point where she had left off.

"We must set to work at once," she said; "this very day, if opportunity offer. Perhaps in the procession—"

"Oh! Ysabel?" interrupted the other. "How I dislike the thought of this procession—making merry as it were, and he in a prison! And we must pass it too—its very doors! I'm sure I shall feel like springing out of the carriage and rushing inside to see him."

"That would be just the way to ensure your not seeing him—perhaps, never more. The very opposite is what you must do, or you'll spoil all my plans. But I'll instruct you better before we start out."

"You insist, then, on our going?"

"Of course, yes; for the very reason—the very purpose we've been speaking of. That's just why I ask you to take me with you. It will never do to offend his High Mightiness, angry as we may be with him. I'm now sorry at having shown temper; but how could I help it, hearing Ruperto called a robber? However, that may be all for the best. So, upstairs; turn out your *guarda-roba*, and your jewel case; array yourself in your richest apparel, and be in readiness for the gilded coach when it comes round. *Carramba!*" she added after drawing out her jewelled watch,—one of Losada's best—and glancing at its dial, "we haven't a moment to spare, I must be off to my toilet too."

She had made a step in the direction of the street, when suddenly turning again she added—

"As a last word, lest I might forget it. When next you appear in the Grand Presence drop that forlorn doleful look. Misery is the weakest weapon either man or woman can make use of—the very worst advocate in any cause. So don't show it, especially in the company of Don Carlos Santander, where in all likelihood you will be before the end of another hour. Try to look cheerful, put on your sweetest smile, though it be a feigned one, as I intend doing for Antonio Lopez de Santa Anna."

She took her departure now; but as she passed out through the *saguan* a cloud could be seen upon her countenance, more than that from the shadow of the arched gateway, telling that she herself needed quite as much as her friend, admonition to be cheerful.

Chapter Twenty Two
In the Sewers

Along with a score of other prisoners, the "chain-gang" of the Acordada, Kearney, Rock, Rivas, and the dwarf were conducted out into the street, and on the Callé de Plateros. Dominguez, the gaoler, went with them—having received orders to that effect—carrying a heavy *cuarta* with hard raw-hide lash knotted at the end. Their escort consisted of two or three files of the prison guard, dirty looking soldiers of the *infanteria*, in coarse linen uniforms, stiff shakoes on their heads, their arm the old-fashioned flint-lock musket.

The scavengers had still their ankle chains on, coupled two and two, these lengthened, however, to give more freedom to their work. One reason for keeping them chained is to economise the strength of the guard, a single sentry thus being as good as a dozen. Of course, it is an additional precaution against escape, a thing which might seem impossible under the muzzles of muskets and bayonets fixed. But to desperadoes such as are some of the Acordada gaol-birds it would not be so if left leg free. More than once had the attempt been made, and with success; for in no city is it easier, or indeed so easy. In the Mexican metropolis there are whole districts where the policeman fears to show his face, and a criminal pursued, even by soldiers in uniform, would have every door thrown open to him, and every opportunity given for stowing himself away. Get he but out into the country, and up to the mountains—on all sides conveniently near—his chances are even better, since the first man there met may be either footpad or *salteador*.

As said, the street to which the scavengers were taken was the Callé de Plateros, where it ends at the Alameda Gate. The covering flags of the *zancas* had been already lifted off, exposing to view the drain brimful of liquid filth the tools were beside—scoops, drags, and shovels having been sent on before.

Soon, on arriving on its edge, Dominguez, who kept close by the two couples in which were the Tejanos, ordered them to lay hold and fall to.

There could be no question of refusal or disobedience. From the way he twirled the *quirt* between his fingers it looked as though he wished there was, so that he might have an excuse for using it. Besides, any hanging back would be rewarded by a blow from the butt of a musket, and, persisted in, possibly a bayonet thrust—like as not to lame the refractory individual for life.

There was no need for such violent measures now. The others of the gang had done scavenger work before; and knowing its ways, went at it as soon as the word was given. *Nolens volens* Kearney and Cris Rock, with their chain partners, had to do likewise; though, perhaps, never man laid hold of labourer's tool with more reluctance than did the Texan. It was a long shafted shovel that had been assigned to him, and the first use he made of the implement was to swing it round his head, as though he intended bringing it down on that of one of the sentries who stood beside.

"Durnashun!" he shrieked out, still brandishing the tool and looking the soldier straight in the face. "If 'twarn't that the thing 'ud be o' no use, an' *you* ain't the one as is to blame, I'd brain ye on the spot, ye ugly yaller-belly. Wage! Let me get back to Texas, and grip o' a good rifle, the Mexikin as kums my way may look out for partickler forked lightnin'!"

Though not comprehending a word of what was said the little manikin of a *militario* was so frightened by the big fellow's gestures as to spring back several feet, with a look of alarm so intense, yet so comical, as to set the Texan off into a roar of laughter. And still laughing, he faced towards the sewer, plunged in his implement, and set to work with the others.

At first the task was comparatively clean and easy—a sort of skimming affair—the scavengers keeping upon the pavement. The necessity had not yet arisen for them going down into the drain.

After a time, however, as the liquid got lower and the sediment at the bottom too stiff to be *conveniently* scooped up, a number of them were ordered to "step in." It was a cruel, brutal order, and Bill Sykes would have declined sending his "bull-dawg" into that sewer after rats. But Dominguez, a sort of Mexican Bill Sykes, had no scruples about this with the unfortunates he had charge of, and with a "*carajo*," and a threatening flourish of his whip, he repeated the order. One or two of the *forzados* took the plunge good-humouredly, even to laughing, as they dropped into the stuff, waist deep, sending the mud in splashes all round. The dainty ones went in more leisurely, some of them needing a little persuasion at the point of the bayonet.

Cris Rock was already down, having gone voluntarily. Only one of each couple had been ordered below; and, much as he disliked the dwarf, he had no wish to see him drowned or suffocated, which the diminutive creature would well-nigh have been in the horrible cesspool. Tall as the Texan was, the stuff reached up to his thighs, the surface of the street itself being on a level with his arm-pits, while only the heads of the others could be seen above the stones.

Neither Kearney nor Rivas had yet taken the plunge. They still stood on the brink, discussing the question of precedence. Not that either wished the other to do the disagreeable; instead, the reverse. Strange as it may appear, knowing or believing him to be a bandit, the young Irishman had taken a liking to the Mexican, and the feeling was reciprocated, so that each was now trying to restrain the other from entering the ugly gulf.

But their friendly contest was cut short by the brutal gaoler; who, advancing, grasped Rivas by the shoulder, and with his other hand pointing downward shouted "*Abajo!*"

There was no help for it but obey; the alternative sure of being something worse. For the man so rudely commanded went down willingly; indeed, with alacrity, to satisfy his impulse of friendship for the *Irlandes*.

Had Carlos Santander been there likely the position would have been reversed, and Kearney compelled to "take the ditch." But the Governor of the Acordada had control of details, and to his hostility and spleen, late stirred by that wordy encounter with Rivas, the latter was no doubt indebted for the partiality shown him by Don Pedro's head turnkey.

In time, all were disposed of: one of each couple down in the sewer, pitching out its sweet contents; the other pressing them back upon the pavement to prevent their oozing in again. Either way the work was now nasty enough; but for those below, it was a task too repulsive to set even the lowest pariah at.

Chapter Twenty Three
The Procession

Disagreeable as was their job, some of the *forzados* made light of it, bandying jests with the street passengers, who did not find it safe to go too near them. A scoopful of the inky liquid could be flung so as to spoil the polish on boots, or sent its splashes over apparel still higher. Even the vigilance of the sentries could not prevent this, or rather they cared not to exercise it. The victims of such practical jokes were usually either of the class *felado*, or the yet more humble aboriginals, accustomed to be put upon by the soldiers themselves, who rather relished the fun.

But only the more abandoned of the gaol-birds behaved in this way, many of them seeming to feel the degradation more than aught else. For among them, as we know, were men who should not have been there. Some may have seen friends passing by, who gave them looks of sympathy or pity, and possibly more than one knew himself under eyes whose expression told of a feeling stronger than either of these—love itself. Indeed this last, or something akin to it, seemed the rule rather than the exception. In Mexico, he must be a deeply disgraced criminal whose sweetheart would be ashamed of him; and every now and then, a brown-skinned "muchacha" might be seen crossing to where the scavengers were at work, and, with a muttered word or two, passing something into a hand eagerly outstretched to receive it. The sentries permitted this, after examining the commodity so tendered, and seeing it a safe thing to be entrusted to the receiver. These gifts of friendship, or *gages d'amour*, were usually eatables from the nearest cook-shop; their donors well knowing that the fare of the Acordada was neither plentiful nor sumptuous.

But beyond these interested ones, few of the pedestrians stopped or even looked at the chain-gang. To most, if not all, it was an ordinary spectacle, and attracted no more attention than would a crossing-sweeper on a London street. Not as much as the latter, as he is often an Oriental. On that particular day, however, the party of scavengers presented a novelty, in having the two Tejanos in it; with a yet greater one in the odd juxtaposition of Cris Rock and his diminutive "mate." In Mexico, a man over six feet in height is a rarity, and as Cris exceeded this by six inches, a rarer sight still was he. The colossus coupled to the dwarf, as Gulliver to Lilliputian—a crooked Lilliputian at that—no wonder that a knot of curious gazers collected around them, many as they approached the grotesque spectacle uttering ejaculations of surprise.

"*Ay Dios!*" exclaimed one. "*Gigante y enano!*" (a giant and a dwarf)— "and chained together! Who ever saw the like?"

Such remarks were continually passing among the spectators, who laughed as they listened to them. And though the Texan could not tell what they said, their laughter "riled" him. He supposed it a slur upon his extraordinary stature, of which he was himself no little proud, while they seemed to regard it sarcastically. Could they have had translated to them the rejoinders that now and then came from his lips, like the rumbling of thunder, they would have felt their sarcasm fully paid back, with some change over. As a specimen:—

"Devil darn ye, for a set of yaller-jawed pigmies! Ef I hed about a millyun o' ye out in the open purairu, I'd gie you somethin' to larf at. Dod-rot me! ef I don't b'lieve a pack o' coycoats ked chase as many o' ye as they'd count themselves; and arter runnin' ye down 'ud scorn to put tooth into yur stinkin' carcasses!"

Fortunately for him, the "yaller-jawed pigmies" understood not a word of all this; else, notwithstanding his superior size and strength, he might have had rough handling from them. Without that, he was badly plagued by their behaviour, as a bull fretted with flies; which may have had something to do with his readiness to go down into the drain. There, up to his elbows, he was less conspicuous, and so less an object of curiosity.

It had got to be noon, with the sun at fire heat; but for all the *forzados* were kept on at work. No rest for them until the task should be completed, and they taken back to their prison quarters at a late hour of the afternoon. The cruel gaoler told them so in a jeering way. He seemed to take a pleasure in making things disagreeable to them, as he strutted to and fro along their line, flourishing his *quirt*, and giving grand exhibition of his "brief authority."

A little after midday, however, there came a change in their favour, brought by unlooked-for circumstances. Groups of people began to gather in the Callé de Plateros, swarming into it from side streets, and taking stand upon the foot-walk. Soon they lined it all along as far as the eye could reach. Not *pelados*, but most of them belonging to a class respectable, attired in their holiday clothes, as on a *dia de fiesta*. Something of this it was, as the scavengers were presently told, though some of them may have had word of it before without feeling any concern about it. Two, however, whom it did concern—though little dreamt they of its doing so—were only made aware of what the crowd was collecting for, when it began to thicken. These were Kearney and Rivas, who, knowing the language of the country, could make out from what was being said around them that there was to be a *funcion*. The foundation-stone of a new church was to be laid in the suburb of San Cosmé the chief magistrate of the State himself to lay it—with all ceremony and a silver trowel. The procession, formed in the Plaza Grande, would, of course, pass through the Callé de Plateros; hence the throng of the people in that street.

Funcions and *fiestas* are of such frequent occurrence in the Mexican metropolis—as indeed everywhere else in that land of the *far niente*—that this, an ordinary one and not much announced, excited no particular interest, save in the suburb of San Cosmé itself—a quarter where a church might be much needed, being a very den of disreputables. Still, a large number of people had put on their best apparel, and sallied forth to witness the procession.

This did not delay long in showing itself. It came heralded by the stirring notes of a trumpet, then the booming of the big drum in a band of music—military. A troop of cavalry—Lancers—formed the advance, to clear the way for what was to follow; this being a couple of carriages, in which were seated the Bishop of Mexico and his ecclesiastical staff, all in grand, gaudy raiments; on such an occasion the Church having precedence, and the post of honour.

Behind came the gilded coach of the Dictator—flanked on each side by guards in gorgeous uniform—himself in it. Not alone, but with one seated by his side, whose presence there caused Florence Kearney surprise, great as he ever experienced in his life. Despite the coat of diplomatic cut and its glittering insignia, he easily recognised his *ci-devant* teacher of the Spanish tongue—Don Ignacio Valverde.

But great as was his astonishment, he was left no time to indulge in it, or speculate how his old "crammer" came to be there. For close behind the Dictator's carriage followed another, holding one who had yet more interest for him than Don Ignacio—Don Ignacio's daughter!

Chapter Twenty Four
Significant Glances

Yes; the lady in the carriage was Luisa Valverde. Too surely she, thought Florence Kearney; for seeing her there was painful to him—a shock—as one who sees the woman he loves in the jaws of some great danger. And so he believed her to be, as a host of unpleasant memories came crowding into his mind like hideous spectres. No imagination either, but a danger real and present before his eyes at that moment, in the person of a man, riding by the side of the carriage in which she sat—Carlos Santander. He it was, in a gold-laced uniform, with a smile of proud satisfaction on his face. What a contrast to the craven, crestfallen wretch who, under a coating of dull green ooze, crawled out of the ditch at Pontchartrain! And a still greater contrast in the circumstances of the two men—fortunes, positions, apparel, everything reversed.

The Hussar colonel appeared not to be one of the regular escorts attending upon the Dictator, but detached, and free to choose his place in the procession. Well had he chosen it, any one would say; for there was a second lady in the carriage, young and beautiful, too; as may be guessed—the Condesa Almonté. But he seemed to have no eyes for her, nor words; his looks and speech all bestowed upon Luisa Valverde. For he was smilingly conversing with her, and she appeared to listen attentively, returning his smiles!

A spectacle to Kearney not only saddening, but maddening. Through his soul, dark as winter now, swept dire bitter misgivings.

"Are they married? No. 'Tis not the behaviour of man and wife. Soon will be—engaged, no doubt. Yes; he has won her heart, after all; likely had it then, when I believed it mine. Such deception? O God!"

These unspoken questions and conjectures passed through his mind rapidly as thought itself.

They were interrupted by his seeing the ladies—the carriage being now nearly abreast—turn their faces towards him in an odd interrogative way. The movement, abrupt and sudden, seemed prompted; and so had it been by him on horseback. Florence Kearney saw him nod in that direction, his lips moving, but the distance was too great to hear what he said.

"*Mira! Los Tejanos!*" were Santander's words, indicating the group of which they formed part. "One of them is, if I mistake not, an old acquaintance of yours, Don Luisa? And how strange!" he added, feigning surprise. "Chained to a criminal—no, let me not call him that—an individual in whom the Condesa Almonté takes an interest, if rumour's to be believed. Is it so, Condesa?"

Neither of them made response, for neither was now listening to him. Each had her eyes upon that which engrossed all her attention, one fixedly gazing at Florence Kearney, the other at Ruperto Rivas. For, by the grace, or rather negligence, of their guards, the latter was now up on the pavement.

What an interchange of glances between the pairs thus brought face to face! What a variety of expression upon their features! For varied and strong were their emotions at this moment—surprise, sadness, sympathy, indignation, and, amidst all, conspicuous above all, looks of unchanged, ever-confiding love!

He who had brought about this odd interview—for it had been pre-arranged—was riding on the left and near side of the carriage, the sewer being on the right and off; which, of course, placed him behind the backs of the ladies as they now were, and hindered his observing their faces. Could he have seen them just then, he might have doubted the success of his scheme, and certainly could not have accounted it a triumph. For the eyes, late turned smilingly upon himself, were now regarding Florence Kearney with earnest, sympathetic gaze.

And the man, to whom this was given, was trying his best to interpret it. He saw that she turned pale as her eyes first fell upon him. That might be but surprise seeing him there, with the consciousness of her own guilt. Or was it pity? If so, he would have spurned it. All the tortures the Acordada could inflict upon him, all the toil and degradation would be easier to bear than that. But no. It could not be pity alone. The sudden start and paling cheek; the look of interest in those eyes, beautiful as ever, and so well remembered; a flash in them that recalled the old time when he believed her heart his; all spoke of something more than mere sympathy with his misfortune. Before the carriage, moving slowly on, had carried her out of his sight, the jealous fancies so late harrowing his soul, seemed to be passing away, as though an angel was whispering in his ear, "She loves you—still loves you!"

Needless to say, he was too much occupied in reading the expression on Luisa Valverde's face to give even a look to the other beautiful one beside it. And alike was he forgetful of the man who stood beside himself. Yet, between these two neglected individuals, glances were being exchanged also in earnest, and watchful glances, which told of their being as much interested in one another as he in Luisa Valverde, or she in him. Better comprehending one another, too, as a physiognomist could have told, observing the play of their features. The first expression on those of the Condesa was surprise, quick changing to indignation, this as suddenly disappearing or becoming subdued, restrained by a thought, or possibly a sign, given by her "dear, noble Ruperto." As evinced by the fond, yet proud, sparkle of her eyes, he was no less dear now, no less noble in that degrading garb, than when she knew him in a gold-laced uniform, splendid as that worn by Santander, and he, in her eyes, ten times more worthy of wearing it. If he had turned bandit, she did not believe it; though, believing it, she would have loved him all the same. Nor in this would she have so much differed from the rest of her sex. Blameable as it may be, love—even that of a lady—has but little to do with the moralities; and of a Mexican lady perhaps less than any other. Certain, that Ruperto Rivas, robber or no, in that crossing of glances with the Condesa Almonté showed no sign of jealousy; instead, full confidence of being beloved by her.

Though the account of this little episode seems long, the actual occurrence—gestures, thoughts, looks, changes of facial expression—was all comprised within a few seconds of time, scarce so much as a minute.

Then the carriage containing the two ladies passed on out of sight, other carriages following, with other ladies in them; more cavalry—Lancers, Hussars, and heavy Dragoons—more music, mingling with the shouts and cheers of the fickle populace, as they swarmed along the foot-walk, every now and then vociferating—

"*Viva, Santa Anna el Illustrissimo! Viva, el Salvador de la Patria!*"

Chapter Twenty Five
A Mysterious Missive

"O! Ysabel! To think of it! In the chain-gang—in the sewers! *Madre de Dios!*"

Thus passionately exclaimed Luisa Valverde, half addressing herself to the Condesa Almonté in her father's house again, to which they had just returned from the ceremony of the procession. They were in the *sala*, seated upon the chair, into which they flung themselves, as if overcome with fatigue.

And weariness it was, but not of the body. Their souls were a-wearied through being unable to give utterance to the thoughts and passions that for hours had been convulsing them. Ever since passing the chain-gang they had been forced to keep up faces, seem as they felt not, smile when they could have wept. This the Condesa had counselled for reasons already hinted at; and now back home, with no one to see or hear, they were giving way to the wild tumult of emotion so long pent up.

For a time the Condesa made no rejoinder, herself as much affected as her friend. Both sat in despairing attitudes, heads drooped, and hands clasping them as though they ached; bosoms rising and falling in laboured undulation, the hearts within them painfully pulsing. All so unlike themselves, in such discordance with their great beauty, and the rich robes they wore. Looking at two such women, one could ill believe it possible for them to be otherwise than happy; yet, at that moment, both were miserable as misery itself.

"Ah, yes!" sighed the Countess, at length, and like as if awakening from some weird dream, its impress still upon her face. "To think of it; and fearful it is to think of. I understand things better now. My Ruperto is indeed in danger—more than I this morning believed. And your Florencio too. I could read his death in the eyes of Don Carlos Santander; and one told me the Tejanos are all to be shot!"

"O Ysabel, say not that! If they kill him, they may kill me! The man I love! Santa Guadalupe—Blessed Virgin! Save, oh, save him from such a fate!"

Against the wall was a picture of this, the patroness Saint of Mexico—for there is one in every Mexican house—and, while speaking, the young girl had risen from her chair, glided across the room, and fallen upon her knees before it. In this attitude she remained for some moments, her hands crossed over her breast, her lips moving as though she muttered a prayer.

Altogether differently acted the Condesa. She was not of the devotional sort, where it seemed unlikely to be of practical service. Good Catholic enough, and observant of all the ceremonies, but no believer in miracles; and therefore distrustful of what Santa Guadalupe, or any other saint, could do for them. She had more belief in the Cromwellian doctrine of keeping the powder dry; and that she meant to practise it, not with powder, but with her purse, was soon made evident by her speech.

"It's no use kneeling there," she said, starting to her feet, and again showing spirit. "Let us pray in our hearts. I've been doing that already, and I'm sure so have you. Something else should be done now—another effort made—this time with money; no matter how much it takes. Yes, Luisa, we must act."

"I want to act," rejoined the other, as she forsook the kneeling posture, with an abruptness not common to devotees; "only tell me how. Can you?"

For some seconds the Condesa let the question remain unanswered. Once more her hand had gone up to her head, the jewelled fingers met and clasped upon her brow—this time to quicken reflection; some scheme, already half conceived, needing further elaboration.

Whatever the plan, it was soon worked out complete, as evinced by her words following.

"*Amiga mia*; is there in your service one we can implicitly trust?"

"José. You know we can trust him."

"True. But he won't do for the first step to be taken: which is, indeed, only to deliver a letter. But it needs being adroitly done, and a woman will be the better for that. Besides, José will be wanted for something else, at the same time. There are two or three of my own female following could be relied on, so far as fidelity is concerned; but, unluckily, they're all known on the Callé de Plateros, as well as the street itself; and there isn't any of them particularly intelligent or dexterous. What we stand in need of now is one possessed of both these qualities—either woman or girl."

"Would Pepita do?"

"You mean the little *mestizo*, who was with you at New Orleans?"

"The same. She's all that; and, besides, devoted to me."

Don Ignacio's daughter had reason to know this, from experience in the Casa de Calvo, in which Pepita had played a part.

"She'll do," said the Countess; "the very individual, from what I've seen of her. Get me pen, ink, and paper—quick! At the same time summon Pepita!"

The Countess was now all action; and, responding to her roused energies, the other rushed towards the bell-pull, and gave it two or three vigorous jerks.

As it chanced, there were writing materials in the room; and, while waiting for the bell to be answered, the Countess made use of them, hastily scribbling some words on a sheet of paper, which she folded without putting into an envelope; instead, twisted it between her finger, as if dissatisfied with what she had written, and designed cancelling it. Far from this her intention, as was soon made manifest.

"*Muchacha!*" she said to Pepita, who, being lady's maid, had answered the bell herself. "Your mistress tells me you can be trusted on a matter which calls not only for confidence, but cleverness. Is that so?"

"I can't promise the cleverness, your ladyship; but for the other, I think the Doña Luisa knows she can rely on me."

"You'd be good at delivering a letter, without letting all the world into the secret, I suppose?"

"I'll do my best, your ladyship, if Duena command it."

"Yes, I wish it, Pepita," interposed Doña Luisa, herself the "Duena."

"*Muy bien Señorita.* Into whose hands is it to be put?"

Though speaking direct to her own mistress, the interrogatory was more meant for the Condesa, between whose fingers and thumb she saw the thing she was to take charge of.

The answer to her query called for some consideration. The note was for Ruperto Rivas; but the girl knew him not; so how could she give it him?

Here was a difficulty not before thought of, for a time perplexing both the ladies. In this case Doña Luisa was the first to see a way out of it, saying in a whisper:—

"Let her give it to Florencio; she knows him, and he can—"

"*Carramba!*" exclaimed the Countess interrupting. "How wonderfully wise you are, *amiga*! The very thing! And it never occurred to me! No, *you* tell her what to do."

"This, Pepita," said her mistress, taking the crumpled sheet from the Condesa, and passing it to her maid, "this is to be delivered to a gentleman you've seen, and should know."

"Where have I seen him, señorita?"

"In New Orleans."

"Do you mean Don Carlos, my lady?"

"No;" the abrupt negative accompanied with a dissatisfied look.

"Who then, señorita?"

"Don Florencio."

"*Ay Dios*! Is he here? I did not know it. But where am I to find him?"

No need to repeat the dialogue as continued. Suffice it that, before leaving the room, Pepita received full instructions where to find Don Florencio, and when found what she was to do and say to him.

So far all this was easy enough. More difficult the commission to be entrusted to José—more dangerous too. But it was made known to him in less than twenty minutes after; receiving his ready assent to its execution—though it should cost him his life, as he said. One motive for his agreeing to undergo the danger was devotion to his young mistress; another to stand well with Pepita, who had a power over him, and as he knew had entered upon her part with an ardent alacrity. But there was a third stimulus to keep up his courage, should it feel like failing—this having to do with the Condesa. Drawing out her grand gold watch—good value for a hundred *dollores*, and holding it up before his eyes, she said:

"That's your reward, José; that or its worth in money."

No need saying more. For the commission he was to execute much preparation was to be made, in all haste too. And in all haste he set to making it—determined to win the watch.

Chapter Twenty Six
The Play of Eyes

The ceremony of laying the foundation-stone had been brief and it was yet only an early hour of the afternoon when the procession passed back along the Callé de Plateros. The scavengers were still at work, and it is scarcely necessary to say that two of their number were earnestly on the lookout for a certain carriage. Sorry plight as they were in, neither felt ashamed or reluctant to come again under those eyes, after the expression they had observed in them. Rivas had hopes that in another exchange of glances with the Condesa, he might see something still further to instruct him; while Kearney, not so confident about his interpretation of those given to himself, longed to have a second reading of them.

Nor was he disappointed. The procession returned sooner than they expected, the looked-for carriage still holding its place in the line; the ladies in it, but now no officer of Hussars, nor any other, riding alongside. Santander, an aide-de-camp as known, had likely been ordered off on some official errand, and likely, too, his chief did not relish seeing him so near that particular equipage. Whatever the cause, his absence gave gratification to the two men noting it. With less constraint glances might now be exchanged—even gestures.

And both were. The look Kearney had given to him was accompanied by a nod of recognition; slight and timid, for it could not well be otherwise under the circumstances. But the eyes spoke more eloquently, telling him of respect undiminished, faith that had never faltered, love strong and true as ever. If he read pity in them too, it was not such as he would now spurn.

To Rivas were accorded signs of a very different sort. He had them not only from eyes, but the movement of a fan and fingers. They seemed satisfactory to him; for as the carriage passed out of sight, he turned to the other and said in a cheerful whisper:

"Keep up heart, *camarado*! I perceive you're not unknown to a friend of my friend. You heard the brute of a gaol-governor taunt me about a certain Condesa?"

"I did."

"Well; that's the lady, alongside her who's just been making eyes at you. An old acquaintance of yours, I see; and I think I could say where it was commenced. Never mind about that now. Enough for you to know that if friendship can get us out of this fix, with gold to back it, we may yet have a chance of giving leg-bail to the turnkeys of the Acordada."

Their dialogue was terminated by Dominguez, who, temporarily absent for a swill at one of the neighbouring *pulquerias*, now returned to the superintendence of his charge, and roughly commanded them to resume their work.

For nearly another hour the work went on, though not so regularly as before. The stream of returning sightseers still lined the foot-walks, many of them showing by their behaviour they had been paying a visit to *pulquerias* too, and more than once. Some stopped to fraternise with the soldiers, and would have done likewise with the *forzados*, if permitted. They were not hindered, however, from holding converse with the former, and extending hospitality to them in the shape of treats; sentry after sentry stealing away from his post after the proffered and coveted toothful. Nor was Dominguez an exception, he too every now and then repeating his visit to the dram-shop.

All this gave the scavengers licence of speech, with some liberty of action, or rather rest from their disagreeable task. And in the interval, while they were thus idling, the young Irishman noticed that the eyes of his chain companion were kept continuously on the foot-walks, now on one side now the other, his face towards the Plaza Grande—as though he expected to see some one coming that way. Kearney himself was regarding the people who came along—but only from curiosity—when his attention was more particularly drawn to one who had come to a stop on the sidewalk nearly opposite. This was a girl of rather diminutive stature, dressed in the ordinary fashion of the common people, short-skirted petticoat, sleeveless *camisa*, arms, ankles, and feet bare; but the head, breast, and shoulders all under one covering—the *reboso*. Even her face was hidden by this, for she was wearing it "tapado," one eye only visible, through a little loop in the folded scarf, which was kept open by the hand that held it. The girl had drawn up in front of a jeweller's window, as though to feast that eye on the pretty things therein displayed. And thus Kearney would not have noticed her, any more than the others, many of them in like garb passing to and fro. But, just as his eye happened to light upon her, he saw that hers—literally a single one—was fixed upon him, regarding him in a way altogether different from that which might be expected on the part of a chance stranger. Her attitude, too, was odd. Though facing nearly square to the shop window, and pretending to look into it, her head was slightly turned, and the eye surely on him.

At first he was puzzled to make out what it could mean, and why the girl should be taking such an interest in him. Possibly, had she been wearing shoes and stockings, he might have come easier to the comprehension of it. But a little brown-skinned, barefooted *muchacha*, in a petticoat of common stuff, and cheap scarf over her shoulders, he could think of no reason why she should have aught to do with him.

Only for a few seconds, however, was he thus in the dark. Then all became clear, the *éclaircissement* giving him a start, and sending the blood in quick rush through his veins—pleasant withal. For the girl, seeing she had caught his attention, relaxed her clasp upon the scarf, partially exposing her face, and the other eye.

Kearney needed not seeing the whole of it for recognition now. Well remembered he those features—pretty in spite of the dark skin—he had often seen wreathed with pleasant smiles, as their owner used to open the door for him in the Casa de Calvo.

Chapter Twenty Seven
A Letter Dexterously Delivered

Pepita it was, though in a different style of dress to what he had been accustomed to see her in; as at New Orleans she had not kept to her national costume. Besides, there was a *soupçon* of shabbiness about her present attire, and then the shoeless feet!

"Dismissed the Valverde service—out of a situation—poor girl!"

He would not have so pityingly reflected, had he seen her as she was but a short half-hour before, in a pretty muslin dress, snow-white stockings, and blue satin slippers. Since then she had made a change in her toilet under direction and by help of the Condesa, who had attired her in a way more befitting the task intended.

Kearney, in full belief of her being a discharged servant, remembering her many little kindnesses to himself in the Casa de Calvo, was about to call her up, and speak a word of sympathy for old time's sake. Dominguez was still absent, and the nearest sentry engaged in a chaffing encounter with some one in the crowd.

Just then he observed a slight tremor of her head, and with a sudden movement of the hand which seemed to say, "No, don't speak to me." She, too, could talk that mute language, so well understood in her country.

So restrained, he kept silent; to see her now glance furtively around, as if to make sure no one else was observing her. She had again closed the scarf over her face, but in the hand that held it under her chin something white—a piece of paper he supposed—appeared; just for one instant, then drawn under. Another significant look accompanied this gesture, saying plain as word could speak it:—

"You see what I've got for you; leave the action all to me."

He did, for he could not do otherwise; he was fixed to this spot, she foot free. And the use she now made of this freedom was to walk straight out into the street, though not as coming to him; instead, her steps, as her eyes were directed towards Cris Rock and the hunchback, who were at work some paces further on. She seemed bent on making a closer inspection of the odd pair, nor would any one suppose she had other object in crossing over to them. No one did, save Kearney himself. Rivas had been again ordered into the sewer, and was at work in it. Besides, he did not know Pepita, though he was the one she most wished to be near. Chiefly for him was the communication she had to make.

It could not be, however, without a demonstration likely to be observed, therefore dangerous. But her wit was equal to the occasion, proving how well the ladies had chosen their letter-carrier.

"*Ay Dios!*" she exclaimed aloud, brushing past the young Irishman, and stopping with her eyes bent wonderingly on the strangely contrasted couple; then aside in *sotto voce* to Kearney, whom she had managed to place close behind her, apparently unconscious of his being there—"A *billetita*, Don Florencio—not for you—for the Señor Rivas—you can give it him—I daren't. Try to take it out of my hand without being seen." Then once more aloud. "*Gigante y enano!*" just as others had said, "*Rue cosa estranja!*" (what a strange thing).

She need not say any more, nor stay there any longer. For while she was speaking the crumpled sheet had passed through the fringe of the scarf, out of her fingers into those of Don Florencio, who had bent him to his work bringing his hand to the right place for the transfer.

Her errand, thus vicariously accomplished with another wondering look at the giant and dwarf, and another "*Ay, Dios!*" she turned to go back to the side walk. But before passing Kearney she managed to say something more to him.

"Carriage will come along soon—two ladies in it—one you know—one dear to you as you to her."

Sweet words to him, though muttered, and he thanked her who spoke them—in his heart. He dared not speak his thanks, even in whisper; she was already too far off, tripping back to the flagged foot-walk, along which she turned, soon to disappear from his sight.

What she had said about the coming of a carriage was to Kearney not altogether intelligible. But, no doubt, the note, now concealed inside his shirt bosom would clear that up; and the next step was to hand it over to him for whom it was intended.

Luckily, Rivas had not been unobservant of what was going on between the girl and his companion. Her look seeming strange to him, had attracted his attention, and though keeping steadily at work, his eyes were not on it, but on them, which resulted in his witnessing the latter part of the little episode, and having more than a suspicion it also concerned himself. He was not taken by surprise, therefore, when Kearney, drawing closer to the edge of the drain, spoke down to him in a half-whisper—

"I've got something for you. Bring the point of your tool against mine, and look out when you feel my fingers."

"*Muy bien*! I understand," was the muttered response.

In a second or two after the shafts of their implements came into collision accidentally, it appeared. He would indeed have been sharp-witted who could have supposed it intentional, and lynx-eyed to have seen that scrap of twisted paper passed from one to the other—the second transfer dexterously done as the first. All any one could have told was, that the two scavengers seemed sorry for what had occurred, made mutual apologies, then separated to the full length of their coupling-chain, and went to work again, looking meek and innocent as lambs.

It was now Rivas' turn to prove himself possessed of quick wit. He had reason to think the letter required immediate reading; and how was this to be done? To be seen at it would surely bring the sentries upon him, even though Dominguez was not there. And for them to get possession of it— that was a calamity perhaps worst of all! Possibly to compromise the writer; and well knew he who that was.

For a time he was perplexed, looking in all directions, and thinking of every way possible for him to read the letter unobserved. But none did seem possible. He could stoop down, so as to be unseen by those passing along the sidewalk; but close to the sewer's edge were two or three of the sentries, who would still command view of him.

All at once a look of satisfaction came over his countenance, as his eyes rested on a side drain, which entered the main one, like many others, from adjacent dwellings. He had just scraped the mud out of its mouth, and was close to it.

The very thing, was his thought—the very place for his purpose. And shortly after he might have been seen standing before it, in bent attitude, his arms busy with his shovel, but his eyes and thoughts busier with a sheet of paper which lay at the bottom of the branch drain, some two or three feet inside it. It was the *billetita*, and though the creases were but hastily pressed out, he contrived to make himself master of its contents. They were but brief and legibly written—the script familiar to him.

"Querido,—Soon after receiving this—say, half an hour—look for a carriage—landau shut up—two ladies inside—pair of large horses— *frisones*—grey. When opposite, be ready—with him who shares your chain. Leave manners in the mud—make a rush, storm the carriage, eject the occupants rudely—violently—and take their places. You can trust the *cochero*. Some danger in the attempt, I know; but more if not made. Your old enemy implacable—determined to have your life. Do this, dearest, and save it—for your country's sake, as also that of Ysabel."

Chapter Twenty Eight
Looking out for a Landau

From the way Rivas treated the "billetita" after he had finished reading it, one unacquainted with its contents might have supposed they had made him either mad angry, or madly jealous. Instead of taking it up tenderly, and treasuring it away, he planted his muddy boot upon it, with a back scrape brought it into the main sewer, still keeping it under the mud and trampling it with both feet, lifted and set down alternately, the while shovelling away, as though he had forgotten all about it. Not so, however. The tread-mill action was neither accidental nor involuntary, but for a purpose. The writer had committed herself in sub-signing a portion of her name, as by other particulars, and should the letter fall into hands he knew of, her danger would be as great as his own.

In a few seconds, however, any uneasiness about this was at an end. The most curious *chiffonier* could not have deciphered a word written on that sheet, which by the churning he had submitted it to must have been reduced to a very pulp.

During all this time no one had taken notice of his proceedings, not even the man chained to him, except by an occasional side glance. For Kearney, well aware of what he was at, to draw attention from him had got up a wordy demonstration with the dwarf—to all appearance a quarrel. There was real anger on the side of the latter; for the "gringo," as he contemptuously called the Irishman, had cruelly mocked his deformity. A cruelty which gave pain to the mocker himself; but he could think of no other way to secure inattention to Rivas, and this efficiently did. Both talking the tongue of the country, their war of words, with some grotesque gestures which Kearney affected, engrossed the attention of all within sight or hearing; so that not an eye was left for the surreptitious reader of the letter.

When the sham quarrel came to an end—which it did soon as he who commenced it saw it should—the knot of spectators it had drawn around dispersed, leaving things as before. But not as before felt Rivas and Kearney. Very different now the thoughts stirring within them, both trying to appear calm while under the greatest agitation. For they had again contrived to bring their ears together, and the latter now knew all about the contents of the Condesa's letter, their purport being fully explained, nor did they draw apart, till a thorough understanding had been established between them as to the action they should take.

All this without loss of time was translated to Cris Rock, who was told also of their resolve to attempt to escape, in which the Texan was but too glad to take part. Kearney would have stayed there, and gone back into the Acordada, loathsome gaol though it was, sooner than leave his old filibustering comrade behind. He could never forget the incident of El Salado, nor cease to feel gratitude to the man who had offered to give up life for him.

But there was no need for Rock being left behind. Rivas himself wished it otherwise, for more than one reason; but one good one, that instead of obstructing their escape he would be an aid to it.

The hunchback alone was not let into their secret. No doubt he too would be glad to get free from his chains, since he was under a sentence of imprisonment for life. But who could tell whether at the last moment he might not purchase pardon by turning out and betraying them? They knew him to be vile enough even for that, and so kept him in the dark about their design.

There was no need of further premeditation or contrivance of plans. That had all been traced out for them in the singular epistle signed "Ysabel," and a few whispered words from one to the other completed the understanding of it, with what was to be done. From the time this was settled out, never looked three pair of eyes more eagerly along a street than did theirs along the Callé de Plateros; never was a carriage more anxiously awaited than a landau which should show itself with hood up, drawn by a pair of grey horses.

It is now well on the afternoon, and the "beauty and fashion" of the Mexican metropolis were beginning to appear in carriages, with chivalry on horseback, along the line of streets leading to the Paseo Nuevo. The procession of the morning would little affect the usual evening display; and already several equipages had rolled past the place where the chain-gang was at work. But as yet appeared not the one so anxiously looked-for, and the half-hour was up!

Still ten minutes more without any sign of it!

More anxious now were the three prisoners, who contemplated escape, though not at all to the same degree, or for the same reason. Kearney feared there had been a failure, from betrayal by the coachman spoken of as so trustworthy; he did not think of suspecting Pepita. The Texan, too, believed some hitch had occurred, a "bit o' crooked luck," as he worded it. Not so Rivas. Though, as the others, chafing at the delay, he still had confidence in the carriage coming, as he had in the directing head of one he expected to see inside it. It was being purposely kept back, he fancied; likely as not, lest it might attract attention by being too early on the street.

Whatever the cause, his conjectures were soon brought to an end—and abruptly—by seeing the thing itself.

"*Bueno!*" he mentally exclaimed, then muttering to the others—"Yonder it comes! *Frisones pardes* coachman in sky-blue and silver—be ready *camarados.*"

And ready they were, as panthers preparing to spring. Rock and Rivas, as Kearney himself, were now out of the sewer and up on the street; all three still making believe to work; while the dwarf seemed to suspect there was something in the wind, but could not guess what.

He knew the instant after, when a strong hand, grasping him by the collar, lifted him off his feet, raising and tossing him further aloft, as though he had been but a rat.

Chapter Twenty Nine
A Clumsy Cochero

Perhaps no people in the world have been more accustomed to spectacular surprises than they who perambulate the streets of the Mexican metropolis. For the half-century preceding the time of which I write, they had witnessed almost as many revolutions as years, seen blood spilled till the stones ran red with it, and dead bodies lying before their doors often for hours, even days, unremoved. As a consequence, they are less prone to curiosity than the dwellers in European cities, and the spectacle or incident that will stir their interest in any great degree must needs be of an uncommon kind.

Rare enough was that they were called on to witness now—such of them as chanced to be sauntering along the Callé de Plateros, where the chain-gang was at work. They first saw a carriage—a handsome equipage of the landau speciality—drawn by a pair of showy horses, and driven by a coachman in smart livery, his hat cockaded, proclaiming the owner of the turnout as belonging to the military or diplomatic service. Only ladies, however, were in it—two of them—and the horses proceeding at a rather leisurely pace. As several other carriages with ladies in them, and liveried coachmen on the boxes, had passed before, and some seen coming behind, there was nothing about this one to attract particular attention; unless, indeed, the beauty of the two "señoritas" inside, which was certainly exceptional. Both were young, and, if related, not likely to be sisters; in contour of features, complexion, colour of eyes and hair, everything different, even to contrast. But alike in that each after her own style was a picture of feminine loveliness of the most piquantly attractive kind; while their juxtaposition made it all the more so, for they were seated side by side.

Such could not fail to draw the eyes of the street passengers upon them, and elicit looks of admiration. So far from courting this, however, they seemed desirous of shunning it. The day was one of the finest, the atmosphere deliciously enjoyable, neither too warm nor too cold; other carriages were open, yet the hoods of theirs met overhead, and the glasses were up. Still, as these were not curtained they could be seen through them. Some saw who knew them, and saluted; gentlemen by raising the hat, lady acquaintances by a nod, a quivering of the fingers. For it was the hour of promenade to the Alameda. Others to whom they were unknown inquired whose carriage it was. But not a few noticed in the faces of its fair occupants an expression which struck them as singular; something of constraint or anxiety—the last so unlike what should have been there.

And so all along the line of street, until the carriage came nearly opposite the entrance gate of the Alameda, still going slowly; at which the pampered, high-spirited horses seemed to chafe and fret. Just then, however, they showed a determination to change the pace, or at all events the direction, by making a sudden start and shy to the right; which carried the off wheels nearly nave-deep into the ridge of mud recently thrown out of the sewer.

Instinctively, or mechanically, the coachman pulled up. No one could suppose designedly; since there was sufficient likelihood of his having an overturn. Still, as the mud was soft, by bearing on the near rein, with a sharp cut of the whip, he might easily clear the obstruction.

This was not done; and the spectators wondered why it was not. They had already made up their minds that the balk was due to the coachman's maladroit driving, and this further proof of his stupidity quite exhausted their patience. Shouts assailed him from all sides, jeers, and angry ejaculations.

"*Burro!*" (donkey) exclaimed one; a second crying out, "What a clumsy *cochero!*" a third, "You're a nice fellow to be trusted with reins! A rope tied to a pig's tail would better become you?"

Other like shafts, equally envenomed, were hurled at Josh's head; for it scarce needs telling that he was the driver of the carriage, and the ladies inside it his mistress and the Condesa Almonté. For all he seemed but little to regard what was being said to him—indeed nothing, having enough on hand with his restive horses. But why did he not give them the whip, and let them have more rein! It looked as if that would start them off all right again, and that was what every one was shouting to him to do, he instead doing the very opposite, holding the animals in till they commenced plunging.

The ladies looked sorely affrighted; they had from the first, for it was all but the occurrence of an instant. Both had risen to their feet, one tugging at the strap to get the sash down, the other working at the handle of the door, which perversely refused to act, all the while uttering cries of alarm.

Several of the passengers rushed to the door in the near side to assist them, that on the off being unapproachable by reason of the open drain. But on this also appeared rescuers—a pair of them—not street promenaders, but two of the chain-gang! All muddy as these were, they were advancing with as much apparent eagerness as the others—more in reality—to release the imperilled señoritas. A proof that humanity may exist even in the breast of a gaol-bird; and the spectators, pleased with an exhibition of it, so rare and unexpected, were preparing to applaud them enthusiastically.

Their admiration, however, received a rude and almost instantaneous check, changing to wild astonishment, succeeded by equally wild indignation. The *forzados* got their door open first; but the ladies, apparently terrified at the rough, unclean creatures, refused to go out that way, and only shrank back. Luckily, the other was by this also opened, and they made through it into the street. But not before the two scavengers had leaped up into the carriage beside them, and, as if angry at their earlier offer being declined, given them a rude shove outward!

That was not all the spectators saw to astonish them. Other incidents followed equally unlooked-for, and with lightning rapidity. One was indeed of simultaneous occurrence; a second couple of the scavengers— the *gigante y enano*—rushing towards the coachman's box, clambering up to it, Rock flinging the dwarf before him as one would an old carpet-bag, and mounting after. Then, jerking the reins and whip out of Josh's hands— letting him still keep his seat, however,—he loosened the one, and laid the lash of the other on the horses' hips, so sharply and vigorously, as to start them at once into a gallop.

Meanwhile, the uncouth couple inside had pulled-to the doors, shutting themselves in, and taken the seats late occupied by the elegantly dressed ladies—a transformation so grotesque as to seem more dream than reality. And so off all went, leaving behind a crowd as much amazed as any that ever witnessed spectacle on the streets of the Mexican metropolis.

Chapter Thirty
The Poor Ladies

Quite a combination of circumstances had favoured the escape of the four *forzados*—the balking of the horses, the absence of Dominguez, and the relaxed vigilance of the guards—from their brains bemuddled with drink. But there was yet another lucky chance that stood them in stead—the point from which they had started. The line of sentries ended at the Alamedas Gate, and, as the one posted there was he who had them in particular charge, once past him they had only to fear a single bullet sent after them.

As it turned out, they did not even get that, fortune favouring them in every way. This sentry, though last on the line outward, was the first encountered by the people returning from the ceremony at San Corme; therefore made most of by passing friends, with the bottle oftener presented to his lips. As a consequence, when the carriage whirled past him he had but an indistinct idea of why it was going so fast, and none at all as to who were in it. With eyes drowned in *aguardiente* he stood as one dazed, looking after, but taking no measures to stop it. When at length some one bawled the truth into his ear and he brought his flint-lock to an unsteady level, it would have been too late—had the piece gone off. Luckily for those on the sidewalk, it did not; missing fire by a flash in the pan, as might have been anticipated.

Never were sentries more completely taken by surprise than they guarding the chain-gang. Nor more disagreeably. They knew they had been neglecting their duty, and might expect severe punishment! possibly set at the very task they were now superintending! Still, they made no attempt to pursue. They were not cavalry; and only mounted men could overtake that landau with its curious load, soon to vanish from their sight. So they stood gazing after it in helpless bewilderment, their faces showing a variety of expressions, surprise, anger, fear, mingled in a most ludicrous manner. Deserting their posts they had gathered into a knot, and it was some time before they had so far recovered their senses as to think of despatching one of their number to the Plaza Grande after cavalry sure to be there.

It was a fine opportunity for others of the gaol-birds to make a bolt; but for the obstructive coupling-chains no doubt some would avail themselves of it. These, however, hindered the attempt. There were no more restive horses, nor blundering coachmen to bring another carriage near enough for a rush.

But the most interesting group now on the ground was that which had collected round the ladies left carriage-less; some offering services, others speaking words of sympathy. "*Las señoritas pobres!*"

"*Pobrecitas!*" —("The poor young ladies!" "Poor things!") were exclamations uttered over and over again.

It was a trying situation for the "poor things" to be in, sure enough. But they acquitted themselves admirably; especially the Condesa, who, young though she was, for courage and coolness had few to equal her. In that emergency no man could have shown himself her superior. Her look of still untranquillised terror, the intermittent flashes of anger in her eyes as she loudly denounced the ruffians who had carried off their carriage, was a piece of acting worthy of a Rachel or Siddons. He would have been a keen physiognomist who could have told that her emotions were counterfeit. Little dreamt the sympathising spectators that while being pushed out of the carriage she had contrived to whisper back to the man so rudely behaving: "Look under the cushions, *querido*! You'll find something. *Dios te guarda!*"

Still less could they have supposed that the other young lady, looking so meek, had at the same time spoken tender words to the second ruffian who had assailed them.

The part the *pobrecitas* were playing, with the sympathy they received, seemed to themselves so comically ludicrous that, but for its serious side, neither could have kept countenance. Alone the thought of the lovers not yet being beyond danger hindered their bursting out into laughter.

And lest this, too, might cease to restrain them they seized upon the earliest pretext to get away from the spot.

Glad were they when some of their gentlemen acquaintances, who chanced to be passing the place, came up and proposed escorting them home. A service accepted and, it need not be said, offered with as much alacrity as it was received.

Their departure had no effect in dispersing the crowd which had gathered by the Alamedas Gate. A spot signalised by an episode so odd and original, was not to be forsaken in that quick inconsiderate way. Instead, the throng grew quicker, until the street for a long stretch was packed full of people, close as they could stand. Only one part of it remained unoccupied, the central list showing the open sewer with its bordering of black mud. In their holiday attire the populace declined invading this, though they stood wedging one another along its edge; their faces turned towards it, with hilarity in their looks and laughter on their lips. It was just the sort of spectacle to please them; the sentries in a row—for they had now sneaked back to their post—appearing terribly crestfallen, while those over whom they stood guard seemed, on the contrary, cheerful—as though expecting soon to be released from their chains. With them it was the *esprit de corps* of the galley slave, glad to see a comrade escape from their common misery, though he cannot escape himself.

All this, however, was tame; but the winding up of the spectacle in a quiet natural way. It would soon have been over now, and the sightseers scattered off to their homes; but just as they were beginning to retire, a new incident claimed their attention. A scene almost as exciting as any that had preceded, though only a single personage appeared in it. This Dominguez, the gaoler, who had been absent all the while at his *pulqueria*, and only just warned of the event that had so convulsed the Callé de Plateros, breaking through the crowd like an enraged bull, rushed along the sewer's edge, nourishing his whip over the heads of the *forzados*, at the same time reviling the sentries for their scandalous neglect of duty! To tell the truth, he was more troubled about his own. He had received particular instructions to be watchful of four prisoners—the very ones that had escaped. Well might he dread the reckoning in store for him on return to the gaol. However could he face his governor?

For some time he strode to and fro, venting his drunken spleen alike on soldiers or scavengers. Some of the former would have retaliated; but they knew him to have authority in high places, and therefore kept silent, sullenly enduring it. Not so the spectators, many of whom, knowing, hated him. Possibly, more than probably, some of them had been under his care. But to all he was now affording infinite amusement. They laughed at his impotent anger, and laughed again, one crying out, "He's as good as a bull in a ring!" another exclaiming, *"Viva el Señor Dominguez rey de las bastoneros!"* ("Hurrah for the Señor Dominguez, king of the turnkeys!")—a sally which elicited roars of applauding laughter.

If angry before, he was now infuriated. Purple in the face, he was making a dash at the man whom he suspected of mocking him, when his foot slipped and down he went into the drain head foremost.

He had altogether disappeared, and was for some seconds out of sight; the laughter, which had become a yelling chorus, all the while continuing. Nor did it cease when he re-appeared; instead, was louder and more uproarious than ever. For his face, late blue with rage, was now black with a limning of the sewer liquid.

But he was less mad than sad, after the ill-timed tumble. The *douche* had tamed, if not sobered him; and his only thought now was how to get away from that place of repeated discomfitures, anywhere to hide and wash himself.

Luck declared for him at last, in the approach of a squadron of Hussars, drawing off from him the eyes of the spectators; who had now enough to do looking out for themselves and their safety. For the Hussars were coming on at a gallop, with drawn sabres.

A crush and a scampering followed, as they forced their way through the crowd, shouting, and striking with the back of their blades. After they had passed, the people were no longer in a humour for laughing at the "King of the turnkeys," nor any one else; neither was he there to be laughed at.

Chapter Thirty One
A Transformation

While the ladies set down upon the street were still plaintively appealing to those around, the carriage from which they had been so unceremoniously ejected was tearing along the Callé de San Francisco, going direct for the Acordada! But nothing could be farther from the thoughts of those in it than a return to that grand gaol, or even approaching its door. All of them knew there was a regular guard there; and instead of a single musket missing fire, they would more likely be saluted with a full volley, sending a shower of bullets about their ears. Bad marksmen as the Mexican soldiers are, they could not all miss. But even if they passed through that unscathed, beyond was the *garita* of San Cosmé, with another guard there. Indeed, go what way they would, there was none leading out into the country without a *garita* to be got through—and for the country they were aiming.

In these gates, however, there was a difference as to the strength of their guard detail, and the possibilities of their being passed. All of which one of the fugitives well understood—Rivas, who, as a matter of course, had assumed direction of everything relating to their flight. When opposite the old convent, which gives its name to the street, he leaned his head out of the carriage window, and said to the *cochero*:—

"Take the route by El Nino Perdido. You know the way; show it to him."

The "him" was Cris Rock, who still had hold of the reins, and who, not understanding Spanish, could not be addressed direct.

The result of the order was, that shortly after, the horses were headed into a side street, indicated to the Texan by a nod perceptible only to himself. It would not do for the real coachman to appear as aiding their escape; though there was no danger of the dwarf observing it—the latter having been crammed down into the boot—where he was held with his head between Rock's huge thighs, as in a vice.

The street into which they had turned was a narrow one running along a dead wall—that of the ancient monastery, which occupies acres of ground.

And in its strip of sidewalk just then there was not a pedestrian to be seen—the very thing Rivas had been wishing for. Again speaking out, he said:—

"Slowly for a bit. I see a *seraph* out there. Tell the Tejanos to put it on."

For the next hundred yards or so—along the dead wall—the horses went at a walk, they inside the carriage, as also one on the box, all the while busy as bees. And when they came out at the end of the quiet street entering upon a more frequented thoroughfare, the brisk pace was resumed; though no one could have believed it the same party, seen but a minute or two before driving at a racecourse speed along the Callé de Plateros. José alone looked the same, in his sky-blue livery and cockaded hat. But the big man by his side had so far effected a change that his mud-stained habiliments were hidden under an ample *seraph*, which covered him from neck to ankles; while the little one was altogether invisible, and under a threat of having his skull kicked in if he attempted to show himself.

Alike quick and complete had been the transformation of the "insides." There now sat two gentlemen, decently, indeed rather stylishly dressed—one wearing a blue cloth cloak with velvet collar; the other a scarlet "manga," with gold bullion embroidery from neck to shoulders.

About the equipage there was little now to make remark upon, or cause it to be regarded with suspicion. Some rich *haciendado*, who had been at the laying of the foundation-stone, on return to his country house, taking a friend along with him. The strapping fellow on the box might be mayor-domo of the estate—they are usually tall men—who had taken a fancy to try his hand at driving, and the coachman had surrendered him the reins. All perfectly natural, and *en règle*, even to the rapid speed at which the horses were put. The driver not accustomed to handling the ribbons would account for this. Besides, the sun was getting low, the *casa de campo* might be a good distance from town, and such a splendid turnout, belated on a country road would be like tempting Providence, and certainly the *salteadores*!

How little would its occupants have regarded an encounter with highwaymen. Perhaps just then they would have welcomed it. Nor much did Rivas anticipate further trouble in the streets of the city. He was familiar with those they were now driving along, and felt no fear of being obstructed there—at least by the people. Had they hung their chain out of the carriage window and exposed the prison dress, no one in that quarter would have cried "Stop thief!" The man who should so cry, would run the risk of having his clamour suddenly silenced.

For all they had apprehensions of the keenest. If they were in no danger while in the streets, they would be when parting from them—at El Nino Perdido. That gauntlet had yet to be run.

But while thinking of it, they had not been idle; instead, all the while planning and preparing for it; Rivas instructing the others as to how they should act.

"A *garita* of the usual kind," he said to Kearney, making known the nature of the anticipated obstruction; "a gate across the road, with a guard-house alongside. There's sure to be a sergeant and eight or ten files in it. If, by good luck, the gate be open, our best way will be to approach gently, then go through at a gallop. If shut, we'll be called upon to show our best diplomacy. Leave all that to me. Failing to fool the guard, we must do battle with it. Anything's better than be taken back to the Acordada. That would be sure death for me; and, if I mistake not, for yourself, Señor."

"I'm sure of it. If we can't get through without, let us fight our way, whatever the result."

"Take this pair, then. They seem the most reliable. You *Americanos* are more skilled in the use of fire-arms than we. With us steel is preferred. But I'll do the best I can with the other pair."

This had reference to two pairs of pistols discovered under the carriage cushions. Nor were they the only weapons there; besides them were two long-bladed knives, and a pearl-handled stiletto—the last a tiny affair, which looked as though taken from the toilet case of a lady.

"See that yours are loaded and in firing order," Rivas added, at the same time looking to his own.

The injunction was not needed, as the Irishman was already examining the weapons put into his hand, with a view to their efficiency.

Both pair of pistols were of the old-fashioned duelling kind—flintlocks, with barrels nearly a foot in length. Like as not the Condesa's father and Don Ignacio Valverde, in days long gone by, had vindicated honour with them.

The inspection was quick and short, as had been all that preceded; pans sprung open, showing them filled with powder; rammers run into the barrels, then drawn out again, and replaced in their thimbles.

"Mine," said Kearney, first to report, "are good for two lives."

"And mine the same," rejoined Rivas, "unless I'm laid low before I can pull the second trigger. Now to dispose of the knives. My countryman, the *cochero*, however trustworthy, mustn't show fight. That would ruin all afterwards. But, if I mistake not, your colossal comrade is the man to make play with one of them in a pinch."

"You may be sure of it. He was in the Alamo with Bowie, and at Goliad with Fanning. Don't fear putting a knife into his hands; he'll make good use of it if we're driven to close quarters."

"Let him have it, then. You give it, and tell him all."

Kearney getting hold of one of the two knives, that seeming best suited for the hands he designed putting it in, passed it on to Cris Rock—not through the carriage window, but a hole cut in the leathern hood by the blade itself. Speaking through the same, he said—

"Cris! we've got to run a gate where there's a guard of soldiers— maybe a dozen or so. You're to drive gently up, and, if you see it open, pass through—then lay on the whip. Should it be shut, approach more briskly, and pull up impatient-like. But do nothing of yourself—wait till I give you the word."

"Trust me, Cap; ye kin do that, I kilk'late."

"I can, Cris. Take this knife, and if you hear pistols cracking behind, you'll then know what to do with it."

"I gie a guess, anyhow," rejoined the Texan, taking hold of the knife, in a hand passed behind him. Then bringing it forward and under his eyes, he added, "'Taint sech a bad sort o' blade eyther, tho' I weesh 'twas my ole bowie they took from me at Mier. Wal, Cap; ye kin count on me makin' use o't, ef 'casion calls, an' more'n one yaller-belly gittin' it inter his guts; notwithstandin' this durnation clog that's swinging at my legs. By the jumping Geehosophat, if I ked only git shet o' that I'd—"

What he would do or intended saying, had to stay unsaid. Rivas interrupted him, pulling Kearney back, and telling him to be ready with the pistols. For they were nearing the place of danger.

Chapter Thirty Two
An Unlooked-for Salute

In a strict military sense the capital of Mexico cannot be called a fortified city. Still, it has defences, one being an *enceinte* wall, which envelops it all round, leaving no straggled suburb, scarce so much as a house, outside. Compact and close stand the dwellings of the modern city as those of ancient Tenochtitlan, whose site it occupies, though the waves of Tezcuco and Xochimilco no longer lap up to its walls.

The *enceinte* spoken of is a mere structure of "adobes," large sun-baked blocks of mud and straw—in short, the bricks of the Egyptians, whose making so vexed Moses and the Israelites. Here and there may be seen a little redoubt, with a battery of guns in it; but only on revolutionary occasions— the wall, so far as defence goes, more concerning the smuggler than the soldier; and less contraband from abroad than infringement of certain regulations of home commerce—chief of them the tax called "alcabala," corresponding to the *octroi* of France, and the *corvée* of some other European countries.

The tax is collected at the "garitas," of which there is one on every road leading out of the city, or rather into it; for it is the man who enters, not he making exit, who is called upon to contribute to the *alcabala*. It is levied on every article or commodity brought from the country in search of a city market. Nothing escapes it; the produce of farm and garden, field and forest—all have to pay toll at the *garitas*, so losing a considerable percentage of their value. The brown aboriginal, his "burro" laden with charcoal, or skins of *pulque*, or himself staggering under a load of planks heavy enough to weigh down a donkey, which he has transported from a mountain forest—ten or twenty miles it may be—is mulcted in this blackmail before he can pass through a *garita*.

Not unfrequently he is unable to meet the demand till he have made sale of the taxed commodity. On such occasions he hypothecates his hat, or *frezada*, leaving it at the gate, and going on bareheaded or bare-shouldered to the market, to redeem the pawned article on return.

Save through these gates there is no access to, or egress from, the Mexican capital; and at each, besides the official having charge of the revenue matters, a soldier-guard is stationed, with a guard-house provided; their duties being of a mixed, three-cornered kind—customs, police, and military. Five or six such posts there are, on the five or six roads leading out from the city, like the radiating limbs of a star-fish; and one of these is the *garita* El Nino Perdido—literally, the gate of the "Lost Child." It is, however, one through which the traffic is of secondary importance; since it is not on any of the main routes of travel. That which it bars is but a country road, communicating with the villages of Mixcoac, Coyoacan, and San Angel. Still, these being places of rural residence, where some of the *familiares principes* have country houses, a carriage passing through the gate of the Lost Child is no rarity. Besides, from the gate itself runs a *Calzada*, or causeway, wide and straight for nearly two miles, with a double row of grand old trees along each side, whose pleasant shade invites, and often receives, visits from city excursionists out for a stroll, ride, or drive. Near the end of the second mile it angles abruptly to the right, in the direction of San Angel—a sharp corner the writer has good reason to remember, having been shot at by *salteadores*, luckily missed, while passing round it on his way from country quarters to the city. A horse of best blood saved *his* blood there, or this tale would never have been told.

Asking the reader's pardon for a personal digression—with the excuse that it may throw light on the scene to follow—it will be understood how easily the guard on duty at the gate might be "thrown off guard" by a carriage passing through it; especially on that day when there were so many, by reason of the grand doings in the city.

Several had just passed, going country-wards; for it was the season of rural sojourn among the "ricos." So, when another appeared, heading in the same direction, the guard-sergeant at Nino Perdido saw nothing amiss, or to be suspicious of; instead, something to inspire him with respect. He had been on guard at the Palace scores of times; and by appearance knew all who were accustomed to pass in and out, more especially those holding authority. Liveries he could distinguish at any distance; and when he saw a carriage approaching along the street, with a coachman in sky-blue and silver, cockaded, he did not need its being near to recognise the equipage of one of the Cabinet Ministers.

Though a non-commissioned officer, he was a man of ambitious aims; dreaming of gold bullion in the shape of epaulettes; and he had long had his eye on the epaulette of an *alferez*—officers of this rank being allowed only one. The good word of a Cabinet Minister, whether war, navy, or *Hacienda*, could give him what he was wishing for, easy at a nod; and here was an opportunity of winning it.

"*Cabo!*" he cried out to his corporal, in a flurry of excitement, "throw open the gate—quick! Fall in, men! Dress up—ready to present arms! See that you do it handsomely!"

It was in his favour, and so he congratulated himself that the carriage came on rather slowly, so that he had ample time to get his half-dozen files well set-up and dressed for the salute.

There was some buttoning of jackets, stocks to be adjusted round shirtless necks, with shakos to be searched for inside the guard-house, and hurriedly clapped on. Still, it was all got through in good time; and, when at length the carriage came abreast, the guard was found standing at "present arms," the sergeant himself saluting in the most gracious manner.

They inside, knowing how, returned the salute in true soldier style, though with a surprised expression upon their faces. No wonder. Where they had anticipated difficulty and danger, they were received with more than civility—accorded military honours!

Chapter Thirty Three
"Is it a Grito?"

The soldiers of the guard had grounded arms, and were sauntering back to their benches, when something came into the sergeant's mind which caused him misgiving.

Was it possible he had been paying honours to those undeserving of them?

He was sure of it being the carriage of Don Ignacio Valverde; his horses and livery too. But nothing more. None of the party was known to him as belonging to Don Ignacio's family or servants. For José was but groom or second coachman, who occasionally drove out his young mistress, but never to the Palace, or other place where the sergeant had been on duty.

Equally a stranger to him was the big fellow on the box, who had hold of the reins, as also one of the gentlemen inside. It occurred to him, however, that the face of the other was familiar—awakening the memories of more than ordinary interest.

"*Mil diablos*!" he muttered to himself as he stood gazing after the retreating equipage. "If that wasn't my old captain, Don Ruperto Rivas, there isn't another man in Mexico more like him. I heard say he had turned *salteador*, and they'd taken him only the other day. *Carria*! what's that?"

The carriage, as yet not over a hundred yards from the *garita*, still going on at a rather moderate pace, was seen suddenly to increase its speed: in fact, the horses had started off at a gallop! Nor was this from any scare or fright, but caused by a sharp cut or two of the whip, as he could tell by seeing the arm of the big man on the box several times raised above the roof, and vigorously lowered again. Extraordinary behaviour on his part; how was it to be accounted for? And how explain that of the gentleman inside, who appeared satisfied with the changed pace? At all events they were doing naught to prevent it, for again and again the whip strokes were repeated. None of the party were intoxicated; at least they had no appearance of it when they passed the gate. A little excited-looking, though no more than might be expected in men returning from a public procession. But an elegant light equipage with horses in full gallop, so unlike the carriage of a Cabinet Minister! What the mischief could it mean?

The guard-sergeant had just asked himself the question, when, hark! a gun fired at the citadela! Soon after another from the military college of Chapultepec! And from the direction of the Plaza Grande the ringing of bells. First those of the Cathedral, then of the Acordada, and the convent of San Francisco, with other convents and churches, till there was a clangour all over the city!

Hark again! A second gun from the citadel, quickly followed by another from Chapultepec, evidently signals and their responses!

"What the *demonio* is it? A *pronunciamento*?" Not only did the sergeant thus interrogate, but all the soldiers under his command, putting the question to one another. It would be nothing much to surprise them, least of all himself. He was somewhat of a veteran, and had seen nigh a score of revolutions, counting *ententes*.

"I shouldn't be surprised if it is," he suggested, adding, as a third gun boomed out from the citadel; "it must be a *grito*!"

"Who's raising it this time, I wonder?" said one of the soldiers, all now in a flurry of excited expectancy.

Several names of noted *militarios* were mentioned at a venture; but no one could say for certain, nor even give a guess with any confidence. They could hardly yet realise its being the breaking out of a *pronunciamento*, since there had been no late tampering with them—the usual preliminary to revolutions.

It might not be, after all. But they would be better able to decide should they hear the rattle of small arms, and for this listened they all ears.

More than one of them would have been delighted to hear it. Not that they disliked the *régime* of the Dictator, nor the man himself. Like all despots he was the soldiers' friend; protested and giving proofs of it, by indulging them in soldierly licence—permission to lord it over the citizen. But much as they liked "El Cojo" (Game leg), as they called him, a *grito* would be still more agreeable to them—promising unlimited loot.

The sergeant had views of his own, and reflections he kept to himself. He felt good as sure there was something up, and could not help connecting it with the carriage which had just passed. He now no longer doubted having seen his old captain in it. But how came he to be there, and what doing? He had been in the city, that's certain—was now out of it, and going at a speed that must mean something more than common. He could get to

San Augustin by that route. There were troops quartered there; had they declared for the Liberals?

It might be so, and Rivas was on his way to meet and lead them on to the city. At any moment they might appear on the *calzada*, at the corner round which the carriage had just turned.

The sergeant was now in a state of nervous perplexity. Although his eyes were on the road his thoughts were not there, but all turned inward, communing with himself. Which side ought he to take? That of the *Liberales* or the *Parti Pretre*? He had been upon both through two or three alternate changes, and still he was but a *sargento*. And as he had been serving Santa Anna for a longer spell than usual, without a single step of promotion, he could not make much of a mistake by giving the Republican party one more trial. It might get him the long-coveted epaulette of *alferez*.

While still occupied with his ambitious dreams, endeavouring to decide into which scale he should throw the weight of his sword, musket, and bayonet, the citadel gun once more boomed out, answered by the canon of Chapultepec.

Still, there was no cracking of rifles, nor continuous rattle of musketry, such as should be heard coincident with that cry which in the Mexican metropolis usually announces a change of government.

It seemed strange not only to him, but all others on guard at El Nino. But it might be a parley—the calm before the storm, which they could not help thinking would yet burst forth, in full fusillade—such as they had been accustomed to.

Listening on, however, they heard not that; only the bells, bells, bells, jingling all over the city, as though it were on fire, those of the cathedral leading the orchestra of campanule music. And yet another gun from the citadel, with the answering one from the "Summer Palace of the Monctezunas."

They were fast losing patience, beginning to fear there would be no *pronunciamento* after all, and no chance of plundering, when the notes of a cavalry bugle broke upon their ears.

"At last!" cried one, speaking the mind of all, and as though the sound were a relief to them. "That's the beginning of it. So, *camarados*! we may get ready. The next thing will be the cracking of carbines!"

They all ran to the stack of muskets, each clutching at his own. They stood listening as before; but not to hear any cracking of carbines. Instead, the bugle again brayed out its trumpet notes, recognisable as signals of command; which, though only infantry men, they understood. There was the "Quick march!" and "Double quick!" but they had no time to reflect on what it was for, nor need, as just then a troop of Hussars was seen defiling out from a side street, and coming on towards them at a charging gallop.

In a few seconds they were up to the gate, which, being still open, they could have passed through, without stop or parley. For all, they made both, the commanding officer suddenly reining up, and shouting back along the line—

"*Alto!*"

The "halt" was proclaimed by the trumpeter at his side, which brought the galloping cohort to a stand.

"*Sargento!*" thundered he at their head to the guard-sergeant, who, with his men re-formed, was again at "Present arms!"

"Has a carriage passed you, guard—a landau—grey horses, five men in it?"

"Only four men, Señor Colonel; but all the rest as you describe it."

"Only four! What can that mean? Was there a coachman in light blue livery—silver facings?"

"The same, Señor Colonel."

"That's it, sure; must be. How long since it passed?"

"Not quite twenty minutes, Señor Colonel. It's just gone round the corner; yonder where you see the dust stirring."

"*Adelante!*" cried the colonel, without waiting to question further, and as the trumpet gave out the "Forward—gallop!" the Hussar troop went sweeping through the gate, leaving the guard-sergeant and his men in a state of great mystification and no little chagrin; he, their chief spokesman, saying with a sorrowful air—

"Well *hombres*, it don't look like a *grito*, after all!"

Chapter Thirty Four
An ill-used Coachman

"Such forethought?" exclaimed Rivas, as the landau went rattling along the road with the speed of a war-chariot, "wonderful!" he went on. "Ah, for cleverness, commend me to a woman—when her will's in it. We men are but simpletons to them. My glorious Ysabel! She's the sort for a soldier's wife. But don't let me be claiming all the credit for her. Fair play to the Señorita Valverde; who has, I doubt not, done her share of the contriving—on your account, Señor."

The Señor so spoken to had no doubt of it either, and would have been grieved to think otherwise, but he was too busy at the moment to say much, and only signified his assent in monosyllables. With head down, and arms in see-sawing motion, he was endeavouring to cut their coupling-chain; the tool he handled being a large file; another of the "something" to be found under the cushions—as found it was! No wonder Don Ruperto's enthusiastic admiration of the providence which had placed it there.

Handy with workmen's tools as with warlike weapons, the young Irishman had laid hold of it as soon as they were safe through the *garita*, and was now rasping away with might and main; the other keeping the chain in place.

It was not a task to be accomplished without time. The links were thick as a man's finger, and would need no end of filing before they could be parted. Still, there was little likelihood of their being interrupted until it could be done. There was nobody on the road, and only here and there some labourers at work in the adjoining fields, too busy to take note of them, or what they were at. The sight of a passing carriage would be nothing strange, and the horses going at a gallop would but lead to the supposition of its being a party of "jovenes dorados" driving out into the country, who had taken too much wine before starting.

But, even though these poor proletarians knew all, there was nothing to be apprehended for any action on their part. Conspiracies and *pronunciamentos* were not in their line; and the storm of revolution might burst over their heads without their caring what way it went, or even inquiring who was its promoter. So the escaping prisoners took little pains to conceal what they were at. Speed was now more to their purpose than strategy, and they were making their best of it, both to get on along the road, and have their legs free for future action.

"We might have passed safely through that gate," said the Mexican, who still continued to do the talking, "even had they known who we were."

"Indeed! how?"

"You saw that sergeant who saluted us?"

"Of course I did, and the grand salute he gave! He couldn't have made it more impressive had it been the Commander-in-Chief of your army, or the Dictator himself who was passing."

"And I fancy it was just something of the kind that moved him. Doubtless, the livery of the coachman, which he would know to be that of Don Ignacio Valverde."

"You think he got us through?"

"Yes. But it wouldn't have done so if he'd known what was up. Though something else might—that is, his knowing *me*."

"Oh! he knows you?"

"He does; though I'm not sure he recognised me in passing, as I did him. Odd enough, his being there just then. He was corporal in a company I once commanded, and I believe liked me as his captain. He's an old schemer, though; has turned his coat times beyond counting; and just as well there's been no call for trusting him. He'll catch it for letting us slip past without challenge; and serve him right, wearing the colours he now does. Ha! they've waked up at last! I was expecting that."

It was the first gun at the citadel which called forth these exclamations, soon followed by the ding-dong of the city bells.

"*Carrai!*" he continued, "we're no doubt being pursued now, and by cavalry; some of those we saw in the procession. It begins to look bad. Still, with so much start, and this fine pair of *frisones*, I've not much fear of their overtaking us, till we reach the point I'm making for; unless, indeed—"

"Unless what?" asked Kearney, seeing he had interrupted himself, and was looking out apprehensively.

"That! There's your answer," said the Mexican, pointing to a puff of smoke that had just shot out from the summit of an isolated hill on which were batteries and buildings. "Chapultepec—a gun!" he added, and the bang came instantly after.

"We'll have it hot enough now," he continued, in a tone telling of alarm. "There's sure to be cavalry up yonder. If they're cleverly led, and know which way to take, they may head us off yet, in spite of all we can do. Lay on the whip," he shouted out to the coachman.

And the whip was laid on, till the horses galloped faster than ever, leaving behind a cloud of dust, which extended back for more than a mile.

The road they were on was the direct route to San Angel; and through this village Rivas had intended going, as he had no reason to believe there were troops stationed in it. But Chapultepec was nearer to it than the point where they themselves were, and cavalry now starting from the latter could easily reach San Angel before them. But there was a branch road leading to Coyoacan, and as that would give them some advantage, he determined on taking it.

And now another gun at the citadel, with the response from Chapultepec, and, soon after, the third booming from both. But meanwhile, something seen at the castle-crowned hill which deepened the anxious expression on the face of the Mexican.

"*Santos Dios!*" he exclaimed; "just as I expected. Look yonder, Señor!"

Kearney looked, to see a stream pouring out from the castle gates and running down the steep causeway which zig-zags to the bottom of the hill. A stream of men in uniform, by their square crowned shakos and other insignia, recognisable as Lancers. They had neither weapons nor horses with them; but both, as Rivas knew, would be at the *Cuartel* and stables below. He also knew that the *Lanzeros* were trained soldiers—a petted arm of the service—and it would not take them long to "boot and saddle."

More than ever was his look troubled now, still not despairing. He had his hopes and plans.

"Drop your file, Señor," he said hurriedly; "no time to finish that now. We must wait for a better opportunity. And we'll have to leave the carriage behind; but not just yet."

By this they had arrived at the embouchure of the branch road coming out from Cayocaon, into which by his direction the horses were headed, going on without stop or slackening of speed. And so for nearly another mile; then he called out to those on the box to bring up.

Rock, anticipating something of the sort, instantly reined in, and the carriage came to a stand. At which the two inside sprang out upon the road, Kearney calling to the Texan—

"Drop the reins, Cris! Down; unhitch the horses. Quick!"

The Free Lances | 139

And quick came he down, jerking the dwarf after, who fell upon all fours; as he recovered his feet, looking as if he had lost his senses. No one heeded him or his looks; the hurry was too great even to stay for unbuckling.

"Cut everything off!" cried Kearney, still speaking to Rock. "Leave on only the bridles."

With the knife late put into his hands the Texan went to work, Kearney himself plying the other, while Rivas held the horses and unhooked the bearing reins.

Soon pole-pieces and hame-straps were severed; and the frisones led forward left all behind, save the bridles and collars.

"Leave the collars on," said Rivas, seeing there was no time to detach them. "Now we mount two and two; but first to dispose of him."

The "him" was José, still seated on the box, apparently in a state of stupor.

"Pull him down, Cris! Tie him to the wheel!" commanded Kearney. "The driving reins will do it."

The Texan knew how to handle tying gear, as all Texans do, and in a trice the unresisting cochero was dragged from his seat and bound, Ixion-like, to one of the carriage wheels.

But Rock had not done with him yet. There was a necessity for something more, which looked like wanton cruelty—as they wished it to look. This was the opening of the poor fellow's mouth, and gagging him with the stock of his own whip!

So, rendered voiceless and helpless, he saw the four forzados, two-and-two, get upon his horses and ride off, the only one who vouchsafed to speak a parting word being the dwarf—he calling back in a jocular way—

"*Adios, Señor cochero*! May your journey be as pleasant as your coach is slow. Ha, ha, ha!"

Chapter Thirty Five
Double Mounted

The labourers hoeing among the young maize plants, and the *tlachiquero* drawing the sap from his magueys, saw a sight to astonish them. Two horses of unusual size, both carrying double, and going at full gallop as if running a race—on one of them two men in cloaks, blue and scarlet; the other ridden by a giant, with a mis-shapen monkey-like creature clinging on the croup behind—harness bridles, with collars dancing loose around their necks—chains hanging down and clanking at every bound they made—all this along field paths, in an out-of-the-way neighbourhood where such horses and such men had never been seen before! To the cultivator of "milpas" and the collector of "aguamiel" it was a sight not only to astonish, but inspire them with awe, almost causing the one to drop his hoe, the other his half-filled hog-skin, and take to their heels. But both being of the pure Aztecan race, long subdued and submissive, yet still dreaming of a return to its ancient rule and glories, they might have believed it their old monarchs, Monctezuna and Guatimozin, come back again, or the god Oatluetzale himself.

In whatever way the spectacle affected them, they were not permitted long to look upon it. For the galloping pace was kept up without halt or slowing; the strange-looking horses—with the men upon their backs, still stranger to look at—soon entered a *chapparal*, which bordered the maize and maguey fields, and so passed out of sight.

"We're near the end of our ride now," said Rivas to Kearney, after they had been some time threading their way through the thicket, the horses from necessity going at a walk. "If 'twere not for this ironmongery around our ankles, I could almost say we're safe. Unfortunately, where we've got to go the chains will be a worse impediment than ever. The file! Have we forgotten it?"

"No," answered Kearney, drawing it from under his cloak, and holding it up.

"Thoughtful of you, *caballero*. In the haste, I had; and we should have been helpless without it, or at all events awkwardly fixed. If we only had time to use it now. But we haven't—not so much as a minute to spare. Besides the lances from Chapultepec, there's a cavalry troop of some kind—huzzars I take it—coming on from the city. While we were cutting loose from the carriage, I fancied I heard a bugle-call in the direction cityward. Of course, with guns and bells signalling, we may expect pursuit from every point of the compass. Had we kept to the roads, we'd have been met somewhere. As it is, if they give us another ten minutes' grace, I'll take you into a place where there's not much fear of our being followed—by mounted men, anyhow."

Kearney heard this without comprehending. Some hiding-place, he supposed, known to the Mexican. It could only mean that. But where? Looking ahead, he saw the mountains with their sides forest-clad, and there a fugitive might find concealment. But they were miles off; and how were they to be reached by men afoot—to say nothing of the chains—with cavalry in hue and cry all around them? He put the question.

"Don't be impatient, *amigo*!" said the Mexican in response; "you'll soon see the place I speak of, and that will be better than any description I could give. It's a labyrinth which would have delighted Daedalus himself. *Mira*! You behold it now!"

He pointed to a *façade* of rock, grey, rugged, and precipitous, trending right and left through the *chapparal* far as they could see. A cliff, in short, though of no great elevation; on its crest, growing yuccas, cactus, and stunted mezquite trees.

"The *Pedregal*!" he added, in a cheerful voice, "and glad am I to see it. I've to thank old Vulcan or Pluto for making such a place. It has saved my life once before, and I trust will do the same now, for all of us. But we must be quick about it. *Adelante*!"

The horses were urged into a final spurt of speed, and soon after arrived at the base of the rocky escarpment, which would have barred them further advance in that direction, had the intention been to take them on. But it was not.

"We must part from them, now," said Rivas. "Dismount all!"

All four slipped off together, Rock taking hold of both bridles, as if he waited to be told what to do.

"We mustn't leave them here," said the Mexican. "They might neigh, and so guide our pursuers to the spot. In another hour, or half that, we needn't care; it'll be dark then—"

He interrupted himself, seeming to reflect, which, the Texan observing, said to Kearney—

"He weeshes the anymals sent off, do he?"

"Just that, Cris."

"I war thinkin' o' thet same, meself. The groun' for a good spell back hez been hard as flint, an' we hain't left much o' trail, nothin' as a set o' bunglin' yaller-bellies air like ter take up. As for startin' the horses, that's easy as fallin' off a log. Let me do it."

"Do it."

"Take holt o' one then, Cap. Unbuckle the neck strap and pull off the bridle, when you see me do so wi' t'other. It is a pity to act cruel to the poor brutes arter the sarvice they've did us; but thar ain't no help for 't. Riddy, air ye?"

"Ready!"

The Texan had taken out his knife; and in another instant its blade was through the horse's ear, the bridle jerked off at the same time. The animal, uttering a terrified snort, reared up, spun round, and broke away in frenzied flight through the thorny *chapparal*. The other, also released, bounded after, both soon passing out of sight.

"*Bueno—bravo!*" cried the Mexican, admiringly, relieved of his dilemma. "Now, señors, we must continue the march afoot, and over ground that'll need help from our hands, too. *Vamonos!*"

Saying which, he took up the bridles, and tossed them over the crest of the cliff; then ascended himself, helping Kearney. There was no path; but some projections of the rock—ledges, with the stems of cactus plants growing upon their—made the ascent possible. The Texan swarmed up after, with hunchback at his heels; as he got upon the top, turning suddenly round, laying hold of the chain, and with a "Jee up," hoisting the creature feet foremost!

Another second and they were all out of sight; though not a second too soon. For as they turned their backs upon the cliff, they could hear behind, on the farther edge of the thicket through which they had passed, the signal calls of a cavalry bugle.

Chapter Thirty Six
The Pedregal

Interesting as is the Mexican Valley in a scenic sense, it is equally so in the geological one; perhaps no part of the earth's crust of like limited area offering greater attractions to him who would study the lore of the rocks. There he may witness the action of both Plutonic and Volcanic forces, not alone in records of the buried past, but still existing, and too oft making display of their mighty power in the earthquake and the burning mountain.

There also may be observed the opposed processes of deposition and denudation in the slitting up of great lakes, and the down wearing of hills by tropical rain storms, with the river torrents resulting from them.

Nor is any portion of this elevated plateau more attractive to the geologist than that known as "El Pedregal"; a tract lying in its south-western corner, contiguous to the Cerro de Ajusco, whose summit rises over it to a height of 6,000 feet and 13,000 above the level of the sea.

It is a field of lava vomited forth from Ajusco itself in ages long past, which, as it cooled, became rent into fissures and honey-combed with cavities of every conceivable shape. Spread over many square miles of surface, it tenders this part of the valley almost impassable. No wheeled vehicle can be taken across it; and even the Mexican horse and mule—both sure-footed as goats—get through it with difficulty, and only by one or two known paths. To the pedestrian it is a task; and there are places into which he even cannot penetrate without scaling cliffs and traversing chasms deep and dangerous. It bristles with cactus, zuccas, and other forms of crystalline vegetation, characteristic of a barren soil. But there are spots of great fertility—hollows where the volcanic ashes were deposited—forming little *oases*, into which the honest Indian finds his way for purposes of cultivation. Others less honest seek refuge in its caves and coverts, fugitives from justice and the gaols—not always criminals, however, for within it the proscribed patriot and defeated soldier oft find an asylum.

In the four individuals who had now entered there was all this variety, if he who directed their movements was what the Condesa Almonté described him. In any case, he appeared familiar with the place and its ways, saying to Kearney, as they went on—

"No thanks to me for knowing all about the Pedregal. I was born on its edge; when a boy bird-nested and trapped armadilloes all over it. Twisted as this path is, it will take us to a spot where we needn't fear any soldiers following us—not this night anyhow. To-morrow they may, and welcome."

Their march was continued, but not without great difficulty, and much exertion of their strength. They were forced to clamber over masses of rock, and thread their way through thickets of cactus, whose spines, sharp as needles, lacerated their skins. With the coupling-chains still on, it was all the more difficult to avoid them.

Luckily, they had not far to go before arriving at the place where their conductor deemed it safe to make a stop. About this there was nothing particular, more than its being a hollow, where they could stand upright without danger of being seen from any of the eminences around. Descending into it, Rivas said—

"Now, Don Florencio, you can finish the little job you were interrupted at, without much fear of having to knock off again."

At which he raised the chain, and held it rested on something firmer than the cushion of a carriage. So placed, the file made better progress, and in a short time the link was cut through, letting them walk freely apart.

"*Caballero*!" exclaimed the Mexican, assuming an attitude as if about to propose a toast; "may our friendship be more difficult to sever than that chain, and hold us longer together—for life, I hope."

Kearney would not have been a son of Erin to refuse reciprocating the pretty compliment, which he did with all due warmth and readiness.

But his work was not over. Rock and Zorillo had yet to be uncoupled; the former, perhaps, longing to be delivered more than any of the four. He had conceived a positive disgust for the hunchback; though, as already said, less on account of the creature's physical than moral deformity, of which last he had ample evidence during the short while they were together. Nor had it needed for him to understand what the latter said. A natural physiognomist, he could read in Zorillo's eyes the evil disposition of the animal from which he drew his name.

As Kearney approached him with the file, the Texan raising his foot, and planting it on a ledge of rock, said—

"Cut through thar, Cap—the link as air nixt to my ankle-clasp."

This was different to what had been done with the other, which had been severed centrally. It was not intended to take off the whole of the chains yet. The Mexican said there was no time for so much filing; that must be done when they got farther on.

"Yer see, Cap," added Rock, giving a reason for the request, "'fore it's all over, who knows I mayn't need full leg freedom 'ithoot any hamper? So gie the dwarf the hul o' the chain to carry. He desarve to hev it, or suthin' else, round his thrapple 'stead o' his leg. This chile have been contagious to the grist o' queer company in his perambulations roun' and about; but niver sech as he. The sight of him air enough to give a nigger the gut ache."

And in his quaint vernacular he thus rambled on all the time Kearney was at work, his rude speech being an appropriate symphony to the rasping of the file.

He at the other end of the coupling-chain lay squatted along the ground, saying not a word, but his eyes full of sparkle and mischief, as those of an enraged rattle-snake. Still, there was fear in his face; for though he could not tell what was being said, he fancied it was about himself, and anything but in his favour. He was with the other three, but not of them; his conscience told him that. He was in their way, too; had been all along, and would be hereafter. What if they took into their heads to rid themselves of him in some violent manner? They might cut his throat with one of the knives he had seen them make such dexterous use of! Reflecting in this fashion, no wonder he was apprehensive.

Something was going to be done to him different from the rest, he felt sure. After the chain had been got apart the other three drew off to a distance, and stood as if deliberating. It must be about himself.

And about him it was—the way to dispose of him.

"I hardly know what we're to do with the little beast," said Rivas. "Leave him here loose we daren't; he'd slip back again, good as certain, and too soon for our safety. If we tie him he will cry out, and might be heard. We're not far enough away. *Oiga!* They're beating up the cover we've just come out of. Yes; they're in the *chapparal* now!"

It was even so, as could be told by the occasional call of a bugle sounding skirmish signals.

"Why not tie and gag him, too?" asked Kearney.

"Sure we could do that. But it wouldn't be safe either. They might find their way here at once. But if they didn't find it at all, and no one came along—"

"Ah! I see," interrupted the Irishman, as the inhumanity of the thing became manifest to him. "He might perish, you mean?"

"Just so. No doubt the wretch deserves it. From all I've heard of him, he does richly. But we are not his judges, and have no right to be his executioners."

Sentiments not such as might have been expected from the lips of a bandit!

"No, certainly not," rejoined Kearney, hastening to signify his approval of them.

"What do *you* think we should do with him, Rock?" he added, addressing himself to the Texan, who quite comprehended the difficulty.

"Wal', Cap; 't 'ud be marciful to knock him on the head at onc't, than leave him to gasp it out with a stopper in his mouth; as ye say the Mexikin thinks he mout. But thar ain't no need for eyther. Why not toat him along? Ef he should bother us I kin heist him on my back, easy enuf. A ugly burden he'd be, tho' 'tain't for the weight o' him."

The Texan's suggestion was entertained, no other course seeming safe, except at the probable sacrifice of the creature's life. And that none of them contemplated for a moment. In fine, it was determined to take him on.

The colloquy now coming to an end, Rivas and the Irishman caught up the pieces of chain still attached to their ankles, each making the end of his own fast round his wrist, so as not to impede their onward march. This done, they all moved on again, the Mexican, of course, foremost, Kearney at his heels. After him, Cris Rock, chain in hand, half leading, half-dragging the dwarf, as a showman might his monkey.

In this way there was no danger of his betraying them. He could shout and still have been heard by those behind. But an expressive gesture of the Texan admonished him that if he made a noise, it would be the last of him.

Chapter Thirty Seven
A Suspicion of Connivance

"Suspicious, to say the least of it! If a coincidence, certainly the strangest in my experience, or that I've ever heard of. A score of other carriages passing, and they to have chosen that one of all! *Carrai!* it cannot have been chance—improbable—impossible!"

So soliloquised the Chief Magistrate of Mexico, after receiving a report of what had occurred in the Callé de Plateros. He had as yet only been furnished with a general account of it; but particularising the prisoners who had escaped, with their mode of making off, as also whose carriage they had seized upon. He had been told, also, that there were two ladies in it, but needed not telling who they were.

All this was made known by a messenger who came post-haste to the Palace, soon after the occurrence. He had been sent by Colonel Santander, who could not come himself; too busy getting the Hussars into their saddles for the pursuit—for he it was who led it. And never did man follow fugitives with more eagerness to overtake them, or more bitter chagrin in their flight.

Not much, if anything, less was that of Santa Anna himself, as he now sat reflecting over it. He, too, had seen the two Texans with Rivas in the sewers; the latter a well-known enemy in war, and, as he late believed, a dangerous rival in love. He had glanced exultingly at him, with the thought of that danger past. The rebel proscribed, and for years sought for, had at length been found; was in his power, with life forfeit, and the determination it should be taken. That but a short hour ago, and now the doomed man was free again!

But surely not? With a squadron of cavalry in pursuit, canon booming, bells ringing, every military post and picket for miles round on the alert, surely four men chained two and two, conspicuous in a grand carriage, could not eventually get off.

It might seem so; still the thing was possible, as Santa Anna had reason to know. A man of many adventures, he had himself more than once eluded a pursuing enemy with chances little better.

He sat chewing the cud of disappointment, though not patiently, nor keeping all the time to his chair. Every now and then he rose to his feet, made stumping excursions round the room, repeatedly touched the bell, to inquire whether any news had been received of the fugitive party.

The aide-de-camp in attendance could not help wondering at all this, having had orders to report instantly whatever word should be brought in. Besides, why should the great Generalissimo be troubling himself about so small a matter as the escape of three or four prisoners, seeming excited as if he had lost a battle.

The cause of this excitement the Dictator alone knew, keeping it to himself. He was still in the dark as to certain details of what had transpired, and had sent for the governor of the Acordada, who should be able to supply them.

Meantime he went about muttering threats against this one and that one, giving way to bitter reflections; one bitterest of all, that there had been a suspicion of connivance at the escape of the prisoners. But to this there was a sweet side as well; so some words uttered by him would indicate.

"Ah, Condesa! You may be clever—you are. But if I find you've had a hand in this, and it can be proved to the world, never was a woman in a man's power more than you'll be in mine. Title, riches, family influence, all will be powerless to shield you. In the cell of a prison where I may yet have the pleasure of paying you a visit, you won't be either so proud or so scornful as you've shown yourself in a palace this same day. *Veremos*—we shall see."

"Don Pedro Arias."

It was an aide-de-camp announcing the Governor of the Acordada.

"Conduct him in."

Without delay the prison official was ushered into the presence, looking very sad and cowed-like. Nor did the reception accorded him have a restoring influence; instead, the reverse.

"What's all this I hear?" thundered out the disposer of punishments and of places; "you've been letting your prisoners bolt from you in whole batches. I suppose by this time the Acordada will be empty."

"*Excellentissimo!* I am very sorry to say that four of them—"

"Yes; and of the four, two of them you had orders to guard most strictly—rigorously."

"I admit it, Sire, but—"

"Sirrah! you needn't waste words excusing yourself. Your conduct shall be inquired into by-and-by. What I want now is to know the circumstances—the exact particulars of this strange affair. So answer the questions I put to you without concealment or prevarication."

The gaol-governor, making humble obeisance, silently awaited the examination, as a witness in the box who fears he may himself soon stand in the dock.

"To begin: why did you send those four prisoners out with the chaingang?"

"By order of Colonel Santander, Sire. He said it was your Excellency's wish."

"Humph! Well, that's comprehensible. And so far you're excusable. But how came it you didn't see to their being better guarded?"

"Sire, I placed them in charge of the chief turnkey—a man named Dominguez—whom I had found most trustworthy on other occasions. Today being exceptional, on account of the ceremonies, he was pressed to take drink, and, I'm sorry to say, got well-nigh drunk. That will explain his neglect of duty."

"It seems there were two ladies in the carriage. You know who they were, I suppose?"

"By inquiry I have ascertained, your Excellency. One was the Countess Almonté the other Don Luisa Valverde, as your Excellency will know, the daughter of him to whom the equipage belonged."

"Yes, yes. I know all that. I have been told the carriage made stop directly opposite to where these men were at work. Was that so?"

"It was, Sire."

"And have you heard how the stoppage came about?"

"Yes, *Excellentissimo*. The horses shied at something, and brought the wheels into a bank of mud. Then the *cochero*, who appears to be a stupid fellow, pulled them up, when he ought to have forced them on. While they were at rest the four *forzados* made a rush, two right into the carriage, the other two up to the box; one of these last, the big *Tejano*, getting hold of the reins and whip, and driving off at a gallop. They had only one sentry to pass in the direction of San Francisco. He, like Dominguez, was too far gone in drink, so there was nothing to stop them—except the guards at the garitas. And, I am sorry to say, the sergeant at El Nino Perdita let them pass through without so much as challenging. His account is that, seeing the carriage belonged to one of your Excellency's Ministers, he never thought of stopping it, and should not. Why should he, Sire?"

This touch of obsequious flattery seemed to mollify the Dictator's wrath, or it had by this otherwise expended itself, as evinced by his rejoinder in a more tranquil tone. Indeed, his manner became almost confidential.

"Don Pedro," he said, "I'm satisfied with the explanation you give, so far as regards your own conduct in the affair. But now, tell me, do you think the ladies who were in the carriage had anything to do with the drawing up of the horses? Or was it all an accident?"

"Will your Excellency allow me a moment to reflect? I had thought something of that before; but—"

"Think of it again. Take time, and give me your opinion. Let it be a truthful one, Don Pedro; there's much depending on it."

Thus appealed to, the gaol-governor stood for a time silent, evidently cudgelling his brains. He made mental review of all that had been told him about the behaviour of the young ladies, both before they were turned out of the carriage and after. He was himself aware of certain relations, friendly at least, supposed to exist between one of them and one of the escaped prisoners, and had thought it strange, too, that particular equipage being chosen. Still, from all he could gather, after ample inquiry, he was forced to the conclusion that the thing was unpremeditated—at least on the part of the ladies.

This was still his belief, after reflecting as he had been enjoined to do. In support of it he stated the facts as represented to him, how the Señoritas had been forced from their carriage, almost pitched into the street, their costly dresses dirtied and damaged, themselves showing wildest affright. Still, this was strange, too, on the part of the Condesa; and, in fine, Don Pedro, after further cross-questioning, was unable to say whether there had been connivance or not.

After giving such an unsatisfactory account of the matter he was dismissed, rather brusquely; and returned to the Acordada, with an ugly apprehension that instead of continuing governor of this grand gaol, with a handsome salary and snug quarters, he might ere long be himself the occupant of one of its cells, set apart for common prisoners.

Chapter Thirty Eight
The Report of the Pursuer

With unappeased impatience the Dictator awaited the return of the pursuing party, or some news of it. The last he in time received at first hand from the lips of its leader, who, after nightfall, had hastened back to the city and reported himself at the Palace.

"You have taken them?" interrogated Santa Anna, as the Hussar officer, no longer in a glitter of gold lace, but dim with sweat and dust, was ushered into his presence.

He put the question doubtingly; indeed, from the expression of Santander's face, almost sure of receiving a negative answer. Negative it was—

"Not yet, Sire; I regret to say they are still at large."

The rejoinder was preceded by a string of exclamatory phrases, ill becoming the Chief of the State. But Santa Anna, being a soldier, claimed a soldier's privilege of swearing, and among his familiars was accustomed to it as any common trooper. After venting a strong ebullition of oaths, he calmed down a little, saying—

"Give me a full account of what you've seen and done."

This was rendered in detail, from the time of the pursuit being entered upon till it had ended abortively, by the coming on of night.

Chancing to be in the Maza, the Colonel said, when word reached him of what had occurred in the Callé de Plateros, he made all haste to pursue with a squadron of Hussars. Why he took so many, was that he might be able to send a force along every road, in case it should be necessary.

He found the *escapados* had gone out by El Nino Perdido, the sergeant on guard there allowing them to go past.

"See that he be put under arrest!"

"He's under arrest now, your Excellency. I had that done as I was returning."

"Proceed with your relation!"

Which Santander did, telling how he had followed the fugitive party along the San Angel Road, and there met a troop of Lancers from Chapultepec. Some field-labourers had seen a carriage turn off towards Coyoacan; and taking that route he soon after came up with it. It was stopped on the roadside: empty, horses gone, the harness strewed over the ground hacked and cut; the *cochero* strapped to one of the wheels, and gagged with the handle of his whip!

When the man was released he could tell nothing more than that the four had mounted his horses, a pair upon each, and galloped off across the country, on a sort of bridle path, as if making for the San Antonio Road.

Turning in that direction, Santander soon discovered that they had entered into a tract of *chapparal*; and while this was being searched for them, the unharnessed horses were observed rushing to and fro in frenzied gallop, riderless of course. When caught, it was seen why they were now excited, one of them having its ear slit, the blood still dropping from the wound.

The *chapparal* was quartered in every direction; but he soon came to the conclusion it was no use searching for them there.

"*Carramba*!" interrupted his listener; "of course not I know the place well. And if you, Señor Colonel, were as well acquainted with that *chapparal*, and what lies alongside it, as one of those you were after, you'd have dropped the search sooner. You needn't tell me more; I can guess the finish; they got off into the Pedregal."

"So it would seem, your Excellency."

"Seem! So it is, *por cierto*. And looking for them there would be so much lost time. Around your native city, New Orleans, there are swamps where the runaway slave manages to hide himself. He'd have a better chance of concealment here, among rocks, in that same quarter you've just come from. It's a very labyrinth. But what did you afterwards? You may as well complete your narrative."

"There is not much more to tell, Sire; for little more could we do. The darkness came on, as we discovered they had taken to the rocks."

"You did discover that?"

"Yes, your Excellency. We found the place where they had gone up over a sort of cliff. There were scratches made by their feet, with a branch broken off one of the cactus plants; some of the sewer mud, too, was on the rock. But there was no path, and I saw it would be useless carrying the pursuit any further till we should have the light of morning. I've taken every precaution, however, to prevent their getting out of the Pedregal."

"What precautions?"

"By completely enfilading it, Sire. I sent the Lancers round by San Geromino and Contreras; the Hussars to go in the opposite direction by San Augustin. They have orders to drop a picket at every path that leads from it, till they meet on the other side."

"Well, Señor Colonel, your strategy is good. I don't see that you could have done better under the circumstances. But it's doubtful whether we shall be able to trap our foxes in the Pedregal. One of them knows its paths too well to let night or darkness hinder his travelling along them. He'll be through it before your pickets can get to their stations. Yes; and off to a hiding-place he has elsewhere—a safer one—somewhere in the Sierras. Confound those Sierras with their caverns and forests. They're full of my enemies, rebels, and robbers. But I'll have them rooted out, hanged, shot, till I clear the country of disaffection. *Carajo*! I shall be master of Mexico, not only in name, but deeds. Emperor in reality!"

Excited by the thought of unrestrained rule and dreams of vengeance— sweet to the despot as blood to the tiger—he sprang out of his chair, and paced to and fro, gesticulating in a violent manner.

"Yes, Señor Colonel!" he continued in tone satisfied as triumphant. "Other matters have hindered me from looking after these skulking proscripts. But our victory over the Tejanos has given me the power now, and I intend using it. These men must be recaptured at all cost—if it take my whole army to do it. To you, Don Carlos Santander, I entrust the task— its whole management. You have my authority to requisition troops, and spend whatever money may be needed to ensure success. And," he added, stepping close to his subordinate, and speaking in a confidential way, "if you can bring me back Ruperto Rivas, *or his head so that I can recognise it*, I shall thank you not as *Colonel*, but as *General* Santander."

The expression upon his face as he said this was truly Satanic. Equally so that on his to whom the horrid hint was given. Alike cruel in their instincts, with aims closely corresponding, it would be strange if the fugitive prisoners were not retaken.

Chapter Thirty Nine
Up the Mountain

"We're going to have a night black as charcoal," said Rivas, running his eye along the outline of the Cordilleras, and taking survey of the sky beyond.

"Will that be against us?" queried the young Irishman.

"In one way, yes; in another, for us. Our pursuers will be sure to ride all round the Pedregal, and leave a picket wherever they see the resemblance of path or trail leading out. If it were to come on moonlight—as luckily it won't—we'd had but a poor chance to get past them without being seen. And that would signify a fight against awkward odds—numbers, arms, everything. We must steal past somehow, and so the darkness will be in our favour."

As may be deduced from this snatch of dialogue, they were still in the Pedregal. But the purple twilight was now around them, soon to deepen into the obscurity of night; sooner from their having got nearly across the lava field, and under the shadow of Ajusco, which, like a black wall, towered up against the horizon. They had stooped for a moment, Rivas himself cautiously creeping up to an elevated spot, and reconnoitring the ground in front.

"It will be necessary for us to reach the mountains before morning," he added after a pause. "Were we but common gaol-birds who had bolted, it wouldn't much signify, and we'd be safe here for days, or indeed for ever. The authorities of Mexico, such as they are at present, don't show themselves very zealous in the pursuit of escaped criminals. But neither you nor I, Señor Kearney, come under that category—unluckily for us, just now—and the Pedregal, labyrinth though it be, will get surrounded and explored—every inch of it within the next forty-eight hours. So out of it we must move this night, or never."

Twilight on the table-lands of the western world is a matter of only a few minutes: and, while he was still speaking, the night darkness had drawn around them. It hindered them not from proceeding onwards, however, the

Mexican once more leading off, after enforcing upon the others to keep close to him, and make no noise avoidable.

Another half-hour of clambering over rocks, with here and there a scrambling through thickets of cactus, and he again came to a stop, all, of course, doing the same. This time to use their ears, rather than eyes; since around all was black as a pot of pitch, the nearest object, rock or bush, being scarcely visible.

For a time they stood listening intently. Not long, however, before hearing sounds—the voices of men—and seeing a glimmer of light, which rose in radiation above the crest of a low ridge at some distance ahead.

"*Un piqûet!*" pronounced Rivas, in a half-whisper.

"*Soto en la puerto—mozo!*" (knave in the door—winner) came a voice in a long-drawn accentuation, from the direction of the light.

"Good!" mutteringly exclaimed the Mexican, on hearing it. "They're at their game of *monté*. While so engaged, not much fear they'll think of aught else. I know the spot they're in, and a way that will take us round it. Come on, *camarados*! The trick's ours!"

Sure enough it proved so. A path that showed no sign of having ever been trodden, but still passable, led out past the gambling soldiers, without near approach to them. And they were still absorbed in their game—as could be told by its calls every now and then drawled out, and sounding strange in that solitary place. Ruperto Rivas conducted his trio of companions clear of the Pedregal, and beyond the line of enfiladement.

In twenty minutes after they were mounting the steep slope of the Cerro Ajusco, amid tall forest trees, with no fear of pursuit by the soldiers, than if separated from them by a hundred long leagues.

After breasting the mountain for some time, they paused to take breath, Rivas saying—

"Well, *caballeros*, we're on safe ground now, and may rest a bit. It's been a close shave, though; and we may thank our stars there are none in the sky—nor moon. Look yonder! They're at it yet. '*Soto en la puerto—mozo!*' Ha, ha, ha!"

He referred to a faint light visible at a long distance below, on the edge of the Pedregal, where they had passed that of a picket fire-camp, which enabled the *monté* players to make out the markings on their cards.

"We may laugh who have won," he added, now seemingly relieved from all apprehension of pursuit.

Nevertheless the fugitive party stayed but a short while there; just long enough to recover wind. The point they were making for was still further up the mountain, though none of them could tell where save Rivas himself. He knew the place and paths leading to it, and well; otherwise he could not have followed them, so thick was the darkness. In daylight it would have been difficult enough, yawning chasms to be crossed *barransas*—with cliffs to be climbed, in comparison with which the escarpments of the Pedregal were but as garden walls.

In a groping way, hand helping hand, all were at length got up and over, as the tolling of distant church bells, down in the valley below, proclaimed the hour of midnight. Just then Rivas, once more making a stop, plucked a leaf from one of the grass plants growing by, and placing it between his lips gave out a peculiar sound, half screech, half whistle—a signal as the others supposed; being assured it was, by the response soon after reaching their ears.

The signal was given again, with some variations; responded to in like manner. Then a further advance up the mountain, and still another halt; this time at hearing the hail:

"*Quien viva!*"

"*El Capitan!*" called out Rivas in answer, and received for rejoinder first an exclamation of delighted surprise, then words signifying permission to approach and pass.

The approach was not so easy, being up a steep incline, almost a cliff. But on reaching its crest they came in sight of the man who had challenged, standing on a ledge of rock. A strange-looking figure he seemed to Kearney and the Texan, wearing a long loose robe, girded at the waist—the garb of a monk, if the dim light was not deceiving them; yet with the air of a soldier, and sentinel-fashion, carrying a gun!

He was at "present arms" when they got up opposite; and wondering, but without saying aught, they passed him—their conductor, after a momentary pause and a muttered word to him, leading on as before.

Another ascent, this time short, but still almost precipitous, and this climbing came to an end.

Chapter Forty
A Faithful Steward

The spot where they had now made stop—final for the night—was still far below the summit of the mountain. It was a sort of platform or bench, formed by the crest of a projecting spur, the cliff rising sheer at its back. Its level surface was only a few acres in extent, supporting a thick growth of tall evergreen pines, the long-leaved species indigenous to Mexico. Centrally there was a place clear of timber, which ran up to the cliff's base, or rather to a building contiguous to it. In front of this they halted, Rivas saying—

"Behold my humble abode, *caballeros*! Let me bid you welcome to it."

There was light enough to let them see a massive pile of mason work outlined against the cliff's *façade*, while too dim for them to distinguish its features. They could make out, however, what appeared to be a pair of windows with pointed arches, and between them a large doorway, seeming more like the mouth of a cavern. Out of this came a faint scintillation of light, and as they drew up to it, a candle could be seen burning inside a sort of covered porch, resembling the lych-gate of a country church. There were some stone benches outside, from one of which a man started up and advanced toward them, as he did so putting the formal question—

"*Quien es?*"

"*Yo, Gregorio!*" was the answer given by Rivas.

"*El Capitan!*" exclaimed the questioner, in a tone also telling of pleased surprise. "And free again! I'm so glad, Don Ruperto! Praise to the Lord for delivering you!"

"Thanks, good Gregorio! And while you're about it, you may as well give part of your praise to a lady, who had something to do with it—indeed, two of them."

"Ah! Señor Capitan, I think I know one of them anyhow, and in all Mexico I can say—ay, swear it—"

"True, true!" interrupted the Captain. "But stay your asseveration. There's no time to talk about the Señoritas now. My friends and I are in want of something to eat. We're as hungry as *coyotes*. What have you got in the larder?"

"Not much, I fear, your worship. And the cook's gone to bed, with everybody else. But they'll only be too delighted to get up when they hear it's your worship come back. Shall I go and rouse them, Señor?"

"No, no. Let them sleep it out. Any cold thing will do for us. We're as much fatigued as famished, and wish to be in bed ourselves as soon as possible. So look out whatever eatables there are, and don't forget the drinkables. I trust the cellar isn't as low as the larder?"

"No, Señor. Of that I can speak with more confidence. Not a cork has been drawn since you left us—I mean of the best wines. Only the common Canario was drunk in your absence."

"In that case, mayor-domo, we may sup satisfactorily, so far as the liquids are concerned, should the solids prove deficient. Bring a bottle of Burgundy, another of the Brown Madeira, and, let me see—yes, one of old Pedro Ximenes. I suppose the brethren have used up all my best cigars?"

"Not one of them, Señor. The Havannahs have been under lock and key, too. I gave out only *puros*."

"What a faithful steward you've proved yourself, Gregorio! Well, along with the wine, let us have a bundle of Imperadores. We haven't tasted tobacco for days, and are all dying for a smoke."

By this time they had entered the porch, and were passing on through a long corridor, still more dimly illuminated. But there was light issuing from a side-door, which stood open. By this Rivas made stop, with word and gesture signifying to the others to pass on inside, which they did. Not all of them, however; only Kearney and Rock. A different disposition he meant making of the dwarf than giving him Burgundy and Madeira to drink, with the smoking of "Emperor" cigars. Pointing to the crooked semblance of humanity, at which Gregorio was gazing with a puzzled air, he whispered to the latter—

"Take the beast back, and shut him up in one of the cells. You may give him something to eat, but see to his being securely kept. Insignificant as he looks, there's mischief in him, and he might take it into his head to stray. You comprehend, Gregorio?"

"I do, your worship. I'll take care to stow him safe."

Saying which, the mayor-domo of the establishment, for such Gregorio was, caught the hunchback by one of his ears—grand auricles they were—and led him away along the corridor, with the prison chain trailing behind.

Rivas did not stay till they were out of sight, but turning, stepped inside the room into which he had ushered the other two.

It was rather a large apartment, but plainly and sparsely furnished; a deal table and half a dozen common chairs, with leathern backs and bottoms, such as may be seen in most Mexican houses. It was better supplied with arms than household effects; several guns standing in corners, with swords hanging against the walls, and a variety of accoutrements—all giving it more the appearance of a guard-house than the reception-room of a gentleman's mansion.

"Now *amigos*" said the Mexican, after rejoining his guests, on whose faces he could not fail to note an odd inquiring expression, "I can at last say to you, feel safe, if I can't assure you of a supper good as I'd wish to give. Still, if I mistake not, 'twill be superior to our prison fare. *Por Dios*! Having to put up with that was punishment enough of itself, without being set to work in the sewers."

"Ah," remarked Kearney, speaking for himself and the Texan, "had you been one of us prisoners from Mier up to Mexico, the diet you complain of would have seemed luxury for Lucullus."

"Indeed! What did they give you to eat?"

"Brown beans only half boiled, *tortillas*, usually cold; and sometimes, for a whole stretch of twenty-four hours, nothing at all."

"*Carramba*!" exclaimed the Mexican. "That was hard usage. But nothing to surprise. Just as Santa Anna might be expected to treat his captive enemies, whether of his own people, or as yourselves, foreigners. More cruel tyrant never ruled country. But his reign, thank Heaven, will not be long. I've reason for saying that, and better still for thinking it."

The little interlude of dialogue was brought to a close by the entrance of the mayor-domo loaded with bottles and glasses. He had orders to bring the wine first, the cigars along with it.

Lumping all down upon the table, he left them to wait upon themselves, while he went off to ransack the pantry soon to return with a sufficiency of viands, and savoury enough to satisfy men who had just come out of the Acordada. There was cold mutton, ham, and venison, maize bread, and "guesas de Guatemala," with a variety of fruit to follow. Verily a supper at which even a gourmand might not cavil; though it was but the *débris* of a dinner, which seemed to have been partaken of by a goodly array of guests.

Not long lingered they over it, before whom it was set a second time. Overcome by the toil and struggle of days, and more the mental worry attendant, even the wine freely quaffed failed to excite them afresh. Rest and sleep they more needed and much desired; all glad when Gregorio again showed his face at the door, saying—

"*Caballeros*, your sleeping rooms are ready."

Chapter Forty One
Anxious Hours

"See, Luisita! Yonder go soldiers!"

"Where?"

"Along the calzada of Nino Perdido—under the trees—by the thick clump—they're galloping!"

"*Santissima*, yes! I see them now. O Ysabel! if they overtake the carriage! *Ay Dios*!"

"*Ay Dios*, indeed! It's to be hoped they won't, though. And I have less fear of it now than ever. It must have gone that way, or the soldiers wouldn't be there; and as it couldn't have stopped at the *garita*, it should now be a good distance on. Keep up your heart, *amiga mia*, as I do mine. They'll soon be safe, if they're not yet."

This exclamatory dialogue was carried on while the alarm bells were still ringing, and the guns booming. The speakers were on the azotea of Don Ignacio's house, up to which they had hastened soon as home—having dismissed their escort below, and left orders for no visitors to be admitted.

In the *mirador*, with opera-glasses to their eyes, they had been scanning the roads which led south and south-west from the city. Only for a few minutes, as they had but just got back, and as the carriage having already rounded the turning to Coyoacan, they saw but the pursuing soldiers. Those were the Hussars, with Santander at their head, though the ladies knew not that.

Fortified by the hopeful speech of the Condesa, the other responded to it with an added word of hope, and a prayer for the safe escape of those they were concerned about.

Then for a while both remained silent, with the lorgnettes to their eyes, following the movements of the soldiers along the road. Soon these were out of sight, but their whereabouts could be told by the cloud of white dust which rose over the trees, gradually drifting farther and farther off.

At length it too disappeared, settling down; and as the bells ceased to ring, and the cannon to be fired, the city, with all around it, seemed restored to its wonted tranquillity.

But not so the breasts of Luisa Valverde and Ysabel Almonté. Far from tranquil they; instead, filled with anxiety, keen as ever. And now, as much on their own account as for those they had been aiding to escape. In their haste to effect this, they had taken no thought of what was to come after. But it was now forced upon them. As they looked back on what they had themselves done—the part they had been playing, with all its details of action—apprehensions hitherto unfelt began to steal over them, growing stronger the longer they dwelt upon them.

But what would be the upshot of all?

What if the carriage got overtaken with the fugitives in it, and beside them those knives and pistols, to say nothing of the file? A gentleman's cloak too, with *mango* and *serape*! Odd assortment of articles for ladies to take out on an airing! They had no fear of the *cochero* betraying them; but this paraphernalia surely would, if it fell into the hands of the pursuers. They might expect investigation, anyhow; but these things, if produced, would bring about an exposure unavoidable.

No wonder at their soon becoming seriously alarmed, henceforth nervously agitated. And they had no one to take council with. Soon after their coming home, Don Ignacio, seeing and hearing of what happened, had sallied forth to make inquiries, and direct pursuit. Furious about his fine carriage and horses carried off, he little dreamt that along with them were his duelling pistols and blue broadcloth cloak.

Nor would it do to tell him of those matters, unless they made up their minds to confess all, and fling themselves on his affection more than his mercy. Of course he was still in the dark about their doings—unsuspicious man—had not even been told who the *forzados* were that had taken away his equipage.

Closeted alone, for some time the alarmed ladies could not think of what they ought to do. They did not yield to despair, however; instead, kept on scheming and considering how they might meet the worst—if the worst came.

But one way seemed plausible—even possible—that depending on Don Ignacio. If they could prevail on him to tell a falsehood, all might be well. Only to say the carriage had been made ready for a journey to his *casa de campo*, whither he had intended to proceed that same evening, taking his daughter and the Condesa along with him. That would explain the presence of the weapons; no uncommon thing—rather the rule—for carriage travellers to take such with them, even going but outside the suburbs of the city. For good reason, there being footpads and robbers everywhere. And the cloaks for protection against the night air!

In this way they groped about, as drowning people clutch at sticks and straws, still without being able to get rid of their apprehensions. Even should Don Ignacio agree to the deception they thought of—he would, no doubt, when made aware of their danger—it was questionable whether it would serve them. For there was a file too—a small matter, but a most conspicuous link in the chain of circumstantial evidence against them. They in the carriage would have been using it, before being taken—if they should be taken. Finally, the worst of all, the relations known to exist between themselves and two of the men attempting escape.

A miserable time it was for them during the remainder of that afternoon and evening; a struggle amid doubts, fears, and conjectures. Nor did Don Ignacio's return home in any way relieve them. They were not yet prepared to surrender up their secret even to him. The time had not come for that. As the hours passed, things began to look better, and the suspense easier to bear. No report from the pursuers, which there would or should have been, were the pursued taken.

Something better still, at length. José back home with the carriage and horses, and nothing besides—no weapons nor spare wraps! All gone off, the tell-tale file along with them.

Pepita brought this intelligence in to the ladies, who longed to have a private interview with the *cochero*. But he had first to deliver his to Don Ignacio, who had sallied out into the stables to receive it.

A strange tale it was, imparted to an angry listener, who, while listening, looked upon his costly harness, patched and mended with ropes, where it had been cut. His fine *frisones* too, abused, possibly injured for good, the ear of one of them well-nigh severed from the head! Slow to wrath though he was, this was enough to make him wrathful, without the further knowledge of his other losses, about which José took care *not* to enlighten him.

At a later hour the circumspect *cochero* told his tale to other ears in terms somewhat different, and with incidents. His master, summoned to the Palace, gave the opportunity so much desired by his young mistress and the Condesa for speaking with him; and he was soon in their presence, getting interrogated with a volubility which made sober reply almost impossible.

His questioners, however, after a time calming down, listened to his narration in a detailed form, though not without repeated interruptions.

He told them about the slow driving of the carriage along the garden wall of San Francisco, the putting on the disguises, and how cleverly they had outwitted the guard at the *garita*.

"Like Ruperto!" at this juncture exclaimed the Countess.

Then, of their onward course along the *calzada*, horses in a gallop, till stopped on the Coyoacan road, with the action taken there—quick as it was varied and strange.

Donna Luisa, in her turn, here interrupted in triumphant exclamation—

"Like Florencio!"

In fine, when made known to them how the fugitives had mounted and ridden off, both cried out together, in terms almost the same—

"Thanks to the Virgin, blessed Mother of God! We now know they are safe."

Their confidence was strengthened by further questioning, for the trusted *cochero* was able to tell them more. How his horses had been caught, and brought back to him by two Hussars, one of whom he chanced to have a speaking acquaintance with. From the soldier he had learnt all about the pursuit, after it had passed beyond him; how they had searched the *chapparal*, but fruitlessly; the latest reports being that the *éscapados* had got into the Pedregal.

That was enough for the Countess, who, springing to her feet and clapping her hands, cried out—

"Joy, Luisita! They're safe, I'm sure. Ruperto knows the Pedregal, every path through it, as well as we the walks of the Alameda. I shall sleep this night better than the last, and you may do the same."

So assured, Luisa Valverde, devout as was her wont, responded with a phrase of thanksgiving, arms crossed over her bosom, eyes turned to the picture of Santa Guadalupe on the wall.

José stood waiting, not for any reward. Recompense for the service he had done them—so modestly declaring it—was not in his thoughts at that moment, though it might be after. But the Condesa was thinking of it then. Sure to promise and contract, she said to him—

"Faithful fellow—courageous as faithful—take this; you've fairly earned it."

Whilst speaking, she drew the jewelled watch from her waist, and, passing the chain over her head, held it out to him.

"And this too!" added the Donna Luisa, plucking a diamond ring from one of her fingers, and presenting it at the same time.

"No!" protested the faithful servitor. "Neither the one nor the other. Enough reward to me to know I've done your ladyship a service—if I have."

"But, good José," urged the Countess, "you must either take my watch or the worth of it in gold *doblones*! That was the understanding, and I shall insist on your adhering to it."

"*Muy bein, Condesa*; I consent to that. But only on the condition that the gentlemen get safe off. Till we're sure of that, I beg your ladyship won't look upon me as a creditor."

"If her ladyship should," here put in a third personage of the sex feminine, who had just entered upon the scene, "if she should, I'll pay the debt myself. I pay it now—there!"

It was Pepita who thus delivered herself, as she did so bounding forward, flinging her arms around his neck, and giving him a sonorous kiss upon the cheek! Then, as she released her lips after the smack, adding—

"I've given you that, *hombre*, for what? Why nothing more than doing your duty. Ha, ha, ha!"

The laughter neither disconcerted nor vexed him. It was not scornful, while the kiss had been very sweet. Long-coveted, but hitherto withheld, he looked upon it as an earnest of many others to follow, with a reward he would more value than all the watches and rings in Mexico—the possession of Pepita herself.

Chapter Forty Two
A Holy Brotherhood

"Where the deuce am I?"

It was Florence Kearney who asked this question, interrogating himself; time, the morning after their retreat up the mountain. He was lying on a low pallet, or rather bench of mason work, with a palm mat spread over it, his only coverlet the cloak he had brought with him from Don Ignacio's carriage. The room was of smallest dimensions, some eight or nine feet square, pierced by a single window, a mere pigeon-hole without sash or glass.

He was yet only half awake, and, as his words show, with but a confused sense of his whereabouts. His brain was in a whirl from the excitement through which he had been passing, so long sustained. Everything around seemed weird and dream-like.

Rubbing his eyes to make sure it was a reality, and raising his head from the hard pillow, he took stock of what the room contained. An easy task that. Only a ricketty chair, on which lay a pair of duelling pistols—one of the pairs found under the carriage cushions—and his hat hanging on its elbow. Not a thing more except a bottle, greasy around the neck, from a tallow candle that had guttered and burnt out, standing on the uncarpeted stone floor beside his own boots, just as he had drawn them off.

Why he had not noticed these surroundings on the night before was due to extreme fatigue and want of sleep. Possibly, the Burgundy, mixed with the Madeira and Old Pedro Ximenes, had something to do with it. In any case he had dropped down upon the mat of palm, and became oblivious, almost on the moment of his entering this strange sleeping chamber, to which the mayor-domo had conducted him.

"Queer crib it is," he continued to soliloquise, after making survey of the room and its containings, "for a bedroom. I don't remember ever having slept in so small a one, except aboard ship, or in a prison-cell. How like the last it looks!"

It did somewhat, though not altogether. There were points of difference, as a niche in the wall, with a plaster cast on a plinth, apparently the image of some saint, with carvings in the woodwork, crosses, and other emblems of piety.

"It must be an old convent or monastery," he thought, after noticing these. "Here in Mexico they often have them in odd, out-of-the-way places, I've heard. Out of the way this place surely is, considering the climb we've had to reach it. Monks in it, too?" he added, recalling the two men he had seen on the preceding night, and how they where habited. "A strange sort they seem, with a *captain* at their head—my prison companion! Well, if it give us sanctuary, as he appears to think it will, I shall be but too glad to join the holy brotherhood."

He lay a little longer, his eyes running around the room, to note that the rough lime-wash on its walls had not been renewed for years; green moss had grown upon them, and there were seams at the corners, stains showing were rainwater had run down. If a monastery, it was evidently not one in the enjoyment of present prosperity, whatever it might have been in the past.

While still dreamily conjecturing about it, the door of his room was gently pushed ajar, and so held by whoever had opened it. Turning his head round, Kearney saw a man in long loose robes, with sandalled feet and shaven crown, girdle of beads, crucifix, cowl, and scapular—in short, the garb of the monk with all its insignia.

"I have come to inquire how you have slept, my son," said the holy man, on seeing that he was awake. "I hope that the pure atmosphere of this, our mountain home—so different from that you've been so lately breathing—will have proved conducive to your slumbers."

"Indeed, yes," rejoined he inquired after, conscious of having slept well. "I've had a good night's rest—the best allowed me for a long time. But where—"

While speaking, he had dropped his feet to the floor, and raised himself erect on the side of the bed, thus bringing him face to face with the friar. What caused him to leave the interrogatory unfinished was a recognition. The countenance he saw was a familiar one, as might be expected after having been so close to his own—within a few feet of it—for days past. No disguise of dress, nor changed tonsure, could hinder identification of the man who had partaken of his chain in the Acordada; for he it was.

"Oh! 'tis you, Don Ruperto!" exclaimed Kearney, suddenly changing tone.

"The same, my son," rejoined the other, with an air of mock gravity.

At which the young Irishman broke out into a loud guffaw, saying:—

"Well, you're the last man I should ever have supposed to be a monk!"

He recalled some strong denunciations of the Holy Brethren he had heard pass the lips of his late fellow-prisoner.

"Ah! Señor Don Florencio, in this our world of Mexico we are called upon to play many parts, and make out home in many places. Yesterday, you knew me as a prisoner, like yourself in a loathsome gaol; to-day, you see me in a monastery. And no common monk, but an Abbot, for know, *amijo mio*, that I am the head of this establishment. But come! As your host I am not now playing the part I should. You must be half famished; besides, your toilet needs attending to. For the first, breakfast will be ready by the time you have looked to the last. Here, Gregorio!" this was a call to the mayor-domo outside, who instantly after appeared at the door. "Conduct this gentleman to the lavatory, and assist him in making his ablutions." Then again to Kearney: "If I mistake not, you will find a clean shirt there, with some other changes of raiment. And may I ask you to be expeditious? It has got to be rather a late hour for breakfast, and the Holy Brethren will be getting a little impatient for it. But, no doubt, your appetite will prompt you. *Hasta Luega!*"

With which salutation—the Mexican custom at parting for only a short while—he passed out of the room, leaving his guest to be looked after by Gregorio.

Surrendering himself to the mayor-domo, Kearney was conducted to an outer room, in which he found a washstand and dressing-table, with towel and other toilet articles—all, however, of the commonest kind. Even so, they were luxuries that had been long denied him—especially the water, a constant stream of which ran into a stone basin from some pure mountain spring.

And, sure enough, the clean shirt was there, with a full suit of clothes; velveteen jacket, *calzoneras calzoncillas*, scarf of China crape—in short, the complete costume of a *ranchero*. A man of medium size, they fitted him nicely; and arrayed in them he made a very handsome appearance.

"Now, your honour," said the individual in charge of him, "allow me to show you the Refectory."

Another turn along the main passage brought them to the door, from which issued a buzz of voices. His host had prepared him to expect company, and on stepping inside this door he saw it in the shape of some twenty-five or thirty men, all in the garb of monks of the same order as Rivas himself.

The room was a large one, saloon shape, with a table standing centrally, around which were benches and chairs. A cloth was spread upon it, with a multifarious and somewhat heterogeneous array of ware—bottles and glasses being conspicuous; for it was after eleven o'clock, and the meal *almuerzo*, as much dinner as breakfast. The viands were being put upon it; three or four Indian youths, not in convent dress, passing them through a hatch that communicated with the kitchen, and from which also came a most appetising odour.

All this the young Irishman took in with a sweep of his eye, which instantly after became fixed upon the friars who had faced towards him. They were standing in two or three groups, the largest gathered round an individual who towered above all of them by the head and shoulders. Cris Rock it was, clean shaven, and looking quite respectable; indeed, better dressed than Kearney had seen him since he left off his New Orleans "store" clothes. The Colossus was evidently an object of great interest to his new acquaintances; and, from the farcical look upon their faces, it was clear they had been doing their best to "draw" him. With what success Kearney could not tell; though, from the knowledge he had of his old comrade's cleverness, he suspected not much. There was just time for him to note the jovial air of the Brethren, so little in keeping with the supposed gravity of the monastic character, when the Abbot entering led him up to them, and gave him a general introduction.

"*Hermanos!*" he said, "let me present another of my comrades in misfortune, the Señor Don Florencio Kearney—an *Irlandes*—who claims the hospitality of the convent."

They all made bow, some pressing forward, and extending hands.

But there was no time for dallying over salutations. By this several dishes had been passed through the hatch, and were steaming upon the table. So the Abbot took seat at its head, Kearney beside him; while the Texan was bestowed at its foot, alongside one who seemed to act as vice-chairman.

If the table-cloth was not one of the finest damask, nor the ware costliest china and cut glass, the repast was worthy of such. In all the world there is no *cuisine* superior to that of Mexico. By reason of certain aboriginal viands, which figured on the table of that Aztec sybarite, Montezuma, it beats the *cuisine* of old Spain, on which that of France is founded, and but an insipid imitation.

The monks of this mountain retreat evidently knew how to live, course after course being passed through the hatch in a variety which seemed as if it would never end. There were pucheros, guisados, tomales, and half a score of other dishes Kearney had never before heard of, much less tasted. No wonder at their dinner of the preceding day having left such *débris* for supper.

And the wines were in correspondence—in quality, profusion, everything. To Kearney it recalled "Bolton Abbey in the olden time." Nor ever could the monks of that ancient establishment on the Wharfe have drunk better wines, or laughed louder while quaffing them, than they whose hospitality he was receiving on the side of the Cerro Ajusco.

Some strange speech, however, he heard passing around him, little in consonance with what might be supposed to proceed from the lips of religious men. But, possibly, just such as came from those of the Tintern and Bolton Brethren when around the refectory table. Not all of it, though. If the talk was worldly, it savoured little of wickedness—far less than that of the cowled fraternity of olden times, if chronicles are to be trusted. And never in convent hall could have been heard such toast as that with which the breakfast was brought to a close, when Rivas, rising to his feet, goblet in hand, the others standing up along with him, cried out—

"*Patria y Libertad!*"

Country and Liberty! Strange sentiment in such a place, and to be received with acclaim by such people!

Chapter Forty Three
What are they?

The repast finished, the Holy Brethren, rising from the table together, forsook the Refectory. Some disappeared into cloisters on the sides of the great hallway, others strolled out in front, and seating themselves on benches that were about, commenced rolling and smoking cigarittos.

The Abbot, excusing himself to his stranger guests, on plea of pressing business, was invisible for a time. So they were permitted to betake themselves apart. Good manners secured them this. The others naturally supposed they might want a word in private, so no one offered to intrude upon them.

Just what they did want, and had been anxiously longing for. They had mutually to communicate; questions to be asked, and counsel taken together. Each was burning to know what the other thought of the company they had fallen into; the character of which was alike perplexing to both.

After getting hold of their hats they sauntered out by the great door, through which they had entered on the night before. The sun was now at meridian height, and his beams fell down upon the patch of open ground in front of the monastery, for a monastery they supposed it must be. A glance backward as they walked out from its walls showed its architecture purely of the conventual style; windows with pointed arches, the larger ones heavy mullioned, and a campanile upon the roof. This, however, without bells, and partially broken down, as was much of the outer mason work everywhere. Here and there were walls crumbling to decay, others half-hidden under masses of creeping plants and cryptogams; in short, the whole structure seemed more or less dilapidated.

Soon they entered under the shadow of the trees; long-leaved evergreen pines loaded with parasites and epiphytes, among these several species of orchids—rare phenomenon in the vegetable world, that would have delighted the eye of a botanist. As they wished to get beyond earshot of those left lounging by the porch, they continued on along a walk which had once been gravelled, but was now overgrown with weeds and grass. It formed a cool arcade, the thick foliage meeting overhead, and screening it from the rays of the sun. Following it for about a hundred yards or so, they again had the clear sky before them, and saw they were on the brow of a steep slope—almost a precipice—which, after trending a short distance right and left, took a turn back toward the mass of the mountain. It was the boundary of the platform on which the building stood, with a still higher cliff behind.

The point they had arrived at was a prominent one, affording view of the whole valley of Mexico, that lay spread out like a picture at their feet. And such a picture! Nothing in all the panoramic world to excel—if equal it.

But as scenery was not in their thoughts, they gave it but a glance, sitting down with faces turned towards one another. For there were seats here also—several rustic chairs under shady trees—it being evidently a favourite loitering place of the friars.

"Well, Cris, old comrade," said Kearney, first to speak, "we've gone through a good deal this day or two in the way of change. What do you think of these new acquaintances of ours?"

"Thar, Cap, ye put a puzzler."

"Are they monks?"

"Wal, them is a sort o' anymals I hain't had much dealin's wi'; niver seed any till we kim inter Mexiko, 'ceptin' one or two as still hangs round San Antone in Texas. But this chile knows little u' thar ways, only from what he's heerin'; an' judgin' be that he'd say thar ain't nerry monk among 'em."

"What then? Robbers?"

"Thar, agin, Cap, I'm clean confuscated. From what we war told o' Mr Reevus in the gaol, they oughter be that. They sayed he war a captain o' *saltadores*, which means highwaymen. An' yet it do 'pear kewrous should be sich."

"From what I know of him," rejoined Kearney, "what I learned yesterday, it would be curious indeed—remarkably so. I've reason to believe him a gentleman born, and that his title of captain comes from his having been an officer in the army."

"That mou't be, an' still wouldn't contrary his havin' turned to t'other. Down by the Rio Grande, thar are scores o' Mexikin officers who've did the same, from lootenants up to kurnels—ay, ginrals. Thar's Canales, who commanded the whole cavalry brigade—the 'Chaperal fox' as we Texans call him—an' thar ain't a wuss thief or cut-throat from Mantamoras up to the mountains. An' what air ole Santy hisself but a robber o' the meanest an' most dastardly sort? So, 'tain't any sign o' honesty their bearing military titles. When they've a war on in thar revolushionary way, they turn sogers, atween times takin' to the road."

"Well, Cris, supposing these to be on the road now, what ought we to do, think you?"

"Neery use thinkin', Cap, since thar's no choice left us. 'Tain't die dog, or eet the hatchet; and this chile goes for chawin' the steel. Whativer they be, we're bound to stick to 'em, an' oughter be glad o' the chance, seein' we haint the shadder o' another. If tuk agin' we'd be strung up or shot sure. Highwaymen or lowwaymen, they're the only ones about these diggin's that kin gie us purtekshun, an' I reck'n we may rely on them for that—so far's they're able."

For a time Kearney was silent, though not thinking over what the Texan had said, much of which had passed through his mind before. The train of his reflections was carried further back, to the point where he was first brought into contact with Rivas, by their legs getting linked together. Then forward throughout the hours and incidents that came after, recalling everything that had occurred, in act as in conversation—mentally reviewing all, in an endeavour to solve the problem that was puzzling them.

Seeing him so occupied, and with a suspicion of how his thoughts were working, the Texan forebore further speech, and awaited the result.

"If we've fallen among banditti," Kearney at length said, "it will be awkward to get away from them. They'll want us to take a hand at their trade, and that wouldn't be nice."

"Sartinly not, Cap; anything but agreeable to eyther o' us. It goes agin the grit o' a honest man to think o' belongin' to a band o' robbers. But forced to jine 'em, that 'ud be different. Besides, the thing ain't the same in Mexico as 'twud be in Texas and the States. Hyar 'tisn't looked on as beein' so much o' a disgrace, s'long's they don't practice cruelty. An' I've heern Mexikins say 'tain't wuss, nor yet so bad, as the way some our own poltishuns an' lawyers plunder the people. I guess it be 'bout the same, when one gits used to it."

To this quaint rigmarole of reasoning—not without reason in it, however,—Kearney only replied with a smile, allowing the Texan to continue; which he did, saying—

"After all, I don't think they're robbers any more than monks; if they be, they're wonderfully well-behaved. A perliter set o' fellers or better kump'ny this chile niver war in durin' the hull coorse of his experience in Texas, or otherwhars. They ain't like to lead us into anythin' very bad, in the way o' cruelty or killin'. So I say, let's freeze to 'em, till we find they ain't worthy of being froze to; then we must gie 'em the slip somehow."

"Ah! if we can," said his fellow-filibuster doubtingly. "But that is the thing for the far hereafter. The question is, what are we to do now?"

"No guess'n at all, Cap, as thar's no choosin' atween. We're boun' to be robbers for a time, or whatsomever else these new 'quaintances o' ours be themselves. Thet's sure as shootin'."

"True," returned the other musingly. "There seems no help for it. It's our fate, old comrade, though one, I trust, we shall be able to control without turning highwaymen. I don't think they are that. I can't believe it."

"Nor me neyther. One thing, howsomever, thet I hev observed air a leetle queery, an' sort o' in thar favour."

"What thing?"

"Thar not hevin' any weemen among 'em. I war in the kitchen this mornin' 'fore ye war up, and kedn't see sign o' a petticoat about, the cookin' bein' all done by men sarvents. Thet, I've heern say, air the way wi' monks; but not wi' the other sort. What do you make o't, Cap?"

"I hardly know, Cris. Possibly the Mexican brigands, unlike those of Italy, don't care to encumber themselves with a following of the fair sex."

"On t'other hand," pursued the Texan, "it seems to contrary their bein' o' the religious sort, puttin' out sentries as they do. Thar wor that one we passed last night, and this mornin' I seed two go out wi' guns, one takin' each side, and soon arter two others comin' in as if they'd been jest relieved from thar posts. Thar's a path as leads down from both sides o' the building."

"All very strange, indeed," said Kearney. "But no doubt we shall soon get explanation of it. By the way," he added, changing tone with the subject, "where is the dwarf? What have they done with him?"

"That I can't tell eyther, Cap. I haven't seen stime o' the critter since he war tuk away from us by that head man o' the sarvents, and I don't wish ever to set eyes on the skunk again. Cris Rock niver was so tired o' a connexshun as wi' thet same. Wagh!"

"I suppose they've got him shut up somewhere, and intend so keeping him—no doubt for good reasons. Ah! now we're likely to hear something about the disposal of ourselves. Yonder comes the man who can tell us!"

This, as the *soi-disant* Abbot was seen approaching along the path.

Chapter Forty Four
The Abbot

"*Amigo,*" said their host, as he rejoined them, speaking to Kearney, who could alone understand him, "permit me to offer you a cigar—your comrade also—with my apologies for having forgotten that you smoked. Here are both Havannahs and Manillas, several brands of each. So choose for yourself."

The mayor-domo, who attended him, carrying a huge mahogany case, had already placed it upon one of the rustic benches, and laid open the lid.

"Thanks, holy father," responded Kearney, with a peculiar smile. "If you have no objection, I'll stick to the Imperadoes. After smoking one of them a man need have no difficulty as to choice."

At which he took an "Emperor" out of the case.

"I'm glad you like them," observed the generous donor, helping him to a light. "They ought to be of good quality, considering what they cost, and where they come from. But, Don Florencio, don't let the question of expense hinder you smoking as many as you please. My outlay on them was *nil*—they were a contribution to the monastery, though not exactly a charitable one."

He said this with a sort of inward laugh, as though some strange history attached to the Imperadoes.

"A forced contribution, then," thought the Irishman, the remark having made a strange, and by no means pleasant impression upon him.

The Texan had not yet touched the cigars, and when with a gesture the invitation was extended to him, he hung back, muttering to Kearney—

"Tell him, Cap, I'd purfar a pipe ef he ked accomerdate me wi' thet 'ere article."

"What says the Señor Cristoforo?" asked the Abbot.

"He'd prefer smoking a pipe, if you don't object, and there be such a thing convenient."

"Oh! *un pipa*. I shall see. Gregorio!"

He called after the mayor-domo, who was returning toward the house.

"Never mind, reverend Father," protested Kearney; "content yourself with a cigar, Cris, and don't give trouble."

"I'm sorry I spoke o' it," said the Texan. "I oughter be only too gled to git a seegar, an' it may be he wudn't mind my chawin', stead o' smokin' it! My stammuck feels starved for a bit o' bacca. What wouldn't I gie jest now for a plug o' Jeemes's River!"

"There, take one of the cigars and eat it if you like; I'm sure he'll have no objection."

Availing himself of the leave thus vicariously accorded the Texan picked out one of the largest in the collection, and, biting off about a third, commenced crunching it between his teeth, as though it was a piece of sugar-stick. This to the no small amusement of the Mexican, who, however, delicately refrained from making remark.

Nor was Cris hindered from having a smoke as well as a "chew,"—the mayor-domo soon after appearing with a pipe, a somewhat eccentric affair he had fished out from the back regions of the establishment.

Meanwhile their host had himself lit one of the "Emperors," and was smoking away like a chimney. A somewhat comical sight at any time, or in any place, is a monk with a cigar in his mouth. But that the Abbot of the Cerro Ajusco was no anchorite they were already aware, and saw nothing in it to surprise them.

Seating himself beside Kearney, with face turned towards the valley, he put the question—

"What do you think of that landscape, Don Florencio?"

"Magnificent! I can't recall having looked upon lovelier, or one with greater variety of scenic detail. It has all the elements of the sublime and beautiful."

The young Irishman was back in his college classics with his countryman Burke.

"Make use of this," said the Abbot, offering a small telescope which he drew out. "'Twill give you a better view of things."

Taking the glass and adjusting it to his sight, Kearney commenced making survey of the valley, now bringing one portion of it within the field of telescopic vision, then another.

"Can you see the Pedregal?" asked the Abbot. "It's close in to the mountain's foot. You'll recognise it by its sombre grey colour."

"Certainly I see it," answered the other, after depressing the telescope. "And the thicket we came through on its further side—quite distinctly."

"Look to the right of that, then you'll observe a large house, standing in the middle of the maguey fields. Have you caught it?"

"Yes; why do you ask?"

"Because that house has an interest for me—a very special one. Whom do you suppose it belongs to; or I should rather say did, and ought to belong to?"

"How should I know, holy father?" asked Kearney, thinking it somewhat strange his being so interrogated. "True," responded the Abbot; "how could you, my son? But I'll tell you. That *magueyal* is mine by right, though by wrong 'tis now the property of our late host, the Governor of the Acordada. His reward at the last confiscation for basely betraying his country and our cause."

"What cause?" inquired the young Irishman, laying aside the glass, and showing more interest in what he heard than that he had been looking at. Country and cause! These were not the words likely to be on the lips of either monk or highwayman.

And that the man who had spoken to him was neither one nor other he had fuller proof in what was now further said.

"A cause, Señor Irlandes, for which I, Ruperto Rivas, am ready to lay down life, if the sacrifice be called for, and so most—I may say all—of those you've just met at *almuerzo*. You heard it proclaimed in the toast, 'Patria y Libertad!'"

"Yes. And a grand noble sentiment it is. One I was gratified to hear."

"And surprised as well. Is not that so, *amigo*?"

"Well, to be frank with you, holy father, I confess to something of the sort."

"Not strange you should, my son. No doubt you're greatly perplexed at what you've seen and heard since you came up here, with much before. But the time has come to relieve you; so light another cigar and listen."

Chapter Forty Five
The Free Lances

"Try a Manilla this time," said the Mexican, as Kearney was reaching out to take a cigar from the case. "Most people believe that the best can only come from Cuba. A mistake, that. There are some made in the Philippine Islands equal—in my opinion, superior—to any Havannahs. I speak of a very choice article, which don't ever get into the hands of the dealers, and's only known to the initiated. Some of our *ricos* import them by way of Acapulco. Those are a fair sample."

The young Irishman made trial of the weed thus warmly recommended; to discover what contradicted all his preconceived ideas in the smoking line. He had always heard it said that the choicest cigars are Havannahs; but, after a few whiffs from that Manilla, which had never seen a cigar shop, he was willing to give up the "Imperadores." His host, lighting one of the same, thus proceeded: "*Pues, caballero*; to give you the promised explanation. That the monks of my community are of an order neither very devout nor austere, you've already observed, no doubt, and may have a suspicion they're not monks at all. Soldiers, every man; most having seen service, and many who have done gallant deeds. When I speak of them as soldiers, you will understand it in its true sense, Señor. With one or two exceptions, all have held commissions in our army, and with a like limitation, I may say all are gentlemen. The last revolution, which has again cursed our country by restoring its chronic tyrant, Santa Anna, of course threw them out; the majority, as myself, being proscribed, with a price set upon their heads."

"Then you're not robbers?"

This was said without thought, the words involuntarily escaping Kearney's lips. But the counterfeit abbot, so far from feeling offence at them, broke out into a laugh, good-humouredly rejoining—

"Robbers, *amigo mio*! who told you we were that?"

The Irishman felt abashed, seeing he had committed himself.

"Don Ruperto," he exclaimed, hastening to make the best of his blunder, "I owe you every apology. It arose from some talk I heard passing around in the prison. Be assured, I neither did nor could believe it."

"Thank you, Señor!" returned the Mexican. "Your apologies are appreciated. And," he added, putting on a peculiar smile, "in a way superfluous. I believe we do enjoy that repute among our enemies; and, to confess the truth, not without some reason."

Kearney pricked up his ears, perplexity, with just a shade of trouble, again appearing upon his face. He said nothing, however, allowing the other to proceed.

"*Carramba*, yes!" continued the proscript. "'Tis quite true we do a little in the plundering line—now and then. We need doing it, Don Florencio. But for that, I mightn't have been able to set so good a breakfast before you; nor wines of such quality, nor yet these delectable cigars. If you look to the right down there, you'll see the *pueblo* of San Augustin, and just outside its suburbs, a large yellow house. From that came our last supply of drinkable and smokeable materials, including those here, mahogany and everything. A forced contribution, as I've hinted at. But, Señor, I should be sorry to have you think we levy blackmail indiscriminately. He from whom they were taken is one of our bitterest enemies; equally an enemy of our country. 'Twas all in the way of reprisal; fair, as you'll admit, when you come to comprehend the circumstances."

"I comprehend them now," returned the listener, relieved, "quite; and I trust you'll accept my apology."

"*Sans arrière pensée*," responded the Mexican, who could speak French, if not English, "I do frankly, freely. No reproach to you for supposing us robbers. I believe many others do, among whom we make appearance. Southward, however, in the State of Oaxaca, we are better known as 'the Free Lances'; a title not so appropriate, either, since our weapons are only at the disposal of the Republic—our lives as well."

"But," questioned Kearney, "may I ask why you are habited as I now see you?"

"For a good reason, *amigo*. It adds to our security, giving all sorts of opportunities. Throughout Mexico, the cowl of the monk is the best passport a man could be provided with. Wearing it, we go about among the mountain villages without suspicion, the people believing that this old monastery, so long abandoned as to have been forgotten, has again become the dwelling-place of a religious order. Of course we don't allow any of the rustics to approach it. Luckily, they are not curious enough to care for that, against the toil of climbing up here. If they attempt it, we have sentinels to stay them. For ourselves, we have learned to play the part of the holy friar, so that there would be difficulty in detecting the counterfeit. As it chances, we have with us one or two who once wore the cowl. These perverts have taught us all the tricks and passwords current among the fraternity. Hitherto they have availed us, and I trust will, till the time arrives for our casting off our cassock, and putting on the soldier's coat. That day is not distant, Don Florencio; nearer than I expected, from what my comrades have told me since we came up. The State of Oaxaca is disaffected; as, indeed, the whole southern side of Acapulco, and a *grito* is anticipated ere long—possibly within a month. Alvarez, who controls in that quarter, will be the man to raise it; and the old Pinto chief will expect to be joined by the 'Free Lances.' Nor will he be disappointed. We are all burning to be at it. So, caballero, you see how it is with us. And now," he added, changing tone and looking his listener earnestly in the face, "I have a question to put to yourself."

"What?" asked the Irishman, seeing that he hesitated putting it.

"Will you be one of us?"

It was now Kearney's turn to hesitate about the answer he ought to make. A proposition fraught with such consequences required consideration. To what would he be committing himself if he consented? And what if he should refuse? Besides, under the circumstances, was he free to refuse? That of itself was a question, a delicate one. He and his comrade, Cris Rock, owed their escape to this strange man, whatever he might be; and to separate from him now, even under full permission, would savour of ingratitude. Still more, after listening to what was further said. For, noting his embarrassment, and deeming it natural enough, the Mexican hastened to relieve him.

"If my proposal be not to your liking, Señor Irlandes, say so; and without fear of offence. All the same, you may rest assured of our protection while you remain with us; and I shall do what I can to get you safe out of the country. At all events, I won't send you back to the Acordada gaol, and the tender care of its governor. So you can speak frankly, without reserve. Are you willing to be one of us?"

"I am!" was the answer, given without further hesitation.

Why should he have either hesitated or said nay? In the heart of a hostile country, an escaped prisoner, his life, as he felt sure, forfeited should he be retaken. Joining Rivas and his Free Lances might be his sole chance of saving it. Even had they been banditti, he could not have done better then.

"Yes, Don Ruperto," he added; "if you deem me worthy of belonging to your brotherhood, be it so. I accept your invitation."

"And your comrade, Don Cristoforo. Will he be of the same mind, think you?"

"Sure to be. I take it I can answer for him. But you shall hear for yourself. Rock!"

He called to the Texan, who, not understanding their dialogue, had sauntered apart, chewing away at the Imperador.

"Wal, Cap; what's up now?" he asked on rejoining them.

"They're no robbers, Cris," said Kearney, speaking freely in their own tongue.

"Gled to hear it. I didn't think they war—noways. Nor monks neyther, I guess?"

"Nor monks."

"What then, Cap?"

"The same as yourself. Patriots who have been fighting for their country, and got defeated. That's why they are here—in hiding."

"Yes, Cap; I see it all, clar as coon's track on a mud bar. Enemies o' ole Santy, who've got beat it thar last risin'."

"Just so. But they expect another rising soon, and wish us to join them. I've agreed, and said so. What say you?"

"Lordy, Cap; what a questun to be axed, an' by yurself! Sure this chile air boun' to stick to ye, whatsomever ye do. Ef they'd been brigants, I shed 'a put my conscience in my pocket, and goe'd in wi' 'em all the same; s'long you're agreed. Nor I wudn't 'a minded turning monk for a spell. But men who intend foughtin' for freedom? Haleluyah! Cris Rock air all thar! Ye may tell him so."

"He consents," said Kearney, reporting to the Mexican; "and willingly as myself. Indeed, Don Ruperto, we ought both to regard it as a grace—an honour—to be so associated, and we shall do the best we can to show ourselves worthy of it."

"*Mil gracias, Señor!* The grace and honour are all given to us. Two such *valientes*, as I know you to be, will be no slight acquisition to our strength. And now, may I ask you to assume the garb which, as you see, is our present uniform? That by way of precaution for the time. You'll find suitable raiment inside. I've given Gregorio orders to get it ready. So you see, *Camarades*, I've been counting upon you."

"Gehosofat!" exclaimed the Texan, when told of the dress he was expected to put on. "What wi' New Orleens store close, an' prison duds, an' the like, this chile hev had a goodish wheen o' changes since he stripped off his ole huntin' shirt. An' now a-goin' in for a monk! Wal; tho' I mayn't be the most sanctified, I reck'n I'll be the tallest in thar mon'stery."

Chapter Forty Six
Saint Augustine of the Caves

One of the pleasantest villages in the valley of Mexico is San Augustin de las Cuevas—*Tlalpam* by Aztec designation—both names due to some remarkable caverns in the immediate neighbourhood. It is some ten or twelve miles from the capital, on the southern or Acapulco road, just where this, forsaking the valley level, begins to ascend the Sierra, passing over which by Cruz del Marques, it continues on through the *tierras calentes* of Cuernavaca and Guerrero to the famed port of the Pacific.

San Augustin is a *pueblo*, endowed with certain municipal privileges. It boasts of an *alcalde-mayor* with other corporate officers, and a staff of alguezils, or policemen.

The heads of departments are mostly men of pure Spanish race—"gente de razon," as they proudly proclaim themselves—though many are in reality of mixed blood, Mestizos. Of this are the better class of shopkeepers, few in number, the *gente de razon* at best forming a scarce discernible element in the population, which is mainly made up of the brown aborigines.

At a certain season of the year, however, paler complexions show in the ascendant. This during carnival time—"*Las Pascuas*." Then the streets of San Augustin are crowded with gay promenaders; while carriages and men on horseback may be seen in continuous stream passing to and fro between it and the capital. In Las Pascuas week, one day with another, half Mexico is there engaged in a gambling orgie, as Londoners at Epsom during the Derby. More like Homburg and Monaco, though; since the betting at Tlalpam is not upon the swiftness of horses, but done with dice and cards. The national game, "monté," there finds fullest illustration, grand marquees being erected for its play—real temples erected to the goddess Fortuna. Inside these may be seen crowds of the strangest composition, in every sense heterogeneous; military officers, generals and colonels, down to the lowest grade, even sergeants and corporals, sitting at the same table and staking on the same cards; members of Congress, Senators, Cabinet Ministers, and, upon occasions, the Chief of the State, jostling the ragged *lepero*, and not unfrequently standing elbow to elbow with the footpad and salteador!—Something stranger still, ladies compose part of this miscellaneous assemblage; dames of high birth and proud bearing, but in this carnival of cupidity not disdaining to "punt" on the *sota* or *cavallo*, while brushing skirts with bare-armed, barefooted rustic damsels, and *poblanas*, more elaborately robed, but with scantier reputation.

After all, it is only Baden on the other side of the Atlantic; and it may be said in favour of San Augustin, the fury lasts for only a few days, instead of a whole season. Then the *monté* banks disappear, with their dealers and croupiers; the great tents are taken down; the gamesters, gentle and simple, scatter off, most going back to the city; and the little *pueblo* Tlalpam, resuming its wonted tranquillity, is scarce thought of till Carnival comes again.

In its normal condition, though some might deem it rather dull, it is nevertheless one of the pleasantest residential villages in the Valley. Picturesquely situated at the foot of the southern Sierras, which form a bold mountain background, it has on the other side water scenery in the curious Laguna de Xochimilco, while the grim Pedregal also approaches it, giving variety to its surroundings.

Besides its fixed population there is one that may be termed floating or intermittent; people who come and go. These are certain "ricos," who chiefly affect its suburbs, where they have handsome houses—*casas de campo*. Not in hundreds, as at San Anjel and Tacubaya, Tlalpam being at a greater and more inconvenient distance from the capital. Still there are several around it of first-class, belonging to *familias principales*, though occupied by them only at intervals, and for a few days or weeks at a time.

One of these, owned by Don Ignacio Valverde, was a favourite place of residence with him; a tranquil retreat of which he was accustomed to avail himself whenever he could get away from his ministerial duties. Just such an interregnum had arisen some time after the stirring incidents we have recorded, and he went to stay at his San Augustin house with his daughter, the Condesa Almonté going with them as their guest. Since their last appearance before the reader, all three had passed through scenes of trial. An investigation had been gone into regarding the Callé de Plateros affair—private, however, before Santa Anna himself, the world not being made the wiser for it. Its results were all in their favour, thanks to the stern, stubborn fidelity of José, who lied like a very varlet. Such a circumstantial story told he, no one could suspect him of complicity in the escape of the *forsados*; far less that his mistress, or the Condesa Almonté had to do with it.

Don Ignacio, too, had done his share to hinder discovery of the truth. For, in the end, it was found necessary to take him into the secret, the missing cloak and pistols, with several mysterious incidents, calling for explanation. But in making a clean breast of it, his daughter had felt no fear of being betrayed by him. He was not the father to deal harshly with his child; besides, it was something more—a real danger. In addition, she knew how he was affected towards the man she had aided to escape—that he held Don Florencio in highest esteem; looked upon him as a dear friend, and in a certain tacit way had long ago signified approval of him for a son-in-law. All these thoughts passed through Luisa Valverde's mind while approaching her father, and steeling herself to make confession of that secret she might otherwise have kept from him.

The result was not disappointing. Don Ignacio consented to the deception, and they were saved. Whatever the suspicions of Santa Anna and his adjutant, both were baffled about that affair, at least for the time.

Alike had they been frustrated in their pursuit of the *escapados*. Despite the most zealous search through the Pedregal and elsewhere, these could not be found, nor even a trace of them. Still, they were not given up. Every town and village in the valley, in the mountains around, and the country outside were visited by soldiers or spies—every spot likely to harbour the fugitives. Pickets were placed everywhere and patrols despatched, riding the roads by night as by day, all proving abortive.

After a time, however, this vigorous action became relaxed. Not that they who had dictated were less desirous of continuing it; but because a matter of more importance than mere personal spite or vengeance was soon likely to declare itself, and threaten their own safety. Talk was beginning to be heard, though only in whispers, and at a far distance from the capital, of a new *pronunciamento* in preparation. And in making counter-preparations, the Dictator had now enough to occupy all his energies; not knowing the day or the hour he might again hear the cry he so dreaded, "Patria y Libertad."

Meanwhile the people had ceased to speak of the stirring episode which had occurred in the Callé de Plateros; thought strange only from the odd circumstances attendant, and the fact of two of the fugitives being *Tejanos*. The city of Mexico has its daily newspapers, and on the morning after a full account of it appeared in *El Diario* and *El Monitor*. For all it was but the topic of a week; in ten days no more heard of it; in a month quite forgotten, save by those whom it specially concerned. So varied are the events, so frequent the changes, so strange the Cosas de Mexico!

Chapter Forty Seven
Over the Cliff

For some time after their arrival at the old monastery, neither Kearney nor Cris Rock saw aught of their late "fourth fellow" prisoner—the hunchback. They cared not to inquire after him; the Texan repeating himself by saying,—"This chile don't want ever to sit eyes on his ugly pictur agin." They supposed that he was still there, however, somewhere about the building.

And so was he, with a chain attached to his leg, the same he had shared with Rock, its severed end now padlocked to a ring bolt; and the apartment he occupied had as much of the prison aspect as any cell in the Acordada. No doubt, in days gone by, many a refractory brother had pined and done penance therein for breach of monastic discipline.

Why the mis-shapen creature was so kept needs little explanation; for the same reason as prompted to bringing him thither. Helpless as he might appear, he was not harmless; and Don Ruperto knew that to restore him to liberty would be to risk losing his own, with something more. Though safely bestowed, however, no severity was shown him. He had his meals regularly, and a bed to sleep on, if but a pallet, quite as good as he had been accustomed to. Moreover, after some time had elapsed, he was relieved from this close confinement during the hours of the day. A clever actor, and having a tongue that could "wheedle with the devil," he had wheedled with the mayor-domo to granting him certain indulgences; among them being allowed to spend part of his time in the kitchen and scullery. Not in idleness, however, but occupied with work for which he had proved himself well qualified. It was found that he had once been "boots" in a *posado*, which fitted him for usefulness in many ways.

In the *cocina* of the old convent his temper was sorely tried, the other "mozos" making cruel sport of him. But he bore it with a meekness very different to what he had shown while in the Acordada.

Thus acquitting himself, Gregorio, who had him in special charge, began to regard him as a useful if not ornamental addition to his domestic staff of the establishment. Notwithstanding, the precaution was still continued of locking him at night and re-attaching the chain to his ankle. This last was more disagreeable than aught else he had to endure. He could bear the jibes of his fellow-scullions, but that fetter sorely vexed him; as night after night he was accustomed to say to the mayor-domo as he was turning the key in its clasp.

"It's so uncomfortable, Señor Don Gregorio," was his constantly recurring formula. "Keeps me from sleeping and's very troublesome when I want to turn over, as I often do on account of the pains in my poor humped shoulders. Now, why need you put it on? Surely you're not afraid of me trying to get away? Ha, ha! that would be turning one's back upon best friends. *Cascaras*! I fare too well here to think of changing quarters. Above all, going into the Acordada; where I'd have to go sure, if I were to show my face in the city again. Oh no, Señor! you don't catch me leaving this snug crib, so long's you allow me to board and bed in it. Only I'd like you to let me off from that nasty thing. It's cold too; interferes with my comfort generally. Do, good Don Gregorio! For this one night try me without it. And if you're not satisfied with the result, then put it on ever after, and I won't complain, I promise you."

In somewhat similar forms he had made appeals for many nights in succession, but without melting the heart of the "Good Don Gregorio."

At length, however, it proved effectual. Among various other avocations he had been a *Zapartero*, of the class cobbler, and on a certain day did service to the mayor-domo by mending his shoes. For which he received payment in the permission to pass that night without being discommoded by the chain.

"It's so very kind of you, Don Gregorio!" he said, when made aware of the grace to be given to him. "I ought to sleep sound this night, anyhow. But whether I do or not, I shall pray for you before going to bed all the same. *Buenas noches!*"

It was twilight outside, but almost total darkness within the cell, as the mayor-domo turned to go out of it. Otherwise he might have seen on the dwarfs features an expression calculated to make him repent his act of kindness, and instantly undo it. Could he have divined the thoughts at that moment passing through Zorillo's mind, the clasp would have quickly closed around the latter's leg, despite all gratitude due to him for the patching of the shoes.

"If I can get out," he commenced in mental soliloquy, as the footfall of the mayor-domo died away in the distant corridor, "out and away from them, my fortune's made; all sorts of good things in store for me. From this time forth I needn't fear to present myself at the door of the Acordada;

walk right into it. No danger of Don Pedro keeping me there now. Instead, I should be sent out again with a free pardon and a full purse. *Chingara*, talk of a cat in the cupboard, here are a score of them—half a hundred! And when I let them out—aha!"

He paused; then rising to his feet, moved across to the door, and laid his ear against it to listen. He heard sounds, but they were sounds of merriment—the counterfeit monks at their evening meal—and did not concern him.

"What a bit of luck it may turn out, after all, my getting coupled to that great brute and brought here! That is, if all goes well, and I can give them the slip. First, to make sure about the possibility of getting out of this hole. *Carrai*! I may be counting my chickens in the eggs."

Leaving the door, he glided across to the window, and set himself square against it, as if to measure its breadth by that of his own body. It was but a slit, unglazed, a single iron bar, placed vertically, dividing the aperture into two. Without removing this he could not possibly pass through. But he had the means to remove it; that file, already known to the reader, which he had contrived to get possession of, and for days kept secret in his cell. First, however, he must see whether it was worth while using it; for during all the time of his being there he had never been allowed an opportunity to approach the window and look out.

Leaning forward into the recess, he thrust his head between the bar and jamb, so far out as to give him a view of the ground below. This was solid rock, the crest of a steep slope, from which the wall rose as above a buttress. But there was a ledge, some ten or twelve feet under the sill, narrow, but wide enough to afford footing, which led off to more level ground. How was he to reach it?

He knew, or he would not have acted as he now did. For without spending another second in the survey, he drew back from the window, plunged his hand under his bed mat, drew forth the file, and commenced rasping away at the bar. Not noisily or in any excited haste. Even if the obstacle were removed, the time had not come for his attempt to pass out. He would wait for an hour after midnight, when all had gone to their beds.

Eaten with rust, the iron was easily sawed through, a clean cut being made near its lower end. Then, laying aside the file, and grasping the bar, he wrenched it out of the solderings. If diminutive in body, his arms were sinewy and strong as those of a coal-heaver.

This task accomplished, he turned to his pallet and taking up the old blanket allowed him for a covering, began to tear it into strips. He meant to make a rope of it to lower himself down outside. But finding it quite rotten, and doubting whether it would bear his weight, he desisted and sat for a time considering. Not long till he bethought himself of something more suitable for his purpose—the chain.

"Bah!" he exclaimed, tossing aside the rags he had commenced splicing together, "why didn't I think of that? Well, it's not too late yet. Good three yards—long enough. And the stupid has left the key behind, which fits both ends. So, Mr Chain, considering the world of worry and trouble you've been to me, it's time, and only fair, you should do me a good turn by way of recompense. After you've done it, I'll forgive you."

While muttering this quaint apostrophe, he commenced groping about over the floor—not for the chain, but the key, which he knew Gregorio had left, after releasing his leg from the clasp. The mayor-domo had either forgotten, or did not think it was worth while taking it away.

Having found it, he felt his way to the ring bolt, and unlocking the clasp at that end, returned to the window, taking the chain with him. Having made one end fast around the stump of the bar, he lowered the other down outside, cautiously, without a tinkle of its links. And now again looking out and below, he was delighted to see that it reached within a foot or two of the ledge. All this done, he once more sat down on the side of the bed, to await the hour of midnight.

But he was not long quiescent, when a thought occurring caused him to resume action.

"Why not try it now?" he mentally interrogated. "They're all in the Refectory, having a fine time of it, drinking their famous wines. Some grand occasion, I heard one of the *mozos* say. There mightn't be a better chance for me than this very minute—maybe not so good. *Carramba!* I'll risk it now."

Quickly at the words he glided back to the window, climbed up into it, and squeezing out through the aperture, let himself down on the chain, link by link, as a monkey making descent of a *lliana* in the forests of the *tierra caliente*.

Soon as he found himself safe landed he let go the chain, and after a minute or so spent in silent reconnaissance of the ledge, commenced moving off along it.

Right he was in choosing that early hour, for the way he must needs take led out into the open ground, in front of the building, where at a later one a watch would have been stationed. There was none there now, and without stop or challenge he passed on and down.

Though they had never allowed him to go outside the building, he perfectly remembered the path by which he and the others had reached it, on that memorable night after their escape from the chain-gang. He recalled the two steep slopes, one above the other, with a narrow shelf between, on which they encountered the sentinel, who had hailed, "*Quien viva?*"

Sure to be one there now, and to such hail what answer could he make?

On this he reflected while descending the upper slope. The darkness due to the overshadowing trees made it necessary for him to go slowly, so giving him time. But it did not hinder his keeping to the path. With his long arms like the tentacles of an octopus he was able to direct his course, now and then using them to grasp overhanging branches, or the parasites dependent therefrom. Withal he went cautiously, and so silently, that the sentinel—for sure enough one was there—heard no noise to warn him of an enemy behind. In his monkish garb, he was standing on the outer edge of the shelf rock, his face turned to the valley, which was just beginning to show silvery white under the rays of a rising moon. Perhaps, like Don Ruperto, he was gazing on some spot, a house endeared to him as the home of his childhood; but from which, as the leader of the Free Lances, he had been bereft by the last confiscation. Possibly he was indulging in the hope of its being soon restored to him, but least of all dreaming of danger behind.

It was there, notwithstanding—in fiendish shape and close proximity. A creature squatted like a toad, human withal, saying to himself—

"What wouldn't I give for a knife with a blade six inches long!"

Then, with a sudden change of thought, seeing the chance to do without the knife, making a dash forward, with the ape-like arms extended, and pushing the sentinel over!

The cry that came from the latter, on feeling the impulse from behind, was stifled as he went whirling to the bottom of the cliff.

Chapter Forty Eight
On down the Mountain

"Dead!" muttered the inhuman wretch, as he stood upon the spot late occupied by his victim, looking down over the cliff. "Dead he must be; unless a man can fall two hundred feet and still live; which isn't likely. That clears the way, I take it; and unless I have the ill luck to meet some one coming up—a straggler—it'll be all right. As sound ascends, I ought to hear them before they could *see* me. I shall keep my ears open."

Saying which he *commenced* the descent of the *second* slope, proceeding in the same cautious way as before.

The path was but a ledge, which, after running fifty yards in a direct line, made an abrupt double back in the opposite direction, all the while obliquing downwards. Another similar zig-zag, with a like length of declivity traversed, and he found himself at the cliff's base, among shadowy, thick standing trees. He remembered the place, and that before reaching it on their way up they had followed the trend of the cliff for more than a quarter of a mile. So, taking this for his guide, he kept on along the back track.

Not far, before seeing that which brought him to a stop. If he had entertained any doubt about the sentinel being dead, it would have been resolved now. There lay the man's body among the loose rocks, not only lifeless, but shapeless. A break in the continuity of the timber let the moonlight through, giving the murderer a full view of him he had murdered.

The sentinel had fallen upon his back, and lay with his face upward, his crushed body doubled over a boulder; the blood was welling from his mouth and nostrils, and the open eyes glared ghastly in the white, weird light. It was a sight to inspire fear in the mind of an ordinary individual, even in that of a murderer. But it had no effect on this strange *lusus* of humanity, whose courage was equal to his cruelty. Instead of giving the body a wide berth, and scared-like stealing past, he walked boldly up to it, saying in apostrophe—

"So you're there! Well, you need not blame me, but your luck. If I hadn't pushed you over, you'd have shot me like a dog, or brained me with the butt of your gun. Aha! I was too much for you, Mr Monk or soldier, whichever you were, for you're neither now.

"Just possible," he continued, changing the form of his monologue, "he may have a purse; the which I'm sure to stand in need of before this time to-morrow. If without money, his weapons may be of use to me."

With a nimbleness which bespoke him no novice at trying pockets, he soon touched the bottom of all those on the body, to find them empty.

"Bah!" he ejaculated, drawing back with a disappointed air, "I might have known there was nothing in them. Whatever cash they've had up there has been spent long ago, and their wine will soon be out too. His gun I don't care for; besides, I see it's broken;—yes, the stock snapped clean off. But this stiletto, it's worth taking with me. Even if I shouldn't need it as a weapon, it looks like a thing Mr Pawnbroker would appreciate."

Snatching the dagger—a silver-hilted one—from the corpse of its ill-starred owner, he secreted it inside his tattered rag of a coat, and without delay proceeded on.

Soon after he came to a point where the path, forsaking the cliff, turned to the left, down the slope of the mountain. He knew that would take him into the Pedregal, where he did not desire to go. Besides his doubts of being able to find the way through the lava field, there was no particular need for his attempting so difficult a track. All he wanted was to get back to the city by the most direct route, and as soon as possible into the presence of a man of whom during late days he had been thinking much. For from this man he expected much, in return for a tale he could tell him. It must be told direct, and for this reason all caution was required. He might fall into hands that would not only hinder him from relating it in the right quarter, but prevent his telling it at all.

Just where the path diverged to the left, going down to the Pedregal, a mass of rocks rose bare above the tops of the trees. Clambering to its summit he obtained a view of what lay below; the whole valley bathed in bright moonlight, green meadows, fields of maize, and maguey, great sheets of water with haze hanging over them, white and gauzy as a bridal veil. The city itself was distinguishable at a long distance, and in places nearer specklings of white telling of some *pueblita*, or single spots where stood a *rancho* or *hacienda*. Closer still, almost under his feet, a clump of those mottlings was more conspicuous; which he recognised as the *pueblo* of San Augustin. A narrow ribbon-like strip of greyish white passing through it, and on to the city, he knew to be the Great Southern or Acapulco Road, which enters the capital by the *garita* of San Antonio de Abad. This route he decided on taking.

Having made note of the necessary bearings, he slipped back down the side of the rock, and looked about for a path leading to the right.

Not long till he discovered one, a mere trace made by wild animals through the underwood—sufficiently practicable for him, as he could work his way through any tangle of thicket. Sprawling along it, and rapidly, despite all obstructions, he at length came out on the Acapulco Road, a wide causeway, with the moon full upon it.

The track was easy and clear even now, too clear to satisfy him. He would have preferred a darker night San Augustin had to be passed through, and he knew that in it were both *serenos* and *alguazils*. Besides, he had heard the *moxos* at the monastery speak of troops stationed there, and patrols at all hours along the roads around. If taken up by these he might still hope to reach his intended destination; but neither in the time he desired, nor the way he wished. He must approach the man with whom he meant seeking an interview, not as a prisoner but voluntarily. And he must see this man soon, to make things effectual, as the reward he was dreaming of sure.

Urged by these reflections, he made no further delay; but taking to the dusty road, moved in all haste along it. In one way the moon was in his favour. The causeway was not straight, for it was still a deep descent towards the valley, and carried by zig-zags; so that at each angle he was enabled to scan the stretch ahead, and see that it was clear, before exposing himself upon it. Then he would advance rapidly on the next turning-point, stop again, and reconnoitre.

Thus alternately making traverses and pauses, he at length reached the outskirts of the *pueblo*, unchallenged and unobserved. But the problem was how to pass through it; all the more difficult at that early hour. He had heard the church clock tolling the hours as he came down the mountain, and he knew it had not struck ten. A beautiful night, the villagers would be all abroad; and how was he to appear in the street without attracting notice— he above all men? His deformity of itself would betray him. An expression of blackest bitterness came over his features as he thus reflected. But it was not a time to indulge in sentimentalities. San Augustin must be got through somehow, if he could not find a way around it.

For this last he had been looking some time, both to the right and left. To his joy, just as he caught sight of the first houses—villa residences they were, far straggling along the road—a lane running in behind them seemed to promise what he was in search of. From its direction it should enable him to turn the village, without the necessity of passing through the *plaza*, or at all entering upon the streets. Without more ado he dodged into the lane.

It proved the very sort of way he was wishing for; dark from being overshadowed with trees. A high park-like wall extended along one side of it, within which were the trees, their great boughs drooping down over.

Keeping close in to the wall he glided on, and had got some distance from the main road, when he saw that which brought him to a sudden stop—a man approaching from the opposite direction. In the dim light, the figure was as yet barely discernible, but there was a certain something in its gait— the confidential swagger of the policeman—which caught the practised eye of Zorillo, involuntarily drawing from him the muttered speech—

"*Maltida sea*! An alguazil!"

Whether the man was this or not, he must be avoided; and, luckily for the dwarf, the means of shunning him were at hand, easy as convenient. It was but to raise his long arms above his head, lay hold of one of the overhanging branches, and draw himself up to the top of the wall; which he did upon the instant. It was a structure of *adobes*, with a coping quite a yard in width, and laid flat along this, he was altogether invisible to one passing below.

The man, alguazil or not, neither saw him nor suspected his being there, but walked tranquilly on.

When he was well beyond earshot the dwarf, deeming himself safe, was about to drop back into the lane, when a murmur of voices prompted him to keep his perch. They were feminine, sweet as the sound of rippling brooks, and gradually becoming more distinct; which told him that those from whom they proceeded were approaching the spot. He had already observed that the enclosure was a grand ornamental garden with walks, fountains, and flowers; a large house on its farther side.

Presently the speakers appeared—two young ladies sauntering side by side along one of the walks, the soft moonlight streaming down upon them. As it fell full upon their faces, now turned toward the wall, the dwarf started at a recognition, inwardly exclaiming—

"*Santissima*! The señoritas of the carriage!"

Chapter Forty Nine
A Tale of Starvation

It was the garden of Don Ignacio's *casa de campo*; the ladies, his daughter and the Condesa. The lovely night, with balm in the air and a bright moon shining through the sky, had drawn them out, and they strolled through the grounds, keeping step, as it were, to that matchless melody, the song of the *czenzontle*. But note of no nightingale was in their thoughts, which were engrossed by graver themes.

"'Tis so strange our never hearing from them, and not a word of them. What do you make of it, Ysabel? Is it a bad sign?"

The question was asked by the Doña Luisa.

"That we haven't heard from them is—in a way," responded the Countess. "Yet that may be explained, too. The probability is, from the roads being all watched and guarded, as we know they are, they'd be cautious about communicating with us. If they've sent a messenger—which I hope they haven't—he must have been intercepted and made prisoner. And then, the message; that might compromise us. But I know Ruperto will be careful. Not to have heard of them is all for the best—the very best. It should almost assure us that they're still free, and safe somewhere. Had they been recaptured, we'd have known before this. All Mexico would be talking about it."

"True," assented Don Ignacio's daughter, with a feeling of relief. "They cannot have been retaken. But I wonder where they are now."

"So I myself, Luisita. I hope, however, not at that old monastery of which Ruperto gave me a description in one of his letters. It's somewhere up in the mountains. But with the country all around so occupied by troops it would seem an unsafe place. I trust they've got over the Sierra, and down to Acapulco. If they have, we needn't feel so very anxious about them."

"Why not, Ysabel?"

"Why not? Ah! that's a question you haven't yet come to understand. But never mind the reason now. You'll know it in good time; and when you do, I've no fear but you'll be satisfied; your father too."

Don Ignacio's daughter was both puzzled and surprised at the strange words. But she knew the Countess had strange ways; and, though a bosom friend, was not without some secrets she kept to herself. This was one of them, no doubt, and she forebore pressing for an explanation.

What the Condesa hinted at was that disaffection in the south, the expected *pronunciamento*, which, if successful, would not only depose the Dictator, but of course also his Cabinet Ministers, her friend's father among them. With some knowledge of coming events, she declined imparting this to the Doña Luisa through delicacy. Right was she, also, in her surmise as to the messenger; none had been intercepted, none having been sent out, just for the reason surmised by her.

They had made a turn or two of the grounds, thus conversing, when both came to a sudden stop, simultaneously uttering exclamations of alarm, "*Santissima!*" and "*Madre de Dios!*"

"What can it be?" gasped Doña Luisa. "Is it a man?"

No wonder she should so doubtingly interrogate, since her question referred to that strange creature on the top of the wall, seeming more ape than human being.

That he was human, however, was to be proved by his being gifted with the power of speech, put forth on the instant after. Before the Countess could make answer to the question (of course overheard by him), he interposed, saying—

"Pray, don't be alarmed, your ladyships, at a poor miserable creature like me. I know that my body is anything but shapely; but my soul—that, I trust, is different. But, Señoritas, surely you remember me?"

While speaking, he had raised himself into an upright attitude, and the moonlight falling upon him showed his shape in all its grotesqueness of outline. This, with his words, at once recalled their having seen him before. Yes; it was the *enano*, whom the big Texan had swung up to the box of their carriage.

Astonishment hindering reply to his interrogatory, he continued—

"Well, your ladyships, I'm sorry you don't recognise me; the more from my being one of your best friends, or, at all events, the friend of your friends."

"Of whom do you speak, sir?" asked the Countess, first to recover composure, the Doña Luisa echoing the interrogatory. Both were alike anxious for the answer, better than half divining.

"Two worthy gentlemen, who, like my poor self, had the misfortune to get shut up in the Acordada; more than that, set to work in the filthy sewers. Thanks to the luck of your ladyship's carriage coming past at a convenient time we all escaped; and so far have been successful in eluding the search that's been made for us."

"You have succeeded—all?" both asked in a breath their eagerness throwing aside reserve.

"Oh yes; as I've said, so far. But it's been hard times with us in our hiding-place; so hard, indeed, we might well have wished ourselves back in the prison."

"How so, sir? Tell us all! You needn't fear to speak out; we'll not betray you."

"*Por Dios*! I'm not afraid of your ladyships doing that. Why should I, since I'm here on account of your own friends, and on an errand of mercy?"

"An errand of mercy?"

"Yes. And one of necessity as well. Ah! that far more."

"Go on, sir! Please tell us what it is!"

"Well, Señoritas, I've been deputed on a foraging expedition. For we're in a terrible strait—all four of us. You may remember there were four."

"We do. But, how in a terrible strait?"

"How? Why, for want of food; starving. Up in the mountains, where we've been hiding for now nearly a month, all we've had to live upon was wild fruits and roots; often eating them raw, too. We daren't any of us venture down, as the roads all round have been beset by spies and soldiers. It's only in sheer desperation I've stolen through them; the Señor Don Ruperto sending me to San Augustin in the hope I might be able to pick up some provisions. I was just slipping the village the back way, when an alguazil coming along made it necessary for me to climb up here and hide myself. The unlucky part of it all is, that even if I get safe in, I haven't the wherewith to buy the eatables, and must beg them. That I fear won't be easy; people are so hard-hearted."

For a time his surprised listeners stood silent, giving way to sad reflections. Florencio and Ruperto starving!

"May I hope," continued the lying wretch, "your ladyships will let me look upon this accidental encounter as a God-send, and that you will give me something to buy—"

"Oh, sir," interrupted the Countess, "we will give you that. Luisa, have you any money in your purse? I haven't in mine—nothing to signify."

"Nor I either—how unfortunate! We must—"

"Never mind money, your ladyships; money's worth will do quite as well. A *reloja*, rings, anything in the way of jewellery. I chance to know a place in the village where I can convert them into cash."

"Here, take this!" cried the Countess, handing him her watch, the same which had been hypothecated to José, but redeemed by a money payment.

"And this!" said the Doña Luisa, also holding out a watch, both of which he speedily took possession of.

"'Tis very generous of your ladyships," he said, stowing them away among his rags; "the proceeds of these ought to support us for a long time, even allowing for the reduced rate I'll have to accept from the pawnbroker. Afterwards we must do the best we can."

As he spoke, his little sparkling eyes were avariciously bent upon certain other objects he saw scintillating in the moonlight—bracelets, rings upon their fingers and in their ears. The hint was hardly needed. Enough for them the thought that more help might be required by those dear to them, and at a time when they could not extend it.

In less than five minutes after both had divested themselves of every article in the way of gold or gems adorning them. They even plucked the pendants from their ears, thrusting all indiscriminately into the outstretched hands of the hunchback.

"*Gracias!—mil gracias!*" he ejaculated, crowding everything into his pocket. "But your ladyships will scarce care to accept thanks from me. 'Twill be more to your satisfaction to know that your generosity will be the saving of valuable lives, two of them, if I mistake not, very dear to you. Oh! won't the Señores Don Ruperto and Don Florencio be delighted at the tale I shall take back—the Virgin seeing me safe! Not for the provisions I may carry, but how I obtained the means of purchasing them. But as time's pressing, Señorita, I won't say a word more, only *Adios!*"

Without waiting for permission to depart, or rejoinder of any kind, he slipped down from the wall, and disappeared on its other side.

It was an abrupt leave-taking, which alike surprised and disappointed them. For they had many questions to ask, and intended asking him—many anxieties they wished set at rest.

Chapter Fifty
An Encounter with Old Acquaintances

Passing out of the San Augustin towards the city, the great National Road, as already said, touches upon the Pedregal, the lava rocks here and there rising cliff-like over it. On the other side are level meadows stretching to the shore of the Laguna de Xochimilco; this last overgrown with a lush aquatic vegetation called the *cinta*, at a distance appearing more pastureland than lake. Excellent pasturage is afforded on the strip between; that end of it adjacent to the *pueblo* being apportioned among several of the rich proprietors of villas, who turn their household stock upon it, as milch kine, and horses kept for the saddle or carriage.

Just about the time when the hunchback was abruptly bidding "Adios" to the ladies, a man might have been seen moving along this part of the road at some half-mile distance from the skirts of the village, with face turned cityward. But that he had no intention of journeying so far was evident both by his gait and the character of his dress. He was going at a slow walk, now and then loitering, as if time was of little consequence. Moreover, he was in his shirt sleeves, and without the universal *serape*, which often serves for both cloak and coat. Otherwise his garb was the ordinary stable wear of a Mexican gentleman's servant; wide velveteen trousers open along the outer seams, and fended with leather at breech and bottoms. "Batos" and a black glaze hat completed his habiliments, with a scarf of China crape, the *chammora*, around his waist. Scanning the face shadowed by the broad rim of his *sombrero*, it was seen to be that of José, Don Ignacio's groom; while his errand along that road could be guessed, by seeing what he carried over his arm—a couple of slip halters. The horses, for whom they were intended, were to be seen standing at a gate, a little further, having browsed their fill; a pair of greys, recognisable as the famous *frisones*; all the easier now from one of them showing a split ear. They had been turned out to cool their hoofs on the soft meadow sward, and he was on his way to take them back to their stable.

Along the other side of the road, for a stretch of some distance, extended the Pedregal, forming a low ridge with a precipitous face towards the causeway. As the *cochero* got up to where his pets were expecting him, he saw a *coyote* standing upon the crest cliff, just opposite the horses, in an attitude and with an air as if it had been holding conversation with them. Solely for frolic's sake, he made a rush towards it, giving a swoop and swinging the halters around his head. Of course, the affrighted animal turned tail, and retreated; instantly disappearing from his sight. The little spurt had carried him in under the shadow of the rocks; and as he faced round to recross the moonlit causeway, he saw coming along it that which, by some mysterious instinct, prompted him to keep his place. After all, no mystery about it; for in the diminutive, crab-like form seen approaching, he recognised the dwarf-hunchback who had shared the box seat with him on that day never to be forgotten.

Nothing had been heard of the creature since, so far as José knew; and therefore it might be supposed his appearance would have been welcome, promising some news of those with whom he had been last seen. But so far from the *cochero* stepping out into the road to receive him, he but drew closer to the cliff, where an embayment in black shadow promised him perfect concealment.

Soon after Zorillo came shuffling along through the dust, keeping close to the shaded side of the road. Having cleared the skirts of the village, however, he was less careful now. Not likely there would be any one abroad at that hour—for it had gone ten—but if so, there was the Pedregal alongside, to which he could retreat. Evidently he had not seen José as when first seen himself he was turning a corner, and the other had been for some time in shadow.

When nearly opposite the meadow gate he also made a stop, with a start, at perceiving the two horses' heads stretched over it, one with a cleft ear! His start came through recognition of them.

"Oho!" he exclaimed, "you there, too, my noble *frisones? Caspita*! this is meeting one's old acquaintances all in a heap! It now only needs to encounter *cochero*, and the party will be complete! Well, I may live in hope to see him too, sometime; and won't there be a reckoning when we're all together again?"

He was about to pass on, when a clattering of hoofs was heard behind, in the direction of the *pueblo*, as if horsemen were issuing out of it. Shortly after, a dark clump was seen rounding the corner, and coming on along the white ribband of road. The sabres clanking against stirrup-irons proclaimed it a cavalry troop.

Like a tarantula retreating to its tree-cave, the dwarf darted in under the cliff, there crouching down—so close to José that the latter could have almost touched him with the tips of his fingers. He had no desire to do so, no thought of it; but the very opposite. His wish was to avoid an encounter; and good reason for it, as he was soon after made aware. Fortunately for him, the hunchback neither saw nor had a suspicion of his proximity. With face turned to the road, he was altogether occupied with the party approaching.

The Hussars turned out—an escort of some eight or ten files, with two officers at its head; these riding side by side, and a little in advance. They were chatting gaily and rather vociferously; the voice of him who spoke loudest being well-known to José. For Colonel Santander, whether welcome or not, was a frequent visitor at the *casa de campo* of Don Ignacio Valverde. And the dwarf now remembered it too, as he did so abandoning all attempt at concealment, and gliding out into the middle of the road.

"*Carajo*!" simultaneously shouted the two officers, as their horses reared up, snorting at the strange shape so suddenly presented before them. "What the *Demonio* is it, if not Satan himself?" added Santander.

"No, *Señor Coronet*," returned Zorillo. "Not the devil; only a poor creature whom God has cursed by making him in a shape that isn't altogether fashionable. But just for that reason I trust being recalled to your Excellency's remembrance—am I not?"

"Ah! You were in the Acordada?"

"*Si, Señor Coronet.*"

"And 'twas you I saw coupled to the Tejano?"

"The same, Señor. In that prosecuted by a like ill, no doubt, the devil all the time directing it."

"But where have you been since, sirrah?"

"Ah! *Excellenza*! that's just it; the very thing I want to tell you. I was on my way to the city in hopes of obtaining an interview with you. What a bit of fortune you passing here: 'twill save me a journey I was ill able to make; for I'm quite worn out, and weak, from being starved up there in the mountains."

"Oh! you've been up there?"

"Yes, Señor Coronel, in hiding with the others. But not like them voluntarily. They took me along with them, whether I would or no, and have kept me ever since—till this night, when an opportunity offered for giving them the slip. It isn't all of four hours since I parted company with them. But if your Excellency wishes to hear the whole story, perhaps you'd like it better in private. If I mistake not, some of it should only reach your own ears."

Santander had been already thinking of this, and turning to the officer by his side, he said—

"Take the men on, Ramirez. Halt at a hundred yards or so, and wait for me."

In obedience to the order the escort moved on, stopping as directed, the dialogue between Santander and the dwarf meanwhile continuing. It was more of a monologue, the latter giving a detailed relation of all that had occurred to him since the time of their escape from the chain-gang, with comments and suggestions added.

After hearing all, Santander rose in his stirrups, his features showing triumph, such as Satan might feel at a world of souls just delivered to him.

"The game is mine at last!" he muttered to himself, "every trick of it. They're in a trap now; and when they go out of it, 'twill be to the *garrota*."

For a moment he sat silent, apparently considering what was his best course to pursue. Then, seemingly having decided, he called out—

"Ramirez! Send a couple of men to me—the corporal and another."

These, detached from the escort, came trotting back along the road.

"Here, *cabo*! Take charge of this curious specimen. Keep him here, and see that you hold him safe till you have my orders for releasing him. Don't stray from this spot as you value your own neck—not an inch."

Saying which he put spurs to his horse, and rejoined his escort. Then commanding, "Forward! at the double quick!" they started off at full gallop towards the city.

Chapter Fifty One
A Grumbling Guard

Part of the dialogue between Santander and the hunchback was overheard by José—enough of it to give him the trembles. Among its revelations was nought relating to himself, or his connivance at the escape of the prisoners. For all, he could see that he was now in as much danger as they who were in hiding. The Colonel of Hussars had gone on to the city, perhaps to complete some duty already engaging him, but as likely to obtain a stronger force. And as his words told, he would return again; and no doubt make direct for the old monastery, the dwarf guiding him.

The first thought of the faithful *cochero* was not about himself, nor his horses. These might stay in the meadow all night, as they were now likely to do. The lives of men were at stake—his own among the number—and his sole purpose now was to get home, report what he had heard to his young mistress and the Condesa; then hasten up the mountain to warn the imperilled ones. As good luck would have it, he knew the place they were in. Son of a *carbonero*, when a boy he had helped his father in the charcoal-burning business; was familiar with the mountain forests, and their paths, and had more than once been at the abandoned monastery. He could easily find the way to it. But the difficulty was to get back to his master's house—even stir from the spot on which he stood. Soon as receiving their orders the two Hussars had dismounted, and tied up their horses, one on each side of the rocky embayment; they themselves, with their curious charge, occupying the space between. It was not possible to pass without being seen by them, and as surely seized.

So long as he kept his place he might feel comparatively safe. The cove was of a three-cornered shape, with luckily a deep dark cleft at its inner angle, into which he had already squeezed himself. While the moon remained low, and the cliff made shadow, there was little likelihood of their seeing him, unless they came close up. Still, the situation was aught but pleasant, and ere long became irksome in the extreme; the conversation to which he was compelled to listen making it so.

The two *Husares* did not seem, to be in the best of temper; the corporal more especially showing signs of dissatisfaction. Groping about for a stone to seat himself on, he grumbled out—

"*Maddita*! What a bore, having to stay here till they get back. Heaven knows when that will be. Like enough not before morning. I thought we were going to pass the night in San Augustin, and had hopes of a chat with that *muchachita* at the house where the colonel visits."

"Pepita, you mean—lady's maid to the Doña Luisa Valverde?"

"Of course I mean her, the pretty dear; and have reason to think she is a bit sweet upon me."

Josh's heart was on fire—his blood boiling. It was with difficulty he restrained himself from springing out upon the soldier and clutching him by the throat. He succeeded, however, in keeping his place, if not his temper; for it would have been sheer madness to show himself there and then. What came after quite tranquillised him.

"Well, *cabo*" returned he of the rank and file, seemingly without fear of speaking plain to the non-commissioned officer, "I should be sorry to dash your hopes; but as a friend I can't help saying I don't think you have much chance in that quarter. She's a step higher, that same Pepita; holds her head far above any of us common soldiers—"

"Common soldiers! I'm a corporal; you forget that, *hombre*. But why do you think my chances are so poor?"

"Because I've heard say there's a man about the establishment to whom she's already given what heart she may have had to give—that they're engaged. The fellow's groom or *cochero*, or something of the sort."

José breathed easier now, noways provoked at having been spoken of as a "fellow."

"Bah!" contemptuously exclaimed the corporal. "What care I for that horse-cleaner and carriage-washer for a rival! I've cut out scores of such before now, and will do the same with him. Lie down there, you devil's imp!" he added, turning savagely upon the dwarf, and venting his spleen by giving the creature a kick. "Down, or I'll break every bone in your body."

"Mercy, master!" expostulated the hunchback. "Don't be so cruel to a fellow-creature."

"Fellow-creature! That's good, ha, ha, ha!" And the brute broke out into a hoarse laugh, till the rocks echoed his fiendish cachinnation.

"Well, your worship," rejoined he thus inhumanly mocked, with an air of assumed meekness; "whatever I am, it pains me to think I should be the cause of keeping you here. But why should you stay, may I ask? You don't suppose I'm going to run away? If I were with you as a prisoner—but I am not. I sought an interview with your Colonel of my own free will. Surely you saw that!"

"True enough, he did," interposed the soldier.

"And what if he did?" growled the corporal.

"Only, Señor, to show that I have no intention to part company with you, nor wish neither. *Por Dios*! don't let me hinder you from having that chat with the *muchachita*. It's but a step back to the *pueblo*, and like as not she'll be on the lookout for you, spite of what your comrade says. Maybe he has an eye to the pretty dear himself, and that's why he wishes to discourage you."

As this rigmarole was delivered in the most comical manner, it put the soldiers in a better humour, both breaking out into laughter.

Of course the corporal had no thought of availing himself of the permission so accorded. Their orders were strict to stay in that spot, and stay they must. The question was, how were they to spend the time. A smoke to begin with; and they drew out their cigarritos, with flint, steel, and tinder.

Soon as the red coal appeared beneath their noses, said the *cabo* to his comrade—

"By the way, Perico, have you your cards with you?"

"Did you ever know me to be without them?"

"How lucky! I quite forgot mine."

"That's because your mind was bent upon Pepita. I saw you giving your moustache an extra twist this evening."

"Oh! bother Pepita. Let's have an *albur* of monté."

"How about light?"

"The moon's clear enough, if it wasn't we could manage with our cigars. Many's the game I've played that way."

"All right! But the stakes? I haven't a *cuartilla*—nay, not so much as a *claco*."

"*Carramba*! Nor I either. I spent the last on a drink just before we got into the saddle. It's bad; but we can bet upon the credit system, and use cartridges for counters."

"Ah, stay!"

At which he turned his eyes upon the dwarf with a look of peculiar significance, cupidity the prevailing expression.

The latter saw it with a heaviness of heart, and a shuddering throughout his frame. All the time apprehensive about the plunder with which his pockets were crammed, he instinctively anticipated what was coming.

Chapter Fifty Two
A Danae's Shower

"Now, I shouldn't wonder," continued the corporal, shifting upon his seat, and facing fully round to the dwarf. "I shouldn't at all wonder but that this diminutive gentleman has some spare cash upon him; and maybe he'll oblige us by a little loan, considering the occasion. What say you, *Señor Enano*?"

"I haven't any," was the ready answer. "And sorry to say it too—that I am."

"It don't look much like he has," observed Perico, with a glance at the hunchback's tattered habiliments.

"Looks are not always to be relied on," persisted the corporal. "Who'd ever suspect a pearl inside an ugly oyster-shell?"

"I haven't, indeed, *Señor Cabo*," once more protested the dwarf with earnest emphasis. "If I had, you'd be welcome to the loan you speak of. No man likes a game of *monté* better than myself. Alas! so far from being in funds, I'm too like your worships—without a *claco*. I've been stripped of everything; and, if you knew my story, you'd pity me, I'm sure."

"What story?" demanded the *cabo*, becoming curious.

"Why, that I've been robbed of all the money I had. It wasn't much, to be sure, only two *pesetas* and a *real*, but still that was better than empty pockets. It happened about half an hour ago. I was on my way to San Augustin, thinking I'd there get some supper, with a night's lodging; when not far from this, two men—footpads I suppose they were—rushed out from the roadside, and made straight at me. One took the right, the other left. But I've good long arms, as you see, pretty strong too; and so I was able to keep them off for a while. Several times they caught hold of my wrists; but I succeeded in jerking them free again. I believe I could have wrestled them both, but that one getting angry, pulled out a long-bladed knife, and threatened to cut my throat with it. *Por dios!* I had to surrender then, seeing he was in earnest."

While giving this somewhat prolix account of an altogether imaginary adventure, he had started to his feet, and accompanied his speech with a series of pantomimic gestures; dancing and flinging his arms about, as he professed to have done while defending himself against the footpads. The grotesqueness of the performance, though seen only in the dim light—for he kept under the shadow—set his listeners to laughing. Little dreamt they why he was treating them to the spectacle, or how cleverly he was outwitting them.

But there was a third spectator of the scene, unknown to all of them, who was aware of it. The *cochero* could not at first tell what were the things striking him in the pit of the stomach, as if he was being pelted with pebbles! But he could see they came from the hands of the hunchback, flung behind in his repeated contortions and gesticulations.

Moreover, that they glistened while passing through the air, and looked whitish where they lay, after falling at his own feet.

"Well; what did they do to you then?" asked the corporal, when he and his comrade had finished their guffaw. "Stripped you clean, as you've said?"

"*Ay, Dios!* Just that, Señor. Took everything I had, except the rags I wear; and to them I might well have made them welcome."

"Now, are you sure they took everything?" questioned the other, still suspicious. The earnestness of the dwarfs affirmation made him so.

"Of course, Señor. Quite sure. I'll swear to it, if you like."

"Oh, there's no need for the formality of an oath. Simpler to search you! and more satisfactory. Draw up here in front of me!"

The hunchback obeyed with an air of confident alacrity. He had no reluctance to being searched now, knowing his pockets were empty. Of which the searcher satisfied himself by groping about among the rags, and sounding every receptacle where coin might be kept.

But if he found no money, an article turned up, which no little surprised himself and his comrade—a stiletto!

"*Caspita!*" he exclaimed, as his hand touched something hard in the waistband of the dwarfs breeches, stuck behind his back. "What have we here? As I live, a dagger!" drawing it out and holding it to the light. "Silver-hilted, too! Yes; it's silver, sure; and blade beautifully chased—worth a *doblone*, at the very least!"

"Half mine," interrupted Perico, putting in his claim.

"All right, *camarado*. We'll settle that by-and-by. Now, you limb of Satan!" he continued to the hunchback, "you told us the footpads had stripped you clean. How do you explain this?"

"Easily enough, your worship. They only thought of trying in my pockets, and the stiletto being there behind where you've found it, luckily they overlooked it."

"Oh, indeed!" doubtingly rejoined the corporal; "and pray how did you become possessed of it, *Señor Enano*? A dagger worth a *doblone* isn't a likely thing for such as you to be owner of—that is, in an honest way."

"I admit, your worship, it isn't likely. For all, I came honestly by the article. It's an heirloom in our family; belonged to my great-great-grandfather, and's descended through several generations. For know, Señor, my ancestors were not deformed like poor me. Some of them were gallant soldiers, as yourself. Indeed, one of them rose to the rank of sergeant—that was my mother's grandfather; but this dagger didn't come down from him, being left in the main line."

"Well," laughingly returned the corporal, after listening to the quaint chapter of explanations, "the future herald of our family won't have to trace it beyond yourself. You're now under our protection, and have no need to warlike weapons. So we, your protectors, will take the liberty of appropriating the historical toy. Get out the cards, Perico! Let us see whether it is to be yours or mine."

"*May bueno!*" responded Perico. "How will you have the game? A single *albur*, or two out of three?"

"Well, as we've only the one stake, and no end of time for winning and losing it, we'd better make it the long game."

"All right—come on! I have the cards spread—*sota y caballo*. How sweet the Queen's face looks in the moonlight! Ah! she's smiling at me, I know, as good as to say—'Worthy Perico, that silver-handled weapon, your corporal tells you is worth all of an *onza*, will ere long be thine.'"

"Well, lay on the Queen if you like. I'll go the Jack, with all his grinning. Now shuffle, and deal off."

By this the two had seated themselves, *vis-à-vis*, just outside the verge where met moonlight and shadow, a suite of cards turned face up between them, the dealing pack in the hands of Perico. The hunchback, on his knees, with neck craned out, was a spectator; but one whose thoughts were not with his eyes. Instead, dwelling upon the valuables he had so cunningly chucked back, making the mental calculation as to how much they might be damaged by breakage, but caring less for that than the danger of their also becoming stakes in that game of *monté*. Could he have known what was going on behind, he would possibly have preferred it so.

The unseen spectator, though silent, was not inactive, but the reverse. From the moment of seeing himself shut up—as it were, in a pen—he had given all his thoughts to how he might escape out of it. It needed none to tell him there was no chance front-wards by the road. A rush he might make past the two soldiers, risking seizure, and surely having the bullets of their carbines sent after him. But even though he got off in that way, what would be the upshot? The hunchback would be certain to recognise him, remembering all. Knowing, too, that his dialogue with the Hussar colonel must have been overheard, he would hasten the very event which he, José, was now all anxious to provide against. The word of warning meant for those now so much needing it might reach them too late.

All these thoughts had passed through the *cochero's* mind before the card-playing commenced. More, too, for he had carefully inspected the cliff overhead, so far as the light would allow, aided by groping. To his joy, he had discovered that there was a possibility of scaling it. A sharp pinnacle of rock was within reach of the swing of his halters; and skilled in the use of the *laso*, over this he had succeeded in flinging the head-stall of one, hooking it fast. It but remained to swarm up the rope, and he was watching for an opportunity, when glittering golden things, like a Danae's shower, came raining against his ribs, to fall at his feet.

He saw no reason for these being left to lie there, but a good one against it; so, stooping cautiously forward, he gathered up all, stowing them away in his pockets. Then turning and taking hold of the halter, with as little noise as possible, he hoisted himself up to the crest of the cliff.

The soldiers engrossed with their game, and the dwarf, though but a spectator, having also become interested in it—none of the three either saw or heard him. And the last he heard of them as he stole silently away was the corporal delightedly calling out—

"*Sota en la puerta, mozo*! The dagger's mine, darling Perico!"

Chapter Fifty Three
A Series of Surprises

The *cochero* had but a confused idea of what he was carrying away with him. By the feel, watches, with chains and bracelets; besides some smaller articles wrapped in bits of paper. The uncertainty of his getting safe up the cliff hindered him from giving them even the most cursory examination, nor did he think of doing this till at sufficient distance from the card-playing party to feel sure he was beyond danger of pursuit. Then the temptation to have a look at the things, which had so strangely and unexpectedly come into his possession, became irresistible; and sitting down upon a ledge of rock, he drew them out into the light of the moon. Two watches were there, both gold, and one with a jewelled case.

"*Carrai*!" he exclaimed, as his eyes fell upon the latter, and became fixed in a stare of blank amazement, "can it be! It is—the Condesa's watch—the very one she would have given me! But how came the hunchback to have it? Surely he must have stolen it. The other, too, with all these things!"

He looked at the second watch, but as it had never been in his hands before, he was unable to identify it. Still, it resembled one he had seen his mistress wearing, and most likely was the same.

The bracelets, chains, necklets, and brooches would be theirs, too; as also the rings and other bijouterie, which the dwarf had found time to do up in paper.

"Stolen them?" continued the *cochero* interrogatively, as he ran his eyes over the varied assortment.

"How could he? The watches he might, but the other things? Why bless me, here are two pairs of ear-rings—and these grand pendants—I'm sure I saw them in the ears of the Condesa this very day. He couldn't have taken them without her knowing it. *Santo Dios*! How ever has he come by them?"

As he thus questioned and reflected, a feeling of apprehension began to creep over him. A little before leaving the house to go after his horses he had observed his young mistress and the Condesa going into the ornamental grounds. And they went alone; Don Ignacio having repaired to a private apartment, where he was accustomed to shut himself up for the examination of State papers, what if the ladies *were* still in the grounds, in some secluded spot, lying dead, where all these adornments had been stripped from their persons!

This horrible tableau did the faithful servant in imagination conjure up. He could not help it. Nor was the thing so very improbable. He had some earlier acquaintance with the desperate character of the dwarf, which later experience confirmed. Besides, there was the state of the country—thieves and robbers all round—men who made light of murder!

With a heaviness of heart—a painful fear that there had been murder—he stayed not to further examine the trinkets; but gathering all up again, and thrusting them back into his pocket, hurried on home.

And when home he went not to his own quarters in the coachyard, but straight into the *patio*—the private court of the house. There he encountered Pepita; soon as he set eyes on her, asking—

"Where are the *Señoritas*?"

"What's that to you?" saucily retorted the maid.

"Nothing, if I only knew they were safe."

"Safe! Why what's the man thinking—talking about? Have you lost your senses, *hombre*?"

"No, Pepita. But the ladies have lost something. Look here!"

He had plunged both his hands into his pockets, and drawn them out again full of things that scintillated in the moonlight—watches and jewellery of different kinds, as she saw. With a woman's curiosity, gliding swiftly forward to examine them, she recognised every article at a glance, amazement overspreading her countenance, as it lately had his.

"*Ay de mi!*" she exclaimed, no longer in jesting tone. "What does it all mean, José?"

"Just what I want to know myself, and why I am asking after the Señoritas. But where are they?"

"In the garden, or the grounds somewhere. They strolled out about an hour ago, and haven't been in since."

"Pray God, they're still alive! Come with me, Pepita. Let us look for them. I have terrible fears."

So appealed to, the girl gave ready assent; and side by side they hastened towards the rear of the house, behind which were the ornamental grounds extending backwards. But they had not far to go before hearing sounds that set their minds at rest, removing all anxiety—the voices of the ladies themselves. They were not only alive, but laughing!

To José and Pepita this seemed strange as anything else—a perfect mystery. Merry after parting with all those pretty things; costly, too—worth hundreds of *doblones*! Withal, they were so; their lightness of heart due to the knowledge thus gained, that their own lovers were still living and safe; and something of merriment, added by that odd encounter with the *enano*, of which they were yet conversing.

If their behaviour mystified their servants, not less were they themselves puzzled when José presented himself before them with hands held out, saying:

"I ask your pardon for intruding, but don't these belong to your ladyships?"

They saw their watches and other effects obtained from them by "false pretences," as they were now to learn.

The revelation that succeeded put an end to their joyous humour; their hearts that had been light for a moment were now becoming heavier than ever. The treachery of the hunchback and his intentions were manifest. He meant to guide Santander and his soldiers to the old monastery, where they would take the *patriotas* by surprise.

"What is to be done, Ysabel?" despairingly asked the Donna Luisa. "How can we give them warning?"

To which the *cochero*, not the Countess, made answer, saying:

"I can do that, *Señorita*."

His confident tone reassured them; more still his making known the design he had already conceived, and his ability to execute it. He was acquainted with the old convent and the paths leading to it—every inch of them.

It needed not their united appeal to urge him to immediate departure. He was off the instant after, and long before the clock of Talpam had struck the midnight hour, well up the mountain road, with eyes looking to the right, in the direction of the Cerro Ajusco.

Chapter Fifty Four
Monks no More

The surmise which had influenced Zorillo to leaving the convent cell earlier than he intended was a correct one. The goings on in the Refectory were, at the time, of an unusual kind—a grand occasion, as he had worded it. There were some fifty men in it; but not one of them now effecting either the garb or the behaviour of the monk. Soldiers all; or at least in warlike guise; a few wearing regular though undress uniforms, but the majority habited as "guerilleros," in the picturesque costumes of their country. They were booted, and belted, swords by their sides, with pistols in holsters hanging against the walls, and spurs ready for buckling on. Standing in corners were stacks of carbines, and lances freshly pennoned, with their blades bright from being recently sharpened—a panoply which spoke of fighting ere long expected to take place.

It may be asked where were their horses, since all the arms and accoutrements seen around were those of cavalry? But horses they had, though not there. Each knew where to lay hands on his own, far or near, stalled in the stable of some sequestered *rancho*, or, it might be, mountain cavern. They were not yet assembled to hearken to the call of "Boot and Saddle." That they would hear at a later hour, and in a different place.

The occasion of their being in such guise and together was because it was to be the last night of their sojourn in the monastery. And they were making it a merry one; the Refectory table was being loaded with the best that was left to them in meals and drinks. Upon it were what bottles remained of those famous wines from the bins of the rich *haciendado*—his forced contribution—and they were fast getting emptied. From the way the *convives* were quaffing, it was not likely that any of the Burgundy, Madeira, or Pedro Ximenes would be left behind—not even a "heel-tap."

It had got to be midnight, and they were still in the midst of the revelry, when Rivas, who headed the table, rose to his feet, in that formal manner which tells of speech to be made or toast proclaimed.

"*Camaradas!*" he said, as soon as the buzz of conversation had ended, "as you're aware, we part from this place to-night; and some of you know whither we are going and for what purpose. But not all; therefore I deem it my duty to tell you. You saw a courier who came up early this morning—bringing good news, I'm glad to say. This despatch I hold in my hand is from an old friend, General Alvarez, who, though he may not boast *sangre-azul* in his veins, is as brave a soldier and pure a patriot as any in the land. You know that. He tells me his *Pintos* are ready for a rising, and only wait for us—the 'Free Lances'—with some others he has summoned to join him in giving the *grito*. By his messenger I have sent answer that we, too, are ready, and will respond to his summons. You all approve of that, I take it?"

"All!" was the exclaim in chorus, without a dissenting voice.

"Moreover," proceeded the speaker, "I've told the General we'll be on the march to-morrow morning, and can meet him at a place he has mentioned the day after. His plan is to attack the town of Oaxaca; and, if we succeed in taking it, then we move direct on the capital. Now *camarados*, I've nothing more to say; only that you're to scatter after your horses, and lose no time in mustering again—the old rendezvous, this side La Guarda."

So ended the speech of the Free Lances' leader; but despite the suggestions of immediate departure, the circle around the table did not instantly break up.

The bottles were not all empty as yet, nor the revellers satisfied to leave them till they should be so. Besides, there was no particular need of haste for another hour or two. So they stuck to the table, smoking, drinking, and toasting many things, as persons, among the latter their lately joined allies—the *Irlandes* and *Tejano*, about whose proved valour on other fields, of which they had heard, the Free Lances were enthusiastically eloquent.

Kearney, speaking in their own tongue, made appropriate response; while Rock, when told he had been toasted, delivered himself in characteristic strain, saying:—

"Feller-citizens,—For since I tuk up yur cause, I reck'n you'll gi'e me leave to call ye so—it air a glad thing to this chile to think he'll soon hev a bit o' fightin'. An' 'specially as it's to be agin ole Santy, the durned skunk. By the jumpin' Geehosofat! if Cris Rock iver gits longside him agin, as he war on't San Jacinty, there wan't be no more meercy for the cussed tyrant, same as, like a set of fools, we Texans showed him thar an' then. Tell them what I sayed, Cap."

With which abrupt wind-up he dropped back upon his seat, gulping down a tumblerful of best Madeira, as though it were table-beer.

Kearney did tell them, translating his comrade's speech faithfully as the *patois* would permit; which heightened their enthusiasm, many of them starting to their feet, rushing round the table, and, Mexican fashion, enfolding the *Tejano* in friendly embrace.

The hugging at an end, there was yet another toast to follow, the same which always wound up the festivals of the "Free Lances," whatever the occasion. Their leader, as often before, now again pronounced it—

"*Patria y Libertad*".

And never before did it have more enthusiastic reception, the cheer that rang through the old convent, louder than any laughter of monks who may have ever made it their home.

Ere it had ceased reverberating, the door of the Refectory was suddenly pushed open, and a man rushed into the room, as he entered, crying out—

"*Traicion!*"

"Treason!" echoed fifty voices as one, all again starting to their feet, and turning faces towards the alarmist. The major-domo it was, who, as the other *mozos*, was half equipped for a journey.

"What mean you, Gregorio?" demanded his master.

"There's one can tell you better than I, Don Ruperto."

"Who? Where is he?"

"Outside, Señor. A messenger who has just come up—he's from San Augustin."

"But how has he passed our sentry."

"Ah! *capitano*; I'd rather he told you himself."

Mysterious speech on the part of the major-domo, which heightened the apprehension of those hearing it. "Call him hither!" commanded Rivas.

No calling was needed; the person spoken of being in the environ close by; and Gregorio, again opening the door, drew him inside.

"The *cochero!*" mentally exclaimed Rivas, Kearney, and the Texan, soon as setting eyes on him.

The *cochero* it was, José, though they knew not his name, nor anything more of him than what they had learned in that note of the Condesa's, saying that he could be trusted, and their brief association with him afterwards— which gave them proof that he could.

As he presented himself inside the room he seemed panting for breath, and really was. He had only just arrived up the steep climb, and exchanged hardly half a dozen words with the major-domo, who had met him at the outside entrance.

Announced as a messenger, neither the Captain of the Free Lances nor Florence Kearney needed telling who sent him. A sweet intuition told them that. Rivas but asked—

"How have you found the way up here?"

"*Por Dios*! Señor, I've been here before—many's the time. I was born among these mountains—am well acquainted with all the paths everywhere around."

"But the sentry below. How did you get past him? You haven't the countersign!"

"He wouldn't have heard it if I had, Señor. *Pobre*! he'll never hear countersign again—nor anything else."

"Why? Explain yourself!"

"*Esta muerto*! He lies at the bottom of the cliff, his body crushed—"

"Who has done it? Who's betrayed us?" interrupted a volley of voices.

"The hunchback, Zorillo," answered José, to the astonishment of all. For in the dialogue between the dwarf and Santander, he had heard enough to anticipate the ghastly spectacle awaiting him on his way up the mountain.

Cries of anger and vengeance were simultaneously sent up; all showing eager to rush from the room. They but waited for a word more.

Rivas, however, suspecting that the messenger meant that word for himself, claimed their indulgence, and led him outside, inviting Kearney to accompany them.

Though covering much ground, and relating to many incidents, the *cochero's* story was quickly told. Not in the exact order of occurrence, but as questioned by his impatient listeners. He ran rapidly over all that happened since their parting at the corner of the Coyoacan road, the latter events most interesting them. Surprised were they to hear that Don Ignacio and his daughter for some time had been staying at San Augustin—the Condesa with them. Had they but known that before, in all probability things would not have been as now. Possibly they might have been worse; though, even as they stood, there was enough danger impending over all. As for themselves, both Mexican and Irishman, less recked of it, as they thought of how they were being warned, and by whom. That of itself was recompense for all their perils.

Meanwhile those left inside the room were chafing to learn the particulars of the treason, though they were not all there now. Some had sallied out, and gone down the cliff to bring up the body of their murdered comrade; others, the major-domo conducting, back to the place where the hunchback should be, but was not. There to find confirmation of what had been said. The cell untenanted; the window bar filed through and broken; the file lying by it, and the chain hanging down outside.

Intelligible to them now was the tale of treason, without their hearing it told.

When once more they assembled in the Refectory, it was with chastened, saddened hearts. For they had come from digging a grave, and lowering into it a corpse. Again gathered around the table, *they* drank the stirrup-cup, as was their wont, but never so joylessly, or with such stint.

Chapter Fifty Five
"Only empty Bottles"

About the time the Free Lances were burying their comrade in the cemetery of the convent the gate of San Antonio de Abad was opened to permit the passage of a squadron of Hussars going outward from the city. There were nigh 200 of them, in formation "by fours"—the wide causeway allowing ample room for even ten abreast.

At their head rode Colonel Santander, with Major Ramirez by his side, other officers in their places distributed along the line.

Soon as they had cleared the *garita*, a word to the bugler, with a note or two from his trumpet quick succeeding, set them into a gallop; the white dusty road and clear moonlight making the fastest pace easily attainable. And he who commanded was in haste, his destination being that old monastery, of which he had only lately heard, but enough to make him most eager to reach it before morning. His hopes were high; at last he was likely to make a *coup*—that capture so much desired, so long delayed!

For nearly an hour bridles were let loose, and spurs repeatedly plied. On along the *calzada* swept the squadron, over the bridge Churubusco, and past the *hacienda* of San Antonio de Abad, which gives its name to the city gate on that side. Thenceforward the Pedregal impinges on the road, and the Hussars still going at a gallop along its edge, another bugle-call brought them to a halt.

That, however, had naught to do with their halting, which came from their commander having reached the spot where he had left the hunchback in charge of the two soldiers.

He need not hail them to assure himself they were still there. The trampling of horses on the hard causeway, heard afar off, had long ago forewarned the corporal of what was coming; and he was out on the road to receive them, standing in an attitude of attention.

The parley was brief, and quick the action which accompanied it.

"Into your saddle, *cabo!*" commanded the colonel. "Take that curiosity up behind you, and bring it along."

In an instant the corporal was mounted, the "curiosity" hoisted up to his croup by Perico, who then sprang to the back of his own horse. Once more the bugle gave tongue, and away they went again.

The cavalcade made no stop in San Augustin. There was no object for halting it there, and delay was the thing its commander most desired to avoid. As they went clattering through the *pueblo*, its people were a-bed, seemingly asleep. But not all. Two at least were awake, and heard that unusual noise—listened to it with a trembling in their frames and fear in their hearts. Two ladies they were, inside a house beyond the village, on the road running south. Too well they knew what it meant, and whither the galloping cohort was bound. And themselves unseen, they saw who was at the head; though they needed not seeing him to know. But peering through the *jalousies*, the moonlight revealed to them the face of Don Carlos Santander, in the glimpse they got of it, showing spitefully triumphant.

He could not see them, though his eyes interrogated the windows while he was riding past. They had taken care to extinguish the light in their room.

"*Virgin Santissima*! Mother of God!" exclaimed one of the ladies, Luisa Valverde, as she dropped on her knees in prayer, "Send that they've got safe off ere this!"

"Make your mind easy, *amiga*!" counselled the Condesa Almonté in less precatory tone. "I'm good as sure they have. José cannot fail to have reached and given them warning. That will be enough."

A mile or so beyond San Augustin the southern road becomes too steep for horses to go at a gallop, without risk of breaking their wind. So there the Hussars had to change to a slower pace—a walk in fact. There were other reasons for coming to this. The sound of their hoof-strokes ascending would be heard far up the mountain, might reach the ears of those in the monastery, and so thwart the surprise intended for them.

While toiling more leisurely up the steep, any one chancing to look in the hunchback's face would there have observed an expression indescribable. Sadness pervaded it, with an air of perplexity, as though he had met with some misfortune he could not quite comprehend.

And so had he. Before leaving the spot where the stiletto was taken from him, he had sought an opportunity to step back into that shady niche in the cliff where he had lost his treasures. The *monté* players, unsuspicious of his object, made no objection. But instead of there finding what he had expected, he saw only a pair of horse-halters: one lying coiled upon the ground, the head-stall of the other caught over the rock above, the rope end dangling down!

An inexplicable phenomenon, which, however, he had kept to himself, and ever since been cudgelling his brains to account for.

But soon after he had something else to think of: the time having arrived when he was called upon to give proof of his capability as a guide. Heretofore it had been all plain road riding; but now they had reached a point spoken of by himself where the *calzada* must be forsaken. The horses, too, left behind; everything but their weapons; the path beyond being barely practicable for men afoot.

Dismounting all, at a command—this time not given by the bugle—and leaving a sufficient detail to look after the animals, they commenced the ascent, their guide, seemingly more quadruped than biped, in the lead. Strung out in single file—no other formation being possible—as they wound their way up the zig-zag with the moonlight here and there, giving back the glint of their armour, it was as some great serpent—a monster of the antediluvian ages—crawling towards its prey. Silently as serpent too; not a word spoken, nor exclamation uttered along their line. For, although it might be another hour before they could reach their destination, less than a second would suffice for their voices to get there, even though but muttered.

One spot their guide passed with something like a shudder. It was where he had appropriated the dagger taken from a dead body. His shuddering was not due to that, but to fear from a far different cause. The body was no longer there. Those who dwelt above must have been down and borne it away. They would now be on the alert, and at any moment he might hear the cracking of carbines—a volley; perhaps feel the avenging bullet. What if they should roll rocks down and crush him and the party behind? In any case there could be no surprisal now; and he would gladly have seen those he was guiding give up the thought of it and turn back. Santander was himself irresolute, and would willingly have done so. But Ramirez, a man of more mettle, at the point of his sword commanded the hunchback to keep on, and the cowardly colonel dare not revoke the order without eternally disgracing himself.

They had no danger to encounter, though they knew not that. Neither vidette nor sentinel was stationed there now; and, without challenge or obstruction, they reached the platform on which the building stood, the soldiers taking to right and left till they swarmed around it as bees. But they found no honey inside their hive.

There was a summons to surrender, which received no response. Repeated louder, and a carbine fired, the result was the same. Silence inside, there could be no one within.

Nor was there. When the Hussar colonel, with a dozen of his men, at length screwed up courage to make a burst into the doorway, and on to the

Refectory, they saw but the evidence of late occupancy in the fragments of a supper, with some dozens of wine bottles "down among the dead men," empty as the building itself.

Disappointed as were the soldiers at finding them so, but still more their commanding officer at his hated enemies having again got away from him. His soul was brimful of chagrin, nor did it allay the feeling to learn how, when a path was pointed out to him leading down the other side, they must have made off. And along such a path pursuit was idle. No one could say where it led—like enough to a trap.

He was not the only one of the party who felt disappointed at the failure of the expedition. Its guide had reason to be chagrined, too, in his own way of thinking, much more than the leader himself. For not only had he lost the goods obtained under false pretences, but the hope of reward for his volunteered services.

Still the dwarf was not so down in the mouth. He had another arrow in his quiver—kept in reserve for reasons of his own—a shaft from which he expected more profit than all yet spent. And as the Hussar colonel was swearing and raging around, he saw his opportunity to discharge it.

With half a dozen whispered words he tranquillised the latter; after which there was a brief conference between the two, its effect upon Santander showing itself in his countenance, that became all agleam, lit up with a satisfied but malignant joy.

When, in an hour after, they were again in their saddles riding in return for the city, a snatch of dialogue between Santander and Ramirez gave indication of what so gratified the colonel of the Hussars.

"Well, Major," he said, "we've done road enough for this day. You'll be wanting rest by the time you get to quarters."

"That's true enough, Colonel. Twice to San Augustin and back, with the additional mileage up the mountains—twenty leagues I take it—to say nothing of the climbing."

"All of twenty leagues it will be when we've done with it. But our ride won't be over then. If I'm not mistaken, we'll be back this way before we lay side on a bed. There's another nest not far off will claim a visit from us, one we're not likely to find so empty. I'd rob it now if I had my way; but for certain reasons, mustn't without permit from headquarters; the which I'm sure of getting! *Carajo!* if the cock birds have escaped, I'll take care the hens don't."

And as if to make sure of it, he dug the spurs deep into the flanks of his now jaded charger, again commanding the "quick gallop."

Chapter Fifty Six
A Day of Suspense

Dawn was just beginning to show over the eastern *Cordilleras*, its aurora giving a rose tint to the snowy cone of Popocatepec, as the Hussars passed back through San Augustin. The bells of the *paroquia* had commenced tolling matins, and many people abroad in the streets, hurrying toward the church, saw them—interrogating one another as to where they had been, and on what errand bound.

But before entering the *pueblo* they had to pass under the same eyes that observed them going outward on the other side; these more keenly and anxiously scrutinising them now, noting every file as it came in sight, every individual horseman, till the last was revealed; then lighting up with joyous sparkle, while they, thus observing, breathed freely.

For the soldiers had come as they went, not a man added to their number, if none missing, but certainly no prisoners brought back!

"They've got safe off," triumphantly exclaimed the Countess, when the rearmost files had forged past, "as I told you they would. I knew there was no fear after they had been warned."

That they had been warned both were by this aware, their messenger having meanwhile returned and reported to that effect. He had met the Hussars on their way up, but crouching among some bushes, he had been unobserved by them; and, soon as they were well out of the way, slipped out again and made all haste home.

He had brought back something more than a mere verbal message—a *billetita* for each of the two who had commissioned him.

The notes were alike, in that both had been hastily scribbled, and in brief but warm expression of thanks for the service done to the writers. Beyond this, however, they were quite different. It was the first epistle Florence Kearney had ever indited to Luisa Valverde, and ran in fervid strain. He felt he could so address her. With love long in doubt that it was even reciprocated, but sure of its being so now, he spoke frankly as passionately. Whatever his future, she had his heart, and wholly. If he lived, he would seek her again at the peril of a thousand lives; if it should be his fate to die, her name would be the last word on his lips.

"*Virgen Santissima*! Keep him safe!" was her prayer, as she finished devouring the sweet words; then, refolding the sheet on which they were written, secreted it away in the bosom of her dress—a treasure more esteemed than aught that had ever lain there.

The communication received by the Condesa was less effusive, and more to the point of what, under present circumstances, concerned the writer, as, indeed, all of them. Don Ruperto wrote with the confidence of a lover who had never known doubt. A man of rare qualities, he was true to friendship as to his country's cause, and would not be false to love. And he had no fear of her. His *liens* with Ysabel Almonté were such as to preclude all thought of her affections ever changing. He knew that she was his—heart, soul, everything. For had she not given him every earnest of it, befriended him through weal and through woe? Nor had he need to assure her that her love was reciprocated, or his fealty still unfaltering; for their faith, as their reliance, was mutual. His letter, therefore, was less that of a lover to his mistress than one between man and man, written to a fellow-conspirator, most of it in figurative phrase, even some of it in cypher!

No surprise to her all that; she understood the reason. Nor was there any enigma in the signs and words of double signification; without difficulty she interpreted them all.

They told her of the anticipated rising, with the attempt to be made on Oaxaca, the hopes of its having a success, and, if so, what would come after. But also of something before this—where he, the writer, and his Free Lances would be on the following night, so that if need arose she could communicate with him. If she had apprehension of danger to him, he was not without thought of the same threatening herself and her friend too.

Neither were they now; instead, filled with such apprehension. In view of what had occurred on the preceding evening, and throughout the night, how could they be other? The dwarf must know more than he had revealed in that dialogue overheard by José. In short, he seemed aware of everything—the *cochero's* complicity as their own. The free surrender of their watches and jewellery for the support of the escaped prisoners were of itself enough to incriminate them. Surely there would be another investigation, more rigorous than before, and likely to have a different ending.

With this in contemplation, their souls full of fear, neither went that morning to matins. Nor did they essay to take sleep or rest. Instead, wandered about the house from room to room, and out into the grounds, seemingly distraught.

They had the place all to themselves; no one to take counsel with, none to comfort them; Don Ignacio, at an early hour, having been called off to his duties in the city. But they were not destined to spend the whole of that day without seeing a visitor. As the clocks of San Augustin were striking 8 p.m. one presented himself at the gate in the guise of an officer of Hussars, Don Carlos Santander. Nor was he alone, but with an escort accompanying. They were seated in the verandah of the inner court, but saw him through the *saguan*, the door of which was open, saw him enter at the outer gate, and without dismounting come on towards them, several files of his men following. He had been accustomed to visit them there, and they to receive his visits, however reluctantly, reasons of many kinds compelling them. But never had he presented himself as now. It was an act of ill-manners his entering unannounced, another riding into the enclosure with soldiers behind him; but the rudeness was complete when he came on into the *patio* still in the saddle, his men too, and pulled up directly in front of them, without waiting for word of invitation. The stiff, formal bow, the expression upon his swarthy features, severe, but with ill-concealed exultation in it, proclaimed his visit of no complimentary kind.

By this both were on their feet, looking offended, even angry, at the same time alarmed. And yet little surprised, for it was only confirmation of the fear that had been all day oppressing them—its very fulfilment. But that they believed it this they would have shown their resentment by retiring and leaving him there. As it was, they knew that would be idle, and so stayed to hear what he had to say. It was—

"*Señoritas*, I see you're wondering at my thus presenting myself. Not strange you should. Nor could any one more regret the disagreeable errand I've come upon than I. It grieves me sorely, I assure you."

"What is it, Colonel Santander?" demanded the Countess, with *sang-froid* partially restored.

"I hate to declare it, Condesa," he rejoined, "still more to execute it. But, compelled by the rigorous necessities of a soldier's duty, I must."

"Well, sir; must what?"

"Make you a prisoner; and, I am sorry to add, also the Doña Luisa."

"Oh, that's it!" exclaimed the Countess, with a scornful inclination of the head. "Well, sir, I don't wonder at your disliking the duty, as you say you do. It seems more that of a policeman than a soldier."

The retort struck home, still further humiliating him in the eyes of the woman he loved, Luisa Valverde. But he now knew she loved not him, and had made up his mind to humble her in a way hitherto untried. Stung by the innuendo, and dropping his clumsy pretence at politeness, he spitefully rejoined—

"Thank you, Condesa Almonté for your amiable observation. It does something to compensate me for having to do policeman's duty. And now let it be done. Please to consider yourself under arrest; and you also, Señorita Valverde."

Up to this time the last named lady had not said a word, the distress she was in restraining her. But as mistress there, she saw it was her turn to speak, which she did, saying—

"If we are your prisoners, Colonel Santander, I hope you will not take us away from here till my father comes home. As you may be aware, he's in the city."

"I am aware of that, Doña Luisa, and glad to say my orders enable me to comply with your wishes, and that you remain here till Don Ignacio returns. I'm enjoined to see to your safe keeping—a very absurd requirement, but one which often falls to the lot of the soldier as well as the *policeman*."

Neither the significant words nor the forced laugh that accompanied them had any effect on her for whom they were intended. With disdain in her eyes, such as a captive queen might show for the common soldier who stood guard over her, the Condesa had already turned her back upon the speaker and was walking away. With like proud air, but less confident and scornful, Luisa Valverde followed. Both were allowed to pass inside, leaving the Hussar colonel to take such measures for their keeping as he might think fit.

His first step was to order in the remainder of his escort and distribute them around the house, so that in ten minutes after the *casa de campo* of Don Ignacio Valverde bore resemblance to a barrack, with sentinels at every entrance and corner!

Chapter Fifty Seven
Under Arrest

Scarce necessary to say that Luisa Valverde and Ysabel Almonté were at length really alarmed—fully alive to a sense of their danger.

It was no more a question of the safety of their lovers, but their own. And the prospect was dark, indeed. Santander had said nothing of the reason for arresting them; nor had they cared to inquire. They divined it; no longer doubting that it was owing to revelations made by the hunchback.

Sure now that this diminutive wretch not only himself knew their secret, but had made it known in higher quarters, there seemed no hope for them; instead, ruin staring them in the face. The indignity to their persons they were already experiencing would be followed by social disgrace, and confiscation of property.

"Oh, Ysabelita! what will they do to us?" was the Doña Luisa's anxious interrogatory, soon as they had got well inside their room. "Do you think they'll put us in a prison?"

"Possibly they will. I wish there was nothing worse awaiting us."

"Worse! Do you mean they'd inflict punishment on us—that is, corporal punishment? Surely they daren't?"

"Daren't! Santa Anna dare anything—at least, neither shame nor mercy will restrain him. No more this other man, his minion, whom you know better than I. But it isn't punishment of that kind I'm thinking of."

"What then, Ysabel? The loss of our property? It'll be all taken from us, I suppose."

"In all likelihood it will," rejoined the Condesa, with as much unconcern as though her estates, value far more than a million, were not worth a thought.

"Oh! my father! This new misfortune, and all owing to me. 'Twill kill him!"

"No, no, Luisita! Don't fear that. He will survive it, if aught survives of our country's liberty. And it will, all of it, be restored again. 'Tis something else I was thinking of."

Again the other asked "What?" her countenance showing increased anxiety.

"What we as women have more to fear than aught else. From the loss of lands, houses, riches of any sort, one may recover—from the loss of that, never!"

Enigmatic as were the words, Luisa Valverde needed no explanation of them, nor pressed for it. She comprehended all now, and signified her apprehension by exclaiming, with a shudder, "*Virgen Santissima*!"

"The prison they will take us to," pursued the Countess, "is a place—that in the Plaza Grande. We shall be immured there, and at the mercy of that man, that monster! O God!—O Mother of God, protect me!"

At which she dropped down upon a couch despairingly, with face buried in her hands.

It was a rare thing for the Condesa Almonté to be so moved—rather, to show despondence—and her friend was affected accordingly. For there was another man at whose mercy she herself would be—one like a monster, and as she well knew equally unmerciful—he who at that moment was under the same roof with them—in her father's house, for the time its master.

"But, Ysabel," she said, hoping against hope, "surely they will not dare to—"

She left the word unspoken, knowing it was not needed to make her meaning understood.

"Not dare!" echoed the Countess, recovering nerve and again rising to her feet. "As I've said, he'll dare anything—will Don Antonio Lopez De Santa Anna. Besides, what has *he* to fear? Nothing. He can show good cause for our imprisonment, else he would never have had us arrested. Enough to satisfy any clamour of the people. And how would any one ever know of what might be done to us inside the Palacio? Ah, *Luisita querida*, if its walls could speak they might tell tales sad enough to make angels weep. We wouldn't be the first who have been subjected to insult—ay, infamy—by *El excellentissimo. Valga me Dios!*" she cried out in conclusion, stamping her foot on the floor, while the flash of her eyes told of some fixed determination. "If it be so, that Palace prison will have another secret to keep, or a tale to tell, sad and tragic as any that has preceded. I, Ysabel Almonté, shall die in it rather than come out dishonoured."

"I, too!" echoed Luisa Valverde, if in less excited manner, inspired by a like heroic resolve.

While his fair prisoners were thus exchanging thought and speech, Santander, in the *sala grande* outside, was doing his best to pass the time pleasantly. An effort it was costing him, however, and one far from successful. His last lingering hope of being beloved by Luisa Valverde was gone—completely destroyed by what had late come to his knowledge—and henceforth his love for her could only be as that of Tarquin for Lucretia. Nor would he have any Collatinus to fear—no rival, martial or otherwise—since his master, Santa Anna, had long since given up his designs on Don Ignacio's daughter, exclusively bending himself to his scheme of conquest— now revenge—over the Condesa. But though relieved in this regard, and likely to have his own way, Carlos Santander was anything but a happy man after making that arrest; instead, almost as miserable as either of those he had arrested.

Still keeping up a pretence of gallantry, he could not command their company in the drawing-room where he had installed himself; nor, under the circumstances, would it have been desirable. He was not alone, however; Major Ramirez and the other officers of his escort being there with him; and, as in like cases, they were enjoying themselves. However considerate for the feelings of the ladies, they made free enough with the house itself, its domestics, larder, and *cocina*, and, above all, the cellar. Its binns were inquired into, the best wine ordered to be brought from them, as though they who gave the order were the guests of an hotel and Don Ignacio's drawing-room a drinking saloon.

Outside in the courtyard, and further off by the coach-house, similar scenes were transpiring. Never had that quiet *casa de campo* known so much noise. For the soldiers had got among them—it was the house of a *rebel*, and therefore devoted to ruin.

Chapter Fifty Eight
The Cochero Dogged

Just after the ladies had been proclaimed under arrest, but before the sentinels were posted around the house, a man might have been seen outside their line, making all haste away from it. He had need, his capture being also contemplated. José it was, who, from a place of concealment, had not only seen what passed, but heard the conversation between Santander and the Señoritas. The words spoken by his young mistress, and the rejoinder received, were all he waited for. Giving him his cue for departure, they also gave him hopes of something more than the saving of his own life. That the last was endangered he knew now—forfeited, indeed, should he fall into the hands of those who had invaded the place. So, instead of returning to the stable-yard, from which he had issued on hearing the *fracas* in front, he retreated rearwards, first through the ornamental grounds, then over the wall upon which the hunchback had perched himself on the preceding night. José, however, did not stay on it for more than a second's time. Soon as mounting to its summit, he slid down on the other side, and ran along the lane in the direction of the main road.

Before reaching this, however, a reflection caused him to slacken pace, and then come to a stop. It was still daylight, and there would be a guard stationed by the front gate, sure to see him along the road. The ground on the opposite side of the lane was a patch of rocky scrub—in short, a *chapparal*—into which in an instant after he plunged, and when well under cover again made stop, this time dropping down on his hands and knees. The attitude gave him a better opportunity of listening; and listen he did—all ears.

To hear voices all around the house, loudest in the direction of the stable-yard. In tones not of triumph, but telling of disappointment. For in truth it was so; the shouts of the soldiers searching for his very self, and swearing because he could not be found. He had reason to congratulate himself in having got outside the enclosure. It was now being quartered everywhere, gardens, grounds, and all.

For the time he felt comparatively safe; but he dared not return to the lane. And less show himself on the open road; as scouting parties were sure of being sent out after him. There was no alternative, therefore, but stay where he was till the darkness came down. Luckily, he would not have long to wait for it. The sun had set, and twilight in the Mexican valley is but a brief interval between day and night. In a few minutes after commencement it is over.

Short as it was, it gave him time to consider his future course of action, though that required little consideration. It had been already traced out for him, partly by the Condesa, in an interview he held with her but an hour before and partly by instructions he had received when up at the old convent direct from the lips of Don Ruperto. Therefore, hurried as was his retreat, he was not making it as one who went blindly and without definite aim. He had this, with a point to be reached, which, could he only arrive at, not only might his own safety be secured, but that of those he was equally anxious about, now more imperilled than himself.

With a full comprehension of their danger, and the hope of being able to avert it, soon as the twilight deepened to darkness he forsook his temporary place of concealment, and, returning to the lane, glided noiselessly along it towards the main road. Coming out upon this, he turned to the left, and without looking behind, hurried up the hill as fast as his limbs could carry him.

Perhaps better for him had he looked behind; and yet in the end it might have been worse. Whether or no, he was followed by a man—if it were a man—and, if a thing, not his own shadow. A grotesque creature, seemingly all arms and legs, moved after, keeping pace with him, no matter how rapidly he progressed. Not overtaking him; though it looked as if able to do so, but did not wish. Just so it was—the stalker being Zorillo.

The stalk had risen rather accidentally. The hunchback—now in a manner attached to the party of Hussars—had been himself loitering near the end of the lane, and saw the *cochero* as he came out on the road. He knew the latter was being sought for, and by no one more zealously than himself. Besides cupidity, he was prompted by burning revenge. The disappearance of his ill-gotten treasure was no longer a mystery to him. The abandoned halters, with the horses for which they had been intended, told him all. Only the *cochero* could have carried the things off.

And now, seeing the latter as he stole away in retreat, his first impulse was to raise the hue and cry, and set the soldiers after. But other reflections, quick succeeding, restrained him. They might not be in time to secure a capture. In the darkness there was every chance of the *mertizo* eluding them. A tract of forest was not far off, and he would be into it before they could come up. Besides, the hunchback had also conjectured that the failure of their over-night expedition was due to José. He must have overheard that conversation with the colonel of Hussars, and carried it direct to those whom it so seriously concerned, thus saving them from the surprise intended. In all likelihood he was now on his way to another interview with them.

If so, and if he, Zorillo, could but spot the place, and bring back report of it to Santander, it would give him a new claim for services, and some compensation for the loss he had sustained through the now hated *cochero*.

Soon as resolved he lost not a moment in making after, keeping just such distance between as to hinder José from observing him. He had the advantage in being behind, as it was all uphill, and from below he could see the other by the better light above, while himself in obscurity. But he also availed himself of the turnings of the road, and the scrub that grew alongside it, through which he now and then made way. His long legs gave a wonderful power of speed, and he could have come up with the *mertizo* at any moment. He knew that, but knew also it would likely cost him his life. For the *cochero* must be aware of what he had done—enough to deserve death at his hands. He might well dread an encounter, and was careful to avoid it. Indeed, but for his belief that he was an overmatch for the other in speed, he would not have ventured after him.

For nearly five miles up the mountain road the stalk was continued. Then he, whose footsteps were so persistently dogged, was seen to turn into a side path, which led along a ravine still upward. But the change, of course, did not throw off the sleuth-hound skulking on his track, the latter also entering the gorge, and gliding on after.

There it was darker, from the shadow of the overhanging cliffs; and for a time the hunchback lost sight of him he was following. Still, he kept on, groping his way, and at length was rewarded by seeing a light—a great blaze. It came from a bivouac fire, which threw its red glare on the rocks around, embracing within its circle the forms of men and horses. Armed men they were, and horses caparisoned for war, as could be told by the glint of weapons and accoutrement given back to the fire's blaze.

There appeared to be over a hundred of them; but the hunchback did not approach near enough to make estimate of their number. Enough for him to know who they were; and this knowledge he obtained by seeing a man of gigantic size standing by the side of the fire—the "big *Tejano!*" He saw, too, that the *cochero* had got upon the ground, his arrival creating an excitement. But he stayed to see no more: his purpose was fulfilled; and turning back down the ravine, he again got out to the road, where he put on his best speed in return for Tlalpam.

Chapter Fifty Nine
Ready to Start

As in all Mexican country houses of the class mansion, that of Don Ignacio Valverde was a quadrangular structure enclosing an inner courtyard—the *patio*. The latter a wide open area, flagged, in its centre a playing fountain, with orange trees and other ornamental evergreens growing in great boxes around it. Along three sides ran a verandah gallery, raised a step or two above the pavement, with a baluster and railing between. Upon this opened the doors of the different chambers, as they would into the hallway of an English house. Being one-storeyed, even the sleeping apartments were entered direct from it.

That into which the ladies had retired was the *cuarto de camara* of Don Luisa herself. No sentry had been stationed at its door; this being unnecessary, in view of one posted at the *patio*. But through a casement window, which opened into the garden at the back, they could see such precaution had been taken. A soldier out there, with carbine thrown lightly over his left arm, was doing his beat backwards and forwards.

As they had no thought of attempting escape, they might have laughed at this had they been in a mood for merriment. But they were sad, even to utter prostration.

Only for a time, however; then something of hope seemed to reanimate the Condesa, and communicate itself to her companion. It was after a report brought in by Pepita; for the lady's maid was allowed to attend upon them, coming and going freely.

"He's got away—safe!" were her words, spoken in a cautious but cheering tone, as for the second time she came into the room.

"Are you sure, Pepita?"

It was the Countess who put the question.

"Quite sure, your ladyship. I've been all around the place, to the stable, grounds, everywhere, and couldn't hear or see anything of him. Oh! he's gone, and so glad I am. They'd have made him prisoner too. Thanks to the Blessed Virgin, they haven't."

The thanksgiving was for José, and however fervent on Pepita's part, it was as fervently responded to by the others, the Condesa seeming more especially pleased at the intelligence.

She better understood its importance, for, but the hour before, she had given him conditional instructions, and hoped he might be now in the act of carrying them out.

Upheld by this hope, which the Doña Luisa, when told of it, shared with her, they less irksomely passed the hours.

But at length, alas! it, too, was near being given up, as the night grew later, nearing midnight. Then the little *mertiza* came in charged with new intelligence; not so startling, since they anticipated it. The *Dueno* had got home, and, as themselves, was under arrest. Astounded by what he had learned on return, and angrily protesting, the soldiers had rudely seized hold of him, even refusing him permission to speak with his daughter.

She had harboured a belief that all might be well on the coming home of her father. The last plank was shattered now. From the chair of the cabinet minister Don Ignacio Valverde would step direct into the cell of a prison! Nothing uncommon in the political history of Mexico—only one of its "cosas."

On their feet they were now, and had come close to the door, which was held slightly open by Pepita. There they stood listening to what was going on outside. The sounds of revelry lately proceeding from the *sala grande* were no more heard. Instead, calls and words of command in the courtyard, with a bustle of preparation. Through the trellis-work they could see a carriage with horses attached, distinguishable as their own. It was the same which had just brought Don Ignacio from the city. But the heads of the *frisones* were turned outward, as if it was intended to take them back. Men on horseback were moving around it; soldiers, as could be seen by their armour gleaming in the moonlight.

Those regarding their movements were not left long in suspense as to their meaning. One of the soldiers on foot, whose sleeve chevrons proclaimed him a corporal, stepped up into the corridor, and advancing along it, halted in front of their door. Seeing it open, with faces inside, he made a sort of military salute, in a gruff voice saying:

"*Señoritas*! Carriage ready. I've orders to conduct you to it without delay."

There was something offensive in the man's manner. He spoke with a thick tongue, and was evidently half intoxicated. But his air showed him in earnest.

"You'll allow us a little time—to put on our cloaks?"

The request came from the Condesa, who for a certain reason was wishful to retard their departure as long as might be possible.

"*Carrai-i!*" drawled out the *cabo*, the same who had won the dagger from darling Perico. "I'd allow such beautiful *doncellas* as you any time—all night—if 'twere only left to me. For myself, I'd far rather stick to these snug quarters, and the company of this pretty *muchacha.*"

At which, leaning forward, with a brutish leer, he attempted to snatch a kiss from Pepita.

The girl shrunk back, but not till she had rebuked him with an angry retort and a slap across the cheek. It stung him to losing temper, and without further ceremony he said spitefully—

"Come, come, I'll have no more dilly-dallying: *nos vamos!*"

There was no alternative but to obey; his attitude told them he would insist upon it, and instantly. Time for cloaking had been a pretence on their part. They were expecting the summons, and the wraps were close at hand. Flinging them around their shoulders, and drawing the hoods over their heads, they issued out upon the corridor, and turned along it—the soldier preceding, with the air of one who conducted criminals to execution.

A short flight of steps led down to the pavement of the court. On reaching these, they paused and looked below. There was still a bustling about the carriage, as if some one had just been handed into it. Several of the soldiers were on foot around it, but the majority were in their saddles; and of these three or four could be distinguished as officers by the greater profusion of gold lace on their jackets and dolmans—for they were all Hussars. One who glittered more than any, seeing them at the head of the stair, gave his horse a prick with the spur, and rode up. Colonel Santander it was, like all the rest somewhat excited by drink; but still not so far gone as to forget gallantry, or rather the pretence of it.

"Ladies," he said, with a bow and air of maudlin humility, "I have to apologise for requiring you to start out on a journey at such a late hour. Duty is often an ungracious master. Luckily, your drive is not to be a very extended one—only to the city; and you'll have company in the carriage. The Doña Luisa will find her father at home."

Neither vouchsafed rejoinder—not a word—scarce giving him the grace of a look. Which a little nettling him, his smooth tone changed to asperity, as addressing himself to the soldier, he gave the abrupt order:

"*Cabo!* take them on to the carriage."

On they were taken; as they approached it, perceiving a face inside, pale as the moonbeams that played upon it. It was a very picture of dejection; for never had Don Ignacio Valverde experienced misery such as he felt now.

"'Tis you, father!" said his daughter, springing up, throwing her arms around him, and showering kisses where tears already trickled. "You a prisoner, too!"

"Ay, *nina mia*. But sit down. Don't be alarmed! It will all come right. Heaven will have mercy on us, if men do not. Sit down, Luisa!"

She sat down mechanically, the Countess by her side; and the door was banged to behind them. Meanwhile, Pepita, who insisted on accompanying her mistress, had been handed up to the box by a *cochero* strange to her; one of the soldiers, pressed into the service for the occasion, a *quondam* "jarvey," who understood the handling of horses as every Mexican does.

All were now ready for the road; the dismounted Hussars had vaulted into their saddles, the "march" was commanded, and the driver had drawn his whip to lay it on his horses, when the animals jibbed, rearing up, and snorting in affright!

No wonder, with such an object suddenly coming under their eyes. An oddly-shaped creature that came scrambling in through the *saguan*, and made stop beneath their very noses. A human being withal; who, soon as entering, called out, in a clear voice,—"Where is the Colonel?"

Chapter Sixty
"Surrender!"

If the carriage horses were startled by the apparition, no less so were the Hussars formed round. Equally frightened these, though not from the same cause. The hunchback—for it was he—had become a familiar sight to them; but not agitated as he appeared to be now. He was panting for breath, barely able to gasp out the interrogation, "Adone 'stael Coronel?"

His distraught air and the tone told of some threatening danger.

"Here!" called out Santander, springing his horse a length or two forward, "What is it, sirrah?"

"The enemy, S'nor Colonel," responded the dwarf, sliding close in to the stirrup.

"Enemy! What enemy?"

"Them we missed catching—Don Ruperto, the Irlandes, the big Tejano."

"Ha!—They!—Where?"

"Close by, S'nor. I saw them round a great camp-fire up in the mountains. They're not there now. I came on to tell you. I ran as fast as ever I was able, but they've been following. I could hear the tramp of their horses behind all the way. They must be near at hand now. Hark!"

"Patria y Libertad!"

The cry came from without, in the tone of a charging shibboleth, other voices adding, "Mueran los tyrannos!"

Instantaneously succeeded by the cracking of carbines, with shouts, and the clash of steel against steel—the sounds of a hand-to-hand fight, which the stamping and snorting of horses proclaimed between cavalry.

Never was conflict of shorter duration; over almost before they in the courtyard could realise its having commenced. The confused sounds of the *mêlée* lasted barely a minute when a loud huzza, drowning the hoof-strokes of the retreating horses, told that victory had declared itself for one side or the other. They who listened were not long in doubt as to which sent up that triumphant cheer. Through the front gate, standing open, burst a mass of mounted men, some carrying lances couched for the thrust, others with drawn sabres, many of their blades dripping blood. On came they into the courtyard, still vociferating: "Mueran los tyrannos!" while he at their head, soon as showing himself, called out in a commanding voice, "Rendite?"

By this a change had taken place in the tableau of figures beside the carriage. The Hussars having reined back, had gathered in a ruck around their colonel, irresolute how to act. Equally unresolved he to order them. That cry, "Country and Liberty," had struck terror to his heart; and now seeing those it came from, recognising the three who rode foremost—as in the clear moonlight he could—the blood of the craven ran cold. They were the men he had subjected to insult, direct degradation; and he need look for no mercy at their hands. With a spark of manhood, even such as despair sometimes inspires, he would have shown fight. Major Ramirez would, and did; for at the first alarm he had galloped out to the gate and there met death.

Not so Santander, who, although he had taken his sword out of its scabbard, made no attempt to use it, but sat shivering in his saddle, as if the weapon was about to drop from his hand.

On the instant after a blade more firmly held, and better wielded, flashed before his eyes; he who held it, as he sprung his horse up, crying out:

"Carlos Santander! your hour has come! Scoundrel! *This time* I intend killing you."

Even the insulting threat stung him not to resistance. Never shone moonlight on more of a poltroon, the glitter and grandeur of his warlike dress in striking contrast with his cowardly mien.

"Miserable wretch!" cried Kearney—for it was he who confronted him—"I don't want to kill you in cold blood Heaven forbid my doing murder. Defend yourself."

"He defend hisself!" scornfully exclaimed a voice—that of Cris Rock. "He dassen't as much as do that. He hasn't the steel shirt on now."

Yet another voice at this moment made itself heard, as a figure, feminine, became added to the group. Luisa Valverde it was, who, rushing out of the carriage and across the courtyard, cried out—

"Spare his life, Don Florencio. He's not worthy of your sword."

"You're right thar, young lady," endorsed the Texan, answering for Kearney. "That he ain't—an' bare worth the bit o' lead that's inside o' this ole pistol. For all, I'll make him a present o' 't—thar, dang ye."

The last words were accompanied by a flash and a crack, causing Santander's horse to shy and rear up. When the fore hoofs of the animal returned to the flags, they but missed coming down upon the body of its rider, now lying lifeless along them.

"That's gin him his quieetus, I reckin," observed Rock, as he glanced down at the dead man, whose face upturned had the full moonlight upon it, showing handsome features, that withal were forbidding in life, but now more so in the ghastly pallor of death.

No one stayed to gaze upon them, least of all the Texan, who had yet another life to take, as he deemed in the strict execution of duty and satisfaction of justice. For it too was forfeit by the basest betrayal. The soldiers were out of their saddles now, prisoners all; having surrendered without striking a blow. But crouching away in a shadowy corner was that thing of deformity, who, from his diminutive size, might well have escaped observation. He did not, however. The Texan had his eyes on him all the while, having caught a glimpse of him as they were riding in at the gate. And in those eyes now gleamed a light of a vengeance not to be allayed save by a life sacrificed. If Santander on seeing Kearney believed his hour was come, so did the dwarf as he saw Cris Rock striding towards him. Caught by the collar, and dragged out into the light, he knew death was near now.

In vain his protestations and piteous appeals. Spite of all, he had to die. And a death so unlike that usually meted out to criminals, as he himself to the commonality of men. No weapon was employed in putting an end to him: neither gun nor pistol, sword nor knife. Letting go hold of his collar, the Texan grasped him around the ankles, and with a brandish raising him aloft, brought his head down upon the pavement. There was a crash as the breaking of a cocoa-nut shell by a hammer; and when Rock let go, the mass of mis-shapen humanity dropped in a dollop upon the flags, arms and legs limp and motionless, in the last not even the power left for a spasmodic kick.

"Ye know, Cap," said the Texan, justifying himself to Kearney, "I'd be the last man to do a cruel thing. But to rid the world o' sech varmint as them, 'cording to my way o' thinking, air the purest hewmanity."

A doctrine which the young Irishman was not disposed to dispute just at that time, being otherwise and better occupied, holding soft hands in his, words exchanging with sweet lips, not unaccompanied by kisses. Near at hand Don Ruperto was doing the same, his *vis-à-vis* being the Condesa.

But these moments of bliss were brief—had need be. The raid of the Free Lances down to San Augustin was a thing of risk, only to have been attempted by lovers who believed their loved ones were in deadly danger. In another hour or less, the Hussars who had escaped would report themselves at San Angel and Chapultepec—then there would be a rush of thousands in the direction of Tlalpam.

So there was in reality—soldiers of all arms, "horse, foot, and dragoons." But on arrival there they found the house of Don Ignacio Valverde untenanted; even the domestics had gone out of it; the carriage, too, which has played such an important part in our tale, along with the noble *frisones*. The horses had not been taken out of it, nor any change made in the company it carried off. Only in the driver, the direction, and *cortège*. José again held the reins, heading his horses up the mountain road, instead of towards Mexico; while, in place of Colonel Santander's Hussars, the Free Lances of Captain Ruperto Rivas now formed a more friendly escort.

Chapter Sixty One
Conclusion

About a month after in San Augustin a small two-masted vessel—a goleta—might have been observed standing on tacks off the coast of Oaxaca, as if working against the land wind to make to the mouth of Rio Tecoyama—a stream which runs into the Pacific near the south-western corner of that State. Only sharp eyes could have seen the schooner; for it was night, and the night was a very dark one. There were eyes sharply on the lookout for her, however, anxiously scanning the horizon to leeward, some of them through glasses. On an elevated spot among the mangroves, by the river's mouth, a party was assembled, in all about a score individuals. They were mostly men, though not exclusively; three female figures being distinguishable, as forming part of the group. Two of them had the air, and wore the dress, of ladies, somewhat torn and travel-stained; the third was in the guise of a maid-servant attending them. They were the Condesa Almonté the Don Luisa Valverde, and her ever faithful Pepita.

Among the men were six with whom the reader has acquaintance. Don Ignacio, Kearney, Rock, Rivas, José, and he who had been major-domo in the old monastery, baptismally named Gregorio. Most of the others, undescribed, had also spent some time in the establishment with the monks while playing the part of Free Lances. They were, in fact, a remnant of the band—now broken up and dispersed.

But why! When last seen it looked as though their day of triumph had come, or was at all events near. So would it have been but for a betrayal, through which the *pronunciamento* had miscarried, or rather did not come off. The Dictator, well informed about it—further warned by what occurred at San Augustin—had poured troops over the Sierras into Oaxaca in force sufficient to awe the leaders of the intended insurrection. It was but by the breadth of a hair that his late Cabinet Minister, and those who accompanied him, were able to escape to the sequestered spot where we find them on the shore of the South Sea. To Alvarez, chief of the Pintos, or "spotted Indians," were they indebted for safe conduct thither; he himself having adroitly kept clear of all compromise consequent on that grito unraised. Furthermore, he had promised to provide them with a vessel in which they might escape out of the country; and it was for this they were now on the lookout.

When Ruperto Rivas, gazing through that same telescope he had given Florence Kearney to make survey of the valley of Mexico, cried out, "La goleta!" every eye around him brightened, every heart beat joyously.

Still more rejoiced were they when, after an hour's tacking against the land breeze, the goleta got inside the estuary of the stream, and working up, brought to by the edge of the mangroves.

Unencumbered with heavy baggage, they were all soon aboard, and in three days after debarked at the port of Panama. Thence crossing the Isthmus to Chagres, another sea-going craft carried them on to the city, where they need no longer live in fear of Mexico's despot.

Back to his old quarters in New Orleans had Don Ignacio repaired; again under the ban of proscription, his estates sequestrated as before. So, too, those of the Condesa Almonté.

But not for all time, believed they. They lived in hope of a restoration.

Nor were they disappointed; for it came. The *pronunciamento* delayed was at length proclaimed, and carried to a successful issue. Once again throughout the land of Anahuac had arisen a "grito," its battle cry "Patria y Libertad!" so earnestly and loudly shouted as to drive the Dictator from his mock throne; sending him, as several times before, to seek safety in a foreign land.

Nor were the "Free Lances" unrepresented in this revolutionary struggle; instead, they played an important part in it. Ere it broke out, they who had fled the country re-entered it over the Texan border, and rejoining their brethren, became once more ranged under the leadership of Captain Ruperto Rivas, with Florence Kearney as his lieutenant, and Cris Rock a sort of attaché to the band, but a valuable adjunct to its fighting force.

Swords returned to their scabbards, bugles no longer sounding war signals, it remains out to speak of an episode of more peaceful and pleasanter nature, which occurred at a later period, and not *so very long* after. The place was inside the Grand Cathedral of Mexico, at whose altar, surrounded by a throng of the land's élite, bells ringing, and organ music vibrating on the air, stood three couples, waiting to be wedded.

And wedded they were! Don Ruperto Rivas to the Condesa Almonté, Florence Kearney to the Doña Luisa Valverde, and—José to Pepita.

Happy they, and happy also one who was but a witness of the ceremony, having a better view of it than most of the spectators, from being the head and shoulders taller than any. Need we say this towering personage was the big Tejano? Cris looked on delightedly, proud of his comrade and *protégé*, with the beautiful bride he had won and was wedding. For all it failed to shake his own faith in single blessedness. In his eyes there was no bride so beautiful as the "Land of the Lone Star," no wife so dear as its wild "purairas." And to them after a time he returned, oft around the camp-fire entertaining his companions of the chase with an account of his adventures in the Mexican valley—how he had there figured in the various rôles of jail-bird, scavenger, friar, and last of all as one of the Free Lances.